Prayers
for the
Dying

Tracy L. Ward

Willow Hill House

Ontario, Canada

The Marshall House Mystery Series

CHORUS OF THE DEAD
DEAD SILENT
THE DEAD AMONG US
SWEET ASYLUM
PRAYERS FOR THE DYING
SHADOWS OF MADNESS

Ebook Edition
ISBN: 978-0-9958914-0-1

Cover Art Copyright © 2016 by Jessica Allain

Edited by Lourdes Venard, Comma Sense Editing

For Mrs. Sue Fox,
Teacher-librarian at Manchester Public School
May your kindness and encouragement resonate on
the following pages.

TRACY L. WARD

Gone From My Sight

By Henry Van Dyke (1852-1933)

I am standing upon the seashore.
A ship, at my side,
spreads her white sails to the moving breeze
and starts for the blue ocean.
She is an object of beauty and strength.

I stand and watch her until, at length, she hangs like a
speck of white cloud just where the sea and sky come to
mingle with each other.

Then, someone at my side says, 'There, she is gone'

Gone where?

Gone from my sight. That is all. She is just as large in mast,
hull and spar as she was when she left my side.
And, she is just as able to bear her load of living freight to
her destined port.

Her diminished size is in me - not in her.
And, just at the moment when someone says,
'There, she is gone,'
there are other eyes watching her coming, and other voices
ready to take up the glad shout, 'Here she comes!'

And that is dying...

Death comes in its own time, in its own way.
Death is as unique as the individual experiencing it.

TRACY L. WARD

Prologue

London, 1868— Robert Crandall could not settle the shaking of his hands even as he pushed the door shut. For a long while he stood there, trying to steady his breathing and hoping to wipe the fear from his features before he would have to turn to his wife.

"Who was that man?" Mary asked from the opposite side of the room.

Robert swallowed back the bile that wreaked havoc on his throat. What little they'd had to eat for supper earlier clawed at him from the inside.

"Robert?"

A muffled cry escaped the baby in her arms, Lucy, swaddled with one chubby leg peeking out from the nearly threadbare blanket. As if sensing her father's unease, she began to wriggle in Mary's arms, letting out a gurgled cry as she stretched out and retracted her limbs.

"What's the matter?" Mary inched toward him, bouncing the now fussy child, but keeping an eye on her husband, who remained at the door.

Robert licked his lips and leaned his forehead into the damp wood of their doorframe. There was little that he could do to redirect the ill winds that had found him that night. They were coming for them unless he did what they asked.

"We have to leave," he said suddenly. He pounded the edge of his fist on the doorframe just above his head and turned. "We'll go to Boston, like your aunt told us to."

Mary scoffed and then reined in a smile as Robert hurried past her. This was not going to be the family reunion she had been asking for. For months he had told her the journey was impossible, that their passage would cost too much and that jobs for the likes of him would be few. She had resigned to remain in London in their ramshackle tenement and hoped somehow they would eek out a living, with him working at the yards and she washing laundry at home. It earned them enough to see the baby fed, at the very least.

As Robert gathered their few belongings he could feel Mary's gaze bearing down on him. She made no attempt to set the baby down to help him. Instead, she stood at the only inside door to their home, questioning him. With an exaggerated exhale of breath, he hung his head low and closed his eyes. She and the baby deserved better than this, better than a late-night escape and hurried passage over the sea.

"I haven't the money to pay what I owe," he said suddenly. He peeked over his shoulder and saw his wife chewing on her lower lip. "And I haven't the strength to fight another match."

They had been married less than a year, the baby already well on the way before they took their vows. She was so young compared to him, and remained innocent in many ways. He'd never raise a hand to her, despite the instructions given to him by the fellows at the shipyard that a regular beating made wives docile. Only if administered from the beginning, they warned. He'd sworn to protect her from all things, but hadn't expected such a formidable foe and so soon.

"You promised me you'd never box again."

He nodded. "That I did. I mean to keep my promise."

Robert snatched a tin music box from a nearby shelf and began wrapping it in a faded cloth.

"They will accept nothing else? You pay or you fight, is that it?"

He avoided her gaze, licking his lips and shaking his head in disbelief. They had quarrelled on the subject many times and it never ended well. "I won't do it, Mary."

"You know they have been looking for her. They will find her eventually. You could erase your debt and save us the heartache."

"She is my sister!"

Mary ducked from the room, and returned having placed the baby in the laundry basket that served as her crib. "Was your sister," she said. "She's all but abandoned us now. You help her escape and then she just deserts us,

4

leaves us to fend for ourselves."

"We have managed." Robert couldn't help but give a slight growl.

"For how long?" She crossed her arms over her chest and glowered at him as he crisscrossed the room.

He stopped his frantic gathering suddenly and stood at his full height. Placing his hands in his pockets, he returned her gaze. "What you ask I cannot do," he said sternly.

Disbelief evident on her features, Mary stepped into the empty space between them. "You'd risk your own life, and mine, for the likes of her? After what she's done?"

"Mary, please—"

"If you won't do what's right for your family I will." With sudden determination, Mary snatched her shawl from the back of a nearby chair and crossed the room in three steps. She might have made it out the door if Robert hadn't placed himself between her and the exit.

"I cannot let you do that," he said. His face was inches from hers. "I took on the debt, not her."

Mary returned his stare with frustration. The silence between them lasted many seconds before a single tear trailed down the crest of Mary's cheek.

"We will find a way," he said softly, hoping a change in tone would calm her mood. He took his wife's face between his rough, workman's hands. Before he was able to kiss her a frantic knock erupted at their door.

They froze in place. Their baby's grunts from the other room morphed into fevered wails. Mary retreated to hush the child while Robert sidled to the door. He hoped the dim light of the room, two candles their only means of illumination, hid their presence.

"Open the door, Crandall," a manic voice called. "It's Jeremiah!"

Almost before Robert could unhook the latch, Jeremiah was pushing his way through. "I saw them leave," he said as he slammed the door shut behind him. "What in the devil are they after?"

The newly married couple exchanged glances, their expression revealing mutual apprehension. They had little enough money as it was; booking passage would require them to sell what precious belongings they had and would leave very little for a new life in America. Staying in London would only mean a much more confined space—six feet under—for all three of them.

"We are leaving for America." Robert locked the door again, but this time he positioned a small table in front of it.

"It cannot be so bad," Jeremiah said, his own tone quick and anxious.

"I haven't enough money to settle my debt and I cannot get back in the ring either."

Mary returned, bouncing the child slightly in her arms. She avoided looking at the men but that didn't stop her from expressing her disapproval.

"How much do ye owe?"

"Twenty pounds and then some."

Mary gasped. "Goodness gracious, Robert Alexander Crandall!"

Jeremiah turned his gaze and ran his hands through his hair. "A mighty sum."

"An impossible sum." Robert felt the panic rise in his chest. "I just don't understand. I had arranged payments, but they always said I was good, you know? Like there was no need to hurry." Robert balled his hands into fists. "I should have insisted when I had the money. But the baby, you see..?" Angered with himself, Robert turned from his friend and his wife and cursed.

Mary gently clutched the back of her baby's head and peered over the soft wisps of hair at her husband's friend. "Tell me this, Jeremiah, what sort of man risks the lives of his wife and child to protect the whereabouts of a known murderer?" Mary sneered at her husband.

"I haven't any choice," Robert snapped. "We must go to Boston."

"Ye do have choices, Robert Crandall. Tell them where she lives and be done with it."

"I will not turn on my sister!" He pounded a hand into the table that separated him from his new wife. Even in the dim light Robert saw his young wife blanch and clutch their baby closer to her bosom.

Jeremiah turned to Robert. "Is it true? They asked for

Julia?"

Robert licked his lips. "Mary seems to think I can have my debt forgiven if I tell them where to find her." He scrunched up his face in an attempt to stave off tears. He raised his hands to his face to hide them from his wife. "I cannot do it, Jeremiah. I will not do it. I swore I would protect her."

"To say nothing of you protecting yer own family," Mary said from across the room.

"Oh, shut up, woman!" Robert snapped, before turning back to his friend.

"I'll tell ye," Jeremiah began, "this is Thaddeus ye are talking about. If they've come fer the debt, it's because they know, Robert. They know what you've been hiding. If you tell them you've known this whole time, what do you think they'll do?"

Robert looked to his wife and child, terrified.

"Even if you don't say a word, they'll find her and when they are done with her they'll come fer you next."

"Their argument is with her. We should have none of it."

"Leave us be, Mary. Let a man think!" Robert waved his wife away and turned from her, sickened that she would suggest he hand over his only living relative to the likes of Thaddeus.

Mary's expression soured further, but she did not leave.

"I have to warn her." Robert went for his jacket.

"Robert, no."

He stopped and put a hand to his face. "Mary's right. I can't risk going to her myself. They're probably in the streets now just waiting for me to leave. I'd just end up taking them right to her."

"I'll go," Jeremiah said without hesitation.

Robert shook his head.

"I'll be back before daybreak," Jeremiah said. "Where is she?"

Robert hesitated, heaving a breath that only weighed down his shoulders more. It had been nearly a year since he last saw her and it had been a great relief to think of her far on the other side of London, protected by her place amongst other uniformed servants.

"She has a good place in a noble house in Belgravia." He crossed the room to the cupboard and pulled a glass jar from its dusty corner. "She has protection. The master's son—"

Mary scoffed as Robert placed the jar on the table. "The same protection Mr. Alderson offered my mother, is it?"

"Mary, please." From the jar Robert pulled out a small wad of faded cloth with a lead figure, molded into the shape of Saint Christopher, wrapped in its folds. "Marshall is the family name. Give her this and she will know it's from me."

Jeremiah twisted the small, slender shape in his two fingers as he eyed it.

"We'll take the first boat the day after tomorrow. If she wants to come with us she'll have to meet us—"

"We can barely afford our own passage!"

"Hush!" Robert was quickly losing his patience. With the weight of the world bearing down on him he wished he had the support of his wife.

"Should I tell her why you are leaving?" Jeremiah asked, stuffing the figure into his pocket.

Robert nodded reluctantly. "She knows who they are. She knows them better than I."

Together they moved the table that barred the door. Jeremiah nodded toward Mary as he pulled the door open just enough to slide through to the hallway. With his friend gone, the quick footfalls down the hall signalling his departure, Robert latched the door and replaced the table in front of it. When he turned to his wife he saw her crying openly, scared for the fate of her tiny child, who had done nothing to deserve such a harried existence.

"We will be all right, Mary," Robert said, heaving a gentle sigh and running a hand over his face. "They won't care enough to follow us across the ocean."

Chapter 1

The wailing reached Ainsley in his dreams first before his consciousness willed him awake. He was out of bed and pulling on his trousers before he'd even been able to fully open his eyes. He glanced to Julia, his sister's lady's maid, who slipped out of the bed on the opposite side.

"It's all right," she said. "Go to him."

All manner of scenario ran through Ainsley's head as he charged down the dark hallway to his father's room. Since the attack, Lord Marshall suffered greatly not only from physical ailments but mental ones as well. He awoke frequently throughout the night, attempting to call out but unable to form the words or even ring the bell rope that hung at the side of his bed.

Once he opened the door, Ainsley saw his father lying perpendicular on the bed, his lower limbs dangling over the edge, his sheets and bedclothes twisted awkwardly. His father moaned in panic.

"Father!" Ainsley came to his side. "Father, it's all right."

Lord Marshall looked up at his son, eyes wide with recognition, his face twisted from his attempts to call for help.

"I'm here," Ainsley said as he pulled his father's limp body toward him. "Lean on me. There you go."

With a grunt and few quick breaths, Ainsley was able to pull his father back into the cushion of the mattress before systematically positioning one leg and then the other in the correct position.

Lord Marshall moaned and began patting at his son's face as Ainsley righted the bedclothes. It was then that Maxwell, the family's butler, appeared, dishevelled and clearly suffering from lack of sleep, much the same as everyone living at Marshall House.

"I'm sorry, sir," Maxwell said, entering the room and placing his oil lantern on the bedside table.

Ainsley shook his head, unwilling to accept any apologies, as none were necessary. The family had endured two weeks of such nights, and worse days, with each person taking up the care of the family's patriarch as required. Everyone was stretched and needing respite. But aside from their new full-time nurse, the staff was short three bodies, including a second footman and two housemaids. The last housemaid to leave was sacked. It was suspected she had been selling information about Lord Marshall's condition to the press.

"What does he require, sir?" Maxwell came alongside the bed and leaned in.

Lord Marshall's eyes darted between the butler and his son, but the soft, subtle trembling in his lips did not cease.

"I'm not sure," Ainsley said, surveying the immediate area around the bed. He lit a few more lanterns and soon the room was bathed in a soft, amber light.

"I will sit with him some more, sir," Maxwell said, repositioning a chair at the bedside.

"No, no," Ainsley answered quickly, adjusting his father's blankets so none of the wrinkles or folds would bother him. "I will read to him some more. He seems to like it."

Ainsley picked up a hardcover he had set aside from the evening before. Other than his work at the hospital, Ainsley seemed to do nothing else but read to his father, an activity that calmed them both while dealing with their present circumstances. All his other interests—drinking, boxing, and gambling—were now a thing of the past. His family needed him more than ever and he needed a clear mind to do it.

Julia appeared at the door then, clutching her housecoat close around her. She paused at the door and looked on with sympathy. "Shall I fetch some tea for you, sir?" she asked.

Ainsley shook his head.

"Where have you come from?" Maxwell asked.

Julia tucked a loose tendril of hair around her ear. "From bed. Same as you, I imagine."

Ainsley smiled, and was glad for the near darkness

that hid his amusement.

"Don't be cheeky," Maxwell snapped, "certainly not in front of His Lordship and his son."

Ainsley watched as Julia's light expression evaporated.

"Forgive me, sir," she said quickly.

No one in the house knew how close Julia and Ainsley were. His sister, Margaret, had guessed not long ago that they were involved, but Ainsley was sure she did not know to what extent. Julia and he had spent many months hiding passionate kisses and meeting late at night for moonlight trysts. He found himself longing to be with her when the harsh reality of his life overwhelmed him. She was his light amongst the dark.

"It's all right, Maxwell. Everyone is just tired," Ainsley said. "You should both return to bed. There will be plenty to do in the morning."

Julia gave Ainsley a mournful nod and retreated back into the darkened hall. Maxwell, however, lingered a moment more before finally agreeing to Ainsley's order. "If you need anything, sir, I can be summoned easily."

"Promise me you will sleep," Ainsley said, slipping into the chair beside his father's bed.

Maxwell bowed, which looked far less dignified in a nightcap and night-robe than it did while he was in a pressed uniform, before quitting the room.

Ainsley offered his father a soft smile. "You see? They squabble when you are not well. All the more reason to get you back on your feet." He squeezed his father's hand before settling back into the chair and opening the book to where they had left off.

There hadn't always been an affinity between them. There was a time when Ainsley would have held no sympathy for the man. A brutal father with exacting standards, Lord Marshall had ruled his family and his fortune with regimentation. Father and son hardly ever saw eye to eye, a reality that had kept them apart for years. As the second son, Ainsley was pleased to allow his older brother, Daniel, to sidle up to their father, as he was the one destined to be head of the family and purveyor of the family purse.

Ainsley himself had no interest in such a fate and

chose to attend an unorthodox university instead against his father's wishes. In fact, his pursuit of meaningful work in medicine caused such an uproar that Ainsley agreed to use his mother's maiden name throughout his studies so as not to tarnish their status amongst the peerage. Lord Marshall had never been pleased with the arrangement, but now that he could only form a few words at most, his protests had died off considerably. Their present circumstances did nothing to dissolve Ainsley's guilt, however. Daily he wrestled with the idea of leaving his chosen profession, if only to be more available to his sister, Margaret, who struggled with their father's needs for care.

Ainsley was jolted from sleep and found himself still in the chair next to his father's bed, the book laying open and face down on his chest as the morning sun streamed in through a slit in the long, heavy drapes. He rubbed his eyes and focused his gaze on his father, who slept soundly in the middle of his bed, undisturbed since the late-night commotion.

Just as he walked out the door to the hall, Margaret appeared. Her eyes barely lifted from the carpet as she hugged a small mound of folded blankets to her chest.

"Good morning, brother," she said.

When their eyes met Ainsley saw how dark and swollen they had become. Her bountiful brown curls were usually arranged neatly but lately she looked as if she had styled it in a rush, allowing the pins to become loose. That day she looked worse than the ones before. Her entire demeanour had changed since their father had returned home from his trip. No longer was she willing to joke with Ainsley and, as the days progressed, she seemed less and less interested in anything beyond their home.

She tried to slip by him, but he stopped her by placing a gentle hand on her shoulder.

"He's sleeping," he said quietly.

Margaret turned slightly to release her shoulder and continued to head into their father's room. Ainsley turned in place and watched from the door as she circled the bed, all the while looking at her father, who slept soundly.

"We really should get someone to help you," he

suggested, careful to keep his voice low. "You cannot keep such vigils all on your own."

Margaret's eyes lifted. "I can manage."

Ainsley slipped both his hands into his pockets. He hated to see her this way. It was not her usual self at all. They all had taken a vested interest in their patriarch, but Margaret seemed obsessed with his care. She was reluctant to let anyone else see to him, even the staff who had catered to his whims for many years.

"Have a good day at the hospital, Peter," she said.

Ainsley watched as she turned and placed the folded blankets on the seat near the window. She kept her back to him for many minutes, a signal that she would say no more.

Ainsley found himself nodding as he walked toward his room at the end of the hall. Such were their lives at Marshall House at present. So much had changed and yet none of it seemed to surprise him. His father, who had been a formidable presence, had been reduced to a mere shell, unable to communicate in the most basic of methods. He was like a stranger to them all, a stranger who required nearly constant care and patience. Despite the demands on them, no one was willing to complain, not openly. After weeks of burdensome work, they all bore the look of exhaustion, but no respite formed on the horizon. With scarcely any improvement in his condition since his return, it grew clearer each day that the father they once knew would not be returning.

Ainsley dressed for work with these thoughts on his mind. He could not expect his sister to continue as she had. He himself could barely muster the strength to face another sleepless night or harrowing setback, though he would certainly try. How much longer would his father linger in such a state?

He took the rounded stairs to the foyer slowly, adjusting his cufflinks as he walked. Movement outside the front door caught his eye. As he passed the long, narrow window, he saw his brother, Daniel, standing outside under the portico.

"Is breakfast being served out here?" Ainsley asked, poking his head through the door.

Daniel didn't bother to generate a smile. He glanced to Ainsley and then returned his stare down the street. When Ainsley stepped out he saw a small crowd of people gathered about four houses down. A single constable stood on guard, trying to keep the onlookers at bay. Ainsley craned his neck around a cement column before he saw a peculiar shape at the gathering's centre. A man, not moving.

He was down the steps before his brother could say anything. As he neared the handful of people he could hear the gasps and murmurs grow louder. Once he was five paces from the scene his suspicion was confirmed when he saw a slim, crimson slash along the man's throat. For a moment, Ainsley stood transfixed, as if he were just another passerby.

The man had been tied to the lamppost, his hands bound in front of him, tied at the wrists, while his feet were separated and tied to the post a few inches from the ground. His shirt was marked with copious amounts of blood that had run down from the wound at his neck. His hair looked as if it had been cut off in haste; nicks in his scalp told Ainsley it had been done with a knife, most likely the same one that had been used on the man's throat.

A woman came alongside him and gasped before turning her head into the chest of her male companion.

After a moment of observation, Ainsley turned to look at their surroundings and saw Julia walking down the street toward them. She carried a large, willow basket laden with items from the nearby bakery. She smiled toward him before he could say anything and then her head turned and she saw the body.

She dropped the basket and took a step back in fright, covering her mouth with her hand and grabbing for Ainsley's arm. "Goodness mercy!" she said, turning away.

Ainsley rubbed her arm in an effort to comfort her, but soon stopped when he realized his brother was still looking at them from the front of Marshall House. Ainsley turned to the bobby, who stood a foot from the dead man. The constable looked far too young to be a member of the force. He regarded the crowd with the stern determination of a hall boy at school.

Ainsley stepped forward to get a closer look but the hall boy pressed back on his chest. "I cannot let you pass, sir," he said with notable uncertainty.

"I'm the morgue surgeon at St. Thomas," Ainsley said quietly so his neighbours would not hear. "Inspector Simms sent word that I was to meet him here." Ainsley blanched at his own lie, and immediately questioned why he had said it. He hadn't worked a case with Inspector Simms at the Yard for over two months and he had no such arrangement, standing or otherwise.

The hall boy looked uncertain and his gaze kept darting to the pavement.

"May I?" Ainsley inched forward and pointed to the body. After a moment of thought, the constable gave a slight nod and Ainsley wasted no time. He inspected the ground quickly before positioning himself right in front of the dead man.

The man's eyes were closed and his head was slouched to the side like an unattended marionette. His bowler hat was held to his chest by the weight of his arms in front of him. The rope used to bind him to the lamppost was as thick as a man's thumb and was fastened in such a way it would take many minutes to unravel it.

Without thought, Ainsley's hand went up to the wound at the man's throat. The cut had been made quickly, but the knife caught on the flesh twice.

Ainsley held the man's chin to turn his head to the side. Something silver in the man's mouth caught his eye. Easing in closer, Ainsley saw what looked like a tiny, round lead ball, but when he lifted his hand to pull it out a familiar voice reached him from the street.

"I said secure the scene, Robertson!" Inspector Simms charged across the street from the police carriage and began pushing the onlookers further away from the scene.

Ainsley pulled his hand away from the corpse and slipped whatever the metal thing was into his trouser pocket. When he turned, Inspector Simms was glaring at him from two paces away.

"My apologies, Inspector," Ainsley said instantly. "Old habits."

Simms said nothing as Ainsley stepped away. He saw

Julia waiting for him near the iron fence down the street and headed straight for her.

From behind him, Ainsley could hear Simms barking orders to other officers who had shown up, and quickly the scene was cordoned off. Ainsley plucked the dropped basket from the pavement and passed it to Julia as they headed back to Marshall House.

Daniel was still under the portico when they approached, smoking a slim cigar. He twisted his mouth in thought. "Perhaps Father would be more comfortable at The Briar," he said, keeping an eye on the ruckus further down the road. The Briar was their country estate near Tunbridge Wells, where their mother resided while she lived. "This neighbourhood will soon be like all the rest." He brought his cigar to his mouth and inhaled.

"Repairs won't be finished for another month," Ainsley reminded him as he walked up the three steps to their front door

Julia turned to head down the servants' stairs that led to the kitchen in the basement. Ainsley's heart lurched when he saw this, but he couldn't stop her, not when his brother was standing over him. After a moment, Ainsley realized he had been watching her far longer than appropriate. He snapped his attention back to his brother and hoped he hadn't noticed. "The roof needed to be completely replaced and much of the plaster inside as well. These are not quick repairs."

Daniel huffed. "The expense, brother," he said with a snarl. "I am only interested in the expense."

"You'll be glad of it in time," Ainsley said. "The house wasn't worth much of anything in that state."

A smile tickled the edges of Daniel's mouth as he surveyed his cigar. "And now with Aunt Louisa and her little...*gems* taking it over it won't be worth much to us at all."

Weeks before, it had been decided that Aunt Louisa and her three boys, recently returned from long residence in India, would stay at The Briar once it was made habitable again. For now they would stay at Marshall House. Nathaniel, her nearly grown son, was more than pleased at the prospect of a prolonged stay in the city.

However, his younger brothers, George and Hubert, who were eight and ten respectively, seemed stifled by the close confines on the Belgravia house and its miniscule yard. To compensate, they spent their days tormenting the servants and running circles around their governess. Aunt Louisa seemed blind to her sons' misdeeds and did very little to correct them.

"We'll stay. For Abraham, you see," Aunt Louisa had said, convinced her presence would help her brother recover from his condition. She pictured herself as a mother to them all, despite the fact that Daniel was now married and Margaret and Peter were completely grown.

It was no secret that Daniel hated the idea of Aunt Louisa taking over their country property, the place where all three of them grew up. He had said once he'd like it sold, but retracted his statement once he saw how much the idea distressed Margaret. She still viewed the property with childlike ideation, something that couldn't be tarnished no matter how many tragedies took place there. Ainsley, however, knew since their mother's death and after their recent misadventure that he and Margaret wouldn't be returning anytime soon.

"It's not like I can take Evelyn there from time to time, could I?" Daniel continued. "And we're still expected to carry the expense."

"Aunt Louisa has nowhere else to go," Ainsley reminded him.

"She can go back to her husband," Daniel answered sharply.

The frustration Ainsley felt for his brother had not improved much over time. Daniel was so much like their father, demanding to the point of cruelty. The fact that Daniel was not actually Lord Marshall's son, but rather the result of a premarital affair their mother had had, still perplexed Ainsley. If anyone should resemble their father, it should be himself, given that they shared a direct bloodline. While Ainsley loathed their father, or at least the memory of the man he once was, Daniel revered him and held him up on the highest pedestal. His brother did not know that he was not Lord Marshall's son. Many months ago Margaret and Peter had decided they were not going to tell him. It was better that way. Daniel could continue to believe he was the direct line of the Marshall name and Ainsley could pursue his career as a surgeon without further expectations to complicate the issue.

Ainsley heaved a heavy-hearted sigh and shook his head at his brother's remark. He had learned not to expect empathy from him because he was disappointed every time. "I have work to do at the hospital." Ainsley forced a smile. "Good to see you again, brother," he said as he passed Daniel and went for the front door.

The door swung open before Ainsley touched the knob, and he realized Maxwell had been standing there waiting for some time.

"I thought you stopped all that nonsense," Daniel said, turning to look at Ainsley in the doorway. When their eyes met Daniel nodded toward the ruckus down the road. "I'd thought you come around for your family's sake." He scraped the top of his cigar on the railing.

Maxwell's gloved hand appeared, his palm upturned as Daniel dropped the cigar end into it. Maxwell closed his fist around it and stepped out of Ainsley's way.

It was all nonsense to Ainsley, who felt the duties of their servants were excessive. Despite footmen to help him dress and coachmen to take him places, Ainsley discovered early on how much freedom he enjoyed when he did things on his own. His brother reveled in the constant attention and most likely could not fathom a life to which one was not completely catered.

"I thought you'd stopped all the nonsense too," Ainsley said.

Daniel returned his comment with a look of bewilderment, but Ainsley was in no mood to continue the conversation. He walked past Maxwell and went for the dining room. He had to be at the hospital shortly and he'd need to start walking soon if he were to get there on time.

Chapter 2

Aunt Louisa was already seated at the breakfast table, a copy of the morning edition of the Daily Telegraph and Courier in her hands. "Good morning, darling," she said, placing her paper to the side. "Another day, another salacious detail regarding Abraham."

"What have they printed now?" he asked, taking a seat opposite his aunt.

Aunt Louisa tried to wave him off, but the look on her face betrayed her worry. "'Tis nothing. I just hate to see the family made into such a mockery for others to jeer at. You'd believe he was an exhibit at the circus the way they talk of him."

Ainsley pulled the paper up and eyed the social pages. "Doctors Bent and Davidson are at a loss to diagnose Lord Marshall's ailment as it does not resemble true apoplexy and appears to be more related to old age than a specific affliction," he read.

"See what I mean? Rubbish."

"Lord Marshall is attended day and night by family members who are further aided by a dedicated nurse and a team of medical doctors who visit the Marshalls' London home on a daily basis." Ainsley tossed the paper aside. "Goodness. It's as if journalists are following our every move."

Aunt Louisa brushed back a curl from her forehead. "I have it in mind to bring a libel suit on that chambermaid, whatever her name was."

"Lisle," Ainsley offered, remembering the girl they had released from their employ not a week prior.

"Yes, that's the one. How dare she sell our secrets to the papers? As if we didn't have enough occupying our thoughts." She huffed and picked up her teacup.

"She's gone now and soon they will have no more to write about."

Aunt Louisa took a sip of tea. "I don't even want to

know what is happening down the street," she said. "Sometimes I fear London is too much for me."

"I'm sure you'll read of it in the papers before long," Ainsley explained.

His aunt was not as aloof as she pretended. She made it a point to know what was going on in all corners of the city, but feigned ignorance whenever a subject came up. Ainsley had caught her a few times offering her informed opinion, but he never held it against her. It was all an act, played out for the benefit of *good society*, which expected women to sit and chat about nonsense, never expecting to touch on any topics of real interest. Margaret also hated the charade and was an admittedly terrible player.

Ainsley waved Cutter, their footman, away and poured his own tea before selecting the few bites he would eat from the plates in front of them.

"My son was looking for you," she said as Ainsley began spreading jam on his biscuit.

"Which one?" he asked.

"Nathaniel, of course. He said he had discovered an interesting place with some friends last evening and he is very keen to show you."

Ainsley raised an eyebrow.

"He wouldn't elaborate, you understand. Certain things a mother is not supposed to know."

Ainsley ate his breakfast quickly and then stood up from his chair.

"Finished so soon?"

"My apologies, Aunt Louisa. I must head to work."

Aunt Louisa sighed and shook her head. "A house full of bodies and no one to dine with."

Ainsley turned to Cutter. "Make sure Margaret receives a plate in Father's room," he said before heading for the hall.

As Ainsley left for work, the body of the man was being loaded into the back of the police carriage. Simms was standing on the sidewalk speaking to Mr. Talbot, the owner and resident of the nearby house. Ainsley had met Mr. Talbot and his wife at some long-forgotten ball. It was Margaret who was far better acquainted with the family thanks to her friendship with Mr. Talbot's daughter, Winifred. Ainsley was acquainted with Miss Winifred as well, though it was a relationship he now greatly regretted.

Ainsley skirted the scene and crossed the street. Curiosity brought him alongside the police carriage, where he saw Sergeant Cooper, whom he recognized from an earlier case.

"Tough case, that," he said casually to Cooper.

"Yeah," Cooper said as he hopped down the carriage steps to the pavement. "You working this one for us then?" he asked, dabbing beads of sweat from his forehead with a handkerchief.

Ainsley fidgeted with the lead figure in his pocket as he looked into the back of the carriage. The body had been covered with a sheet. He didn't wish to lie outright, but there was nothing wrong with leading them back toward him. "It's being brought to St. Thomas then?"

Cooper shrugged. "We'll have it there before ten." He pointed his thumb over his shoulder. "We'll leave when he's done his dithering." The sergeant laughed at his disparaging remark. Simms was many things, a ditherer was not one of them.

Ainsley glanced up. "In this heat, you'd be better off taking him there now."

Cooper looked up to the heavens, squinting against the direct summer sun. It was barely nine o'clock and the temperature was rising rapidly. London had been sweltering under a relentlessly dry few weeks, a phenomenon that had everyone asking when the rains would return. A few wondered if they ever would.

Ainsley stepped closer and lowered his voice. "Once a person passes away their internal organs begin a process of bloating. The intestinal gases—"

Cooper's face began to contort as Ainsley spoke. "All right, all right. I'll take him there myself." He began walking toward the front of the carriage. "Care to join me?" he asked.

Ainsley looked past the horses to Simms, who was scribbling hurriedly in his notebook. "Yes," Ainsley answered. "Then I can get started right away."

He smiled at his own cleverness and ignored the

nagging guilt that found him by the time the carriage reached Westminster Bridge. He would have a little less than an hour with the body before Simms noticed it had been directed to the wrong place—and then what? Simms would undoubtedly come looking for it. He'd have to be quick to ensure the extraction of as many details as possible.

When the carriage pulled up outside St. Thomas, Ainsley hopped down and went straight for the back door of the carriage. He didn't bother waiting for a porter and together he and Sergeant Cooper brought the body down to the basement.

Luckily, the autopsy table was empty and they were able to deposit the man there straightaway. Barely in the room for two minutes, Sergeant Cooper covered his nose at the smell. Ainsley was quick to pull a pack of cigarettes from a nearby shelf. He removed one and lit it. He offered the pack to Cooper. "Helps with the smell," he explained.

Cooper nodded and took one. After it was lit he waved the smoking end under his nostrils and breathed deeply. "How can you stand it, doctor?"

"It's not usually this wretched." Ainsley turned to take his leather apron from the hook near the sink. "It's this weather, you see. Even down here it gets quite warm."

"Is it cooking them?" Cooper asked, daring to look under the sheet at a nearby table. At least twenty corpses lay in even rows about the room, awaiting their turn with the surgeon. Only after Ainsley examined them could he issue a death certificate and hopefully some peace for their grieving families.

"Not cooking them," Ainsley answered, hurriedly readying his tools. "At this time of year the decomposition process is accelerated. Our job goes much smoother if we can keep the ambient temperature low. It allows us more time, you see."

With his tools ready, Ainsley turned to his subject and pulled back the sheet. The man's arms were still bound in front of him and his hat remained wedged between his forearms and his body. The cut at his throat was clearly visible now that the corpse was reclined.

Cooper edged away from the autopsy table. Intrigued

by Ainsley's work, he slipped into one of the aisles and walked toward a cloaked body.

"I wouldn't go over there—" Ainsley cringed at the sticky sound of Cooper's shoe touching a pool of bile and coagulated blood that had spilt on the floor.

"Ah, God!" Cooper retreated quickly to the main aisle. "I'll leave you to it then, doctor," he said, backing toward the door. "Send word once you know anything about our man, yeah?"

"Wash your hands," Ainsley called without looking up from the body. "There's some carbolic soap next to the sink in the closet down the hall."

Cooper waved his thanks as he pushed through the doors that led from the room. Ainsley smiled. The antics of laymen in the morgue never ceased to amuse him.

With the cigarette perched in his mouth, Ainsley leaned over the body. With his tweezers, he pulled back the severed skin at the throat to have a closer look at the damage done beyond the dermis. He could hear the familiar *tick tick tick* of his pocket watch, which only became more exaggerated as time went on. Any minute Simms would come bursting through that door, demanding the return of his dead man, and Ainsley would be forced to comply.

The throat wound was delivered by a dull blade, which left tear marks, and didn't pierce too far into the neck. The damage was enough, though, to end the man's life, but it would have been far from instant. A major artery was severed entirely while another had only been nicked. Ainsley pulled away and surveyed the man's shirt and coat. He ran his hand along the dark linen fabric and felt the blood that had gushed from his wound and dried. Ainsley scrunched up the fabric in his fist. It felt far too malleable to have soaked up all the blood. The fibers would be stiff and rigid if all the blood from his wound had collected there.

Ainsley closed his eyes and recalled the scene. The pavement hadn't a drop of blood on it. He turned his attention to the coarse rope that held the man's hands together. Pulling a magnifying glass from the cache of tools behind him, Ainsley leaned in close. The rope was clean.

He stood up and leaned into the table with his fists.

Either the majority of the blood gushed forward or he was held from behind as he bled out.

The door to the morgue opened violently, slamming into a nearby table. Ainsley paused and readied himself for a confrontation with Simms. When he turned he saw a middle-aged woman standing just inside the doors. Her hands shook as she placed her handkerchief over her mouth and nose.

A porter ran in just behind her and grabbed her arm. "I'm sorry, sir," he said. "She got past me."

The woman, who had red hair and a pale complexion, sobbed openly. She hid her face with her handkerchief while the other clutched a pendant dangling at her neck. The porter began tugging at her, trying to convince her to leave. Ainsley raised a hand to stop him and began walking down the main aisle toward them.

"I'm sorry," she said, her mouth twisted in emotional agony. She kept her gaze on Ainsley as he walked toward her. "He wouldn't let me in." Her eyes darted past Ainsley and scanned the room, a glint of apprehension in her eyes.

"What is it?" Ainsley asked. "What are you looking for?"

"My daughter has been missing for three days," she said, lowering her handkerchief briefly.

Ainsley nodded and waved the porter away. "It's all right, Sam," he said. "I can take it from here."

Sam clenched his jaw and finally nodded before turning to leave.

"Oh, what a god-awful smell," she said. She closed her eyes as if to steel herself against the stench. If she were a man, Ainsley would have offered her a cigarette as well.

"How old is your daughter?" Ainsley asked.

"Fourteen this September," the woman said, her words laced with pride. "She works as a scullery maid in Clerkenwell. She's a good girl, she is. A proper girl."

Ainsley smiled. "Perhaps you'd like to wait outside the doors while I look."

"If it's all the same, I'd like to see for myself. I've enquired at all the other hospitals. No one has her. I thought... maybe."

He nodded. "Yes, ma'am. I'll see what I can find. Can I

ask your name?"

"Mrs. Adelaide Wagner."

Systematically, Ainsley went from table to table checking the papers provided for each corpse, pulling back the sheets of those without paperwork. As he searched, Mrs. Wagner wandered up and down the main aisle, all the while giving a detailed description of her daughter. "Red hair like my own, though not as curly," she said. "She had a sprinkling of freckles, on her nose mostly, with a few on her cheeks. They move when she smiles."

Ainsley's heart lurched at the last detail. If her daughter was in the morgue such a description would only remain a memory. After a good half hour, Ainsley had looked under every sheet but found no one who even closely matched Mrs. Wagner's daughter's description.

"She's not here, ma'am—" When he looked up Mrs. Wagner was standing at his examination table, enthralled by the body he had just been working with. Her eyes raised when she realized Ainsley was watching her.

"Poor fellow," she said, sniffling. She raised her handkerchief to her nose again. "I'll never understand what brings men to do such things to others. I only hope my daughter does not share his fate." Overwhelmed at the thought, Mrs. Wagner cried openly. "Thank you for taking the time to look."

Ainsley followed her out the door and after a few steps he guided her to a row of chairs along the wall. She sat down without a word and buried her face in her hands.

There was a time when he wouldn't have wanted so much contact with a family member of the deceased. When he had begun his position at St. Thomas he'd avoided any such interaction and went to great lengths to ensure he never saw the other side of a cadaver's existence. It was a habit gained from medical school. A calm detachment served all the medical students well, especially when there were concerns about the origins of their specimen. It was often better not to ask.

The last year, however, had softened him considerably. Starting with the death of his own mother the previous Christmas, Ainsley realized that death could not be isolated. To understand the death he needed to understand the life lived. It was becoming an obsession. He needed to know how, but most of all why.

"Are there any family members who can help you?" he asked after a time.

Mrs. Wagner nodded as she pulled the handkerchief away from her face. "Yes. I have a son, who is more dear to me than anything. He takes good care of my daughter and me. He's all we have left." She sniffled into her handkerchief. "I had another son," she explained. "But he was murdered."

And that was when Ainsley realized why she had come to the morgue so soon, assuming her daughter had met with a similar end.

"I just don't know what to do. No one will help me. Even the police have thrown up their hands." She closed her eyes and bowed her head.

Ainsley looked down the hall to his superior's office. The door was closed, but he knew Dr. Crawford was inside. "Will you wait right here a moment?" Ainsley asked. "I'll go ask my supervisor."

Mrs. Wagner's gaze followed him as he stood and walked the length of the hall. He hadn't said many words to Dr. Crawford in recent weeks. It was enough to know his old position had remained vacant and that Dr. Crawford voiced no objections to his return.

"Come in."

Ainsley pushed his way through. Dr. Crawford sat behind his desk, a sour expression the only acknowledgement of Ainsley's intrusion. The seasoned surgeon, once commanding and unforgiving, had turned to the drink to drown out the sorrows that seemed destined to plague him during his final years at the hospital. It wasn't entirely Dr. Crawford's fault—Ainsley knew this—but that did not garner any sympathy from the Board of Governors. Crawford's demeanor toward Ainsley was neutral at best and that was about as much as Ainsley could hope for, given the circumstances.

"What is it?"

"There is a woman here searching for a missing fourteen-year-old." Ainsley watched as Crawford remained still. "It's her daughter, sir."

Pressing his lips together, Crawford turned in his chair and quickly thumbed through a dossier. "There's no unidentified woman that young," he said.

"Perhaps her age was misidentified." Ainsley stepped forward.

Crawford looked unimpressed by Ainsley's insistence. "You have a look then," he said, slapping the file on Ainsley's chest. "But get out of my office."

Ainsley fumbled as some of the papers tried to slide from the folder. "Thank you, sir," he said as he turned. Dr. Crawford was waving at Ainsley dismissively with one hand and reaching for a half-drunk bottle of scotch with the other when Ainsley closed the door behind him.

The hallway was empty and the woman was gone. The chair where she had sat remained uniform among the others as if it had never been disturbed. "Mrs. Wagner?"

Ainsley's throat went dry. Had he only imagined her? He was no stranger to unearthly visits, though none of them had lasted so long. He spied Sam at a doorway at the end of the hall and hurried toward him.

Sam turned as Ainsley neared him, revealing a large bundle of soiled and stained sheets destined for the laundry at the other end of the hospital basement. Sam hoisted the heavy bundle onto his shoulder with a grunt.

"Did you see Mrs. Wagner leave?" Ainsley asked, as he pulled himself to the wall to allow Sam room to walk by.

"No, sir," Sam said. "Last I saw her she was with you." Sam took two steps before turning to face Ainsley. "Funny woman, that. She didn't want me to check Dr. Crawford's files. Said she wanted to see for herself."

Ainsley glanced to the files still anchored at his chest. He nodded absentmindedly and thanked Sam for his help.

"Where is he?" The unmistakable voice of Inspector Simms boomed down the hall. Ainsley took a deep breath and steeled himself against Simms's wrath. He ducked into the morgue and was halfway down the aisle to the examination table when Simms burst through the door.

"Where is he?" he repeated more sternly.

Two constables circled around Simms and charged down the aisle. Ainsley backed away and was surprised when they flew past him to the examination table. They wrapped the body in the sheet once again and positioned themselves at the head and feet to carry him from the room.

"Inspector Simms," Ainsley said and hurried toward the detective before he had a chance to leave. "I took the liberty of—"

Simms rounded on him and forced him back into one of the tables. "You are always taking liberties, aren't you?" he charged, his nose merely inches from Ainsley's own. "I have no room in my work for men like you."

"Men like me?"

"Yes!" Simms scowled. "I warned you, now don't force me to make good on my promise." He poked Ainsley hard on the chest with his pointed finger, his expression revealing his wish to do far worse. "If I see you within ten yards of another crime scene I will see you are properly charged. Have I made myself clear?"

"But Simms, I think—"

Simms shoved Ainsley then, sending him back into the occupied table and further into the space beside it. The corner jabbed Ainsley in the kidney as he stumbled backward. The file and the papers it held spilled out onto the floor. "I don't give a damn what you think. Not anymore!" Simms bellowed, towering over him.

Ainsley's fists tightened at his side as he leaned into the table. If they were going to have it out, fist to fist, then Ainsley would not back down, though he really hoped it wouldn't come to that.

The door opened again and Ainsley expected to see one of the constables returning. Both he and Simms were surprised to see Julia standing there. Simms adjusted his jacket on his shoulders. He heaved a breath and looked to Ainsley.

"Don't let your arrogance hinder your common sense, Dr. Ainsley," Simms said, plucking his hat from the ground and brushing off the dust. "You don't work for me anymore." He turned for the door and nodded at Julia. "Miss Kemp."

"Inspector Simms." Julia bit her lip as the detective passed her and walked out the door.

Ainsley leaned into the table a moment longer to catch his breath. He deserved every ounce of disdain Simms dealt him. There was no excuse for what Ainsley had done and he didn't dare justify it.

"I wish you'd tell me what happened between the two of you," Julia said, stepping toward him. "You used to work so well together."

Ainsley straightened his stance and felt a stab of pain in his left flank. He rubbed his backside and knew he'd develop a bruise. "Just posturing," he said dismissively. "Simms doesn't work well with others."

As Julia stepped toward him Ainsley glanced to the door, making sure they were alone, before leaning in to plant a kiss on the crest of her cheek. When he pulled away, breathing in the scent of her, he saw a budding smile on her lips.

"You should visit me more often," he said, bending over to pull the dossier and scattered papers from the floor. "But I have a feeling you have not come merely for a kiss." He winced as he began to walk down the main aisle toward his tools and now-empty examination table. He slapped the file down next to his tools.

"Ms. Katherine didn't show up this morning," Julia said, following him.

That was the third nurse they'd lost in as many weeks.

"Lady Margaret didn't wish me to bother you, but I came anyway."

As Ainsley washed his hands, he sensed Julia coming up along beside him. "Who is with Father now?" he asked, reaching for the towel.

"Lady Margaret, of course."

He circled the examination table, all the while aware of how Julia's eyes followed him.

"She does not sleep," Julia continued. "I have scarcely seen her eat more than a thimbleful of anything in the last three days. I am worried for her and I think you should be too."

"Has she asked you to tell me these things?" Ainsley asked.

"No, of course not."

"We must tread carefully," Ainsley said, reclaiming the file folder. "I promised Margaret I wouldn't jeopardize your trust. She needs your discretion in all things."

Julia wrinkled her nose at the accusation. "Have I been anything but discreet?"

Ainsley gave a slow exhale. "That isn't what I mean. We had an agreement."

Muscles in Julia's neck flexed as he spoke.

"She won't say anything about us to Father or Daniel, but she needs you as her lady's maid. That means you aren't permitted to tell me—"

"Yes, I understand. This isn't about anything like that." Julia rounded the examination table. "There is something else at play, more than just Lord Marshall's condition."

Ainsley took a seat on the high stool at the desk near the window and slapped the papers down. Julia came to his side. "I believe it involves Dr. Davies."

Recently appointed to the University of Edinburgh, Dr. Jonas Davies was one of Ainsley's colleagues from medical school. Equal parts adversary and confidante, Davies had helped Ainsley on more than one occasion, proving his loyalty to not only Ainsley, but also the entire Marshall family. Ainsley had long known Jonas was smitten with Margaret. Only recently had Margaret spoken of her mutual affection. Their friend's removal from London took place near the exact time Lord Marshall returned to the city suffering the recent attack of apoplexy. The Marshalls had become so all consumed with their patriarch's condition that a proper send-off was near impossible.

Reminded of his own shortcomings as a friend, Ainsley rubbed his forehead. "I wrote to him," he said, trying to reassure himself that he meant well, "but I have yet to put it in the post."

"Lady Margaret doesn't talk about him any longer," Julia said.

"She used to speak of him often?"

Julia raised her eyebrows. "I'm not supposed to say, remember?"

Caught by his own principles, Ainsley shook his head.

"She needs a break from all this," Julia said, "a reliable person to take the lead on Lord Marshall's care. It should never have been placed on Margaret's shoulders alone."

"She isn't alone," Ainsley interjected. "We are all helping as best we can."

"Yes but..." Julia hesitated. "Daniel is free to come and go as he pleases, and you escape to your work. Where is Lady Margaret's reprieve?"

Ainsley nodded, finally understanding what Julia was telling him. "All right," he said, "I will make enquiries. See if we can find someone on a more permanent basis. You wouldn't have anyone you can recommend, would you, seeing as you seem to have all the answers?"

Julia smiled. "Unfortunately, I do not," she said. "Perhaps Mrs. Holliwell knows if one of the girls has taken some nursing courses."

Mrs. Holliwell was head mistress at the foundling home where Julia herself was raised and where Ainsley's mother had been patron.

"Perhaps."

Julia took two steps closer to him, close enough that her body was pressed into his. "Thank you," she said softly.

Ainsley watched as she placed her hand on top of his and pulled it toward her lips. After kissing his knuckles, she leaned in to grace his cheek with her own. Ainsley relished the feeling of her bare skin brushing his and began planting kisses on her cheek. As she melted in his arms, he left a trail of kisses down her neck to her collar. Holding her to him, he kept her from pulling away or slipping to the floor. She wrapped her arms around his shoulders and buried her face in his neck as he doted on her, licking the skin at her throat and shoulder.

She was the first to come to her senses, pushing him from her and murmuring for him to stop. "Someone may come in," she said unconvincingly.

Ainsley found himself smiling as he moved his attentions toward her bosom.

"Peter. Peter!" She slapped him furiously now, tapping his chest quickly to get his attention. He pulled away in time to see Crawford enter at the back of the room. Once she was released from his grasp, Julia stepped back and plucked a small jar from the top of his desk. "What is this then?" she asked, clearing her throat somewhat to hide the slight shake in her voice. She held the jar up to the light streaming through the window.

Ainsley thrust his hands in his pockets and stood up. "That is a growth removed from a man's testicle," he explained. "He died in great agony."

With subdued revulsion, Julia returned the jar to Ainsley's desk. "Oh."

Crawford stopped a few paces from them and eyed Julia suspiciously. "Women do not belong in the morgue," he said.

From the corner of his eye, Ainsley watched Julia square her shoulders and elevate her chin slightly. "I imagine at least half of us in here are of the fairer sex," she corrected.

A scowl slid over Crawford's face as Ainsley bowed his head slightly, stifling a laugh.

"Who are you and why are you here?" Crawford asked, any ounce of patience vanishing quickly.

Before Julia could reply, Ainsley stepped forward, placing himself between her and his supervisor. "She came to see me, sir," he said. "I didn't see the harm in allowing her entrance."

"We haven't the time to dally," Crawford glowered. "Can't you see they are turning to mush before our very eyes?" He turned in place to survey the room. "Get them out, Ainsley. Get them out and in the ground before we have an epidemic on our hands."

Ainsley nodded, agreeing with his supervisor's emphasis on speed. There would always be more bodies and the living begging for answers from them. The longer it took to process, the higher likelihood that any evidence that could bring those answers was melting away in the summer heat. "Yes, sir," he said. "I will hasten to finish."

Crawford grunted and began to turn but stopped, taken aback by Ainsley's agreeance. So rare was such an occurrence Ainsley was sure Crawford would remain to argue with him out of habit alone. "Good," the senior doctor said after a pause. "Thank you." He pointed his thumb over his shoulder at Julia as he turned. "And get her out of here."

The couple released a unified breath as the door closed behind him. "Do you think he knows?" Julia asked.

"I highly doubt it," Ainsley answered. "These days he barely pays attention to anything beyond his bottle of brandy." Without much thought, he began turning the small lead statue in his pocket over with his hand. He saw Julia's gaze drawn to it as she turned to face him.

"What's that?" she asked.

Ainsley's hand quickly enveloped the statue in a fist but he did not pull it out. "What do you mean?"

"In your pocket," Julia said, smiling at first. "I know you took something from that man."

He bit down on his inner cheek and his eyes shot up to the ceiling.

"No point in hiding it," she said, smiling from one side of her mouth. She stepped toward him, eyeing him as if a jaguar readying to pounce on its prey. She pressed an open palm into his chest as her torso collided with his. Looking up at him, she smiled and used her other hand to trail down his arm to the hand that was still in the pocket of his trousers. "I just want to see it," she said softly, "please."

"Damn it." Ainsley pulled out his hand and opened it, palm up.

Julia nearly giggled at her triumph and quickly stepped back with the small figurine in her hand. "It looks like a religious relic," she said almost immediately. Within seconds, however, her celebratory expression vanished and was replaced by something far more serious. "It's Saint Christopher," she said.

Ainsley shrugged. "What does that mean?"

"He's the patron saint of travellers," Julia explained, rolling the figure over in her hand. Ainsley watched as she bit her lower lip.

"How do you know that?" Ainsley asked.

"My brother and I were raised Catholic before being sent to the orphanage," she said. Julia rarely spoke of her life in the foundling home and had never mentioned what life was like before. Ainsley had always imagined she was very young when she was placed in Mrs. Holliwell's care.

"You are Catholic?" Ainsley asked, somewhat cautiously.

Julia nodded. "You are sure you found this on the man?"

"Yes," Ainsley said. "You saw me."

She closed her eyes momentarily before giving it back to Ainsley. "I should go," she said, offering a forced smile. "Ms. Nelson will be wondering what is taking me so long." She gave him a quick kiss on the cheek before retreating down the main aisle.

"Let me give you a few shillings for a hansom," Ainsley offered, following her.

"No, it's all right," she said, turning at the door. "I walk quickly."

"But the heat."

Julia laughed. "You are such a sweet man," she said. "I will be fine." She blew him a kiss and was gone before Ainsley could say another word.

Chapter 3

Margaret sat in her father's room, which in recent weeks had become her hideaway from the rest of London. While seated in the red, high back, upholstered chair placed between the window and the bed, Margaret could will herself to concentrate on one single, solitary thing—her father's recovery—and stave off the bitterness and heartache that fought to overwhelm her.

The previous year had done its worst and tested the young heiress in more ways than she ever dreamed imaginable. There was once a time, when she was cooped up at The Briar, that she craved interesting things, anything to break the monotony of her country existence. She had cursed her mother's reclusive nature and her father's bitter avoidance of them. She had envied Peter his medical degree, which included his recently won position at the hospital, and had even spat a curse at her eldest brother, Daniel, for being so well suited to his role as the future earl. Margaret had begun to begrudge anyone who led even a slightly more entertaining life than her and, now, ten months on and possessing many stories of her own, she was ready for it to return to the way it had once been—painfully predictable and dull as tombs.

Not one month before, she had been the happiest of women, convinced the man who stole her heart would manage to steal her away as well. She wanted to go with him and had found herself counting the hours until such a time as he could whisk her away to Scotland as they had planned. She'd even packed a small valise with a modest, if somewhat austere, trousseau tucked in its folds. The bag remained hidden in the shadows under her bed, still packed. Any hope she had had of one day making a journey north with it had vanished in the days following her father's return to London.

How could she have left him in such a state? The once noble peer, member of the House of Lords and Earl of

Moncliff, had been reduced to nothing more than a murmuring invalid who could neither eat nor use the chamber pot on his own. With a deceased mother and only brothers to call family, Margaret knew rather quickly that the lion's share of their father's care would fall to her. At first, she did not mind. She saw it as a duty, the mere repayment of lifelong support bestowed upon her since birth, but as the days passed she feared the reality was becoming far worse than she imagined.

They could not keep a staff of nurses, once promised to them by their family physicians. Attending chamber pots and administering sponge baths was far less appealing to the current generation of young women, it would seem. Wooed to the profession by Nightingale and her contemporaries, many girls, once it was realized they would not be attending the wounds of strapping young men in uniform, left the service and took up jobs in the factories instead.

"It's noble work, miss," Katherine had said when Margaret met her in the hallway the evening before, "steady work with only slightly worse pay. And I won't be expected to see to anyone else's business, if you know what I mean. That should be worth its weight in gold, don't you think?"

Margaret could not find the words to agree. She did not care to argue and allowed the girl to leave. She had said nothing to Peter the night before, knowing there was little that could be done for it so late in the day. Margaret had taken on so much of her father's care that it almost seemed a blessing to do so without the distracting flutter of someone else in the room.

From her chair by the window, Margaret was granted a sufficient amount of light by which to read, which she did, out loud, as a way to quiet her mind and subdue the restless spirit of her father, who was not yet used to his immobility.

A few grunts often escaped her father while she droned on. That day he seemed particularly unsettled.

> *"He who repeats a tale after man,*
> *Is bound to say, as nearly as he can,*
> *Each single word, if he remembers it,*

However rudely spoken or unfit,
Or else the tale he tells will be untrue,
The things invented and the phrases new."

Lord Marshall writhed and squirmed, using the good side of his body to roll to the edge of the bed. Margaret lowered *The Canterbury Tales* and let out a huff as she watched her father struggle with such a simple task.

"Pretty dull, isn't it?" she asked, forcing a smile.

Lord Marshall stopped his wriggling when Margaret stood. She placed the book down on the bedside table and stepped toward him. He watched intently as she came to his side, as if mesmerized by her presence and the long shadow she cast over him. A pat of drool formulated on the edge of his dry and cracked mouth.

"I don't have to read," Margaret offered, stooping down to help him back into his place in the middle of the bed. Margaret could not imagine anything else she could do to help pass away the hours.

Lord Marshall's mouth opened and closed quickly, with only short huffs accompanying them. His neck twisted in an odd way as he tried to look at her, his eyes wild.

"I wish you wouldn't fuss so," she said, taking a seat on the side of the bed. Using one hand, she lifted his head while the other adjusted his pillow. "Maybe we should try some more speech work, like Dr. Davidson suggested."

Margaret brought her face inches from her father's and began to form shapes with her mouth, imitating some of the easiest sounds of human speech. "Mmmm," she repeated slowly before pausing to give her father a chance to reply. "Mmmmargaret." She smiled at the thought of hearing her father say her name again, but the eager anticipation vanished when haggard sounds came from him, none of which sounded like an 'M'.

She patted the side of her father's cheek, as if to subdue his frantic attempts to speak. "It's all right, Father," she said, fighting back tears. "Dr. Davidson did say it would take time."

Dr. Davidson had said a great number of things, most of which Peter disagreed with. During the family's first meeting with him, Ainsley practically embarrassed her with all his pointed questions and contradictory theories.

"Peter, calm down. Who's the doctor here?" Aunt Louisa had said, raising an eyebrow and wriggling in her seat, eager to restore the doctor's evaporating patience.

The truth was the doctor knew only slightly more than Ainsley, who quickly devoured any book referencing the condition. The family soon realized not much was known about apoplexy. Some suffers regained mobility and speech while others where chairbound, requiring nearly constant care. Their father's attack had been significant. Lord Benedict had said the Barbadian doctors suggested Lord Marshall had suffered several attacks in quick succession. This would complicate his recovery. The Marshalls had started off hopeful but grew less so with each passing day. Conversations changed from discussing his recovery to deciding what would ultimately make him more comfortable. All the while, Lord Marshall looked on, frustration building in his eyes and contorting his lax facial features into a near permanent scowl.

Margaret tried not to look at her father with pity. She knew it must unsettle him to see so many people look to him as if he were a disappointment and not the man he was.

"Perhaps we should have a turn in the garden," she said, pulling forth a lighthearted tone. "I'd go for a walk along the pavement—"

Lord Marshall's eyes popped open in a panic.

"—but Daniel said there was some sort of commotion a few houses down. At the Talbots', I think." Margaret had pressed her brother for the true reason, but she wasn't about to relay that to her father, who already had enough worries. "I'll have Cutter and Maxwell come help get you in your chair."

She squeezed his hand, a ritual she performed each time she meant to leave the room. Sometimes she lingered a moment or two longer in the hopes that he would squeeze back an acknowledgement, but he never did.

It did not take long for Cutter and Maxwell to respond to her summons. Within minutes, they plucked Lord Marshall from his bed and transferred him to a high back wheeled chair fitted with cushions for both his underside and his backside. A strap had been fitted, however, to hold up his torso and keep him from tumbling out, which had been a common enough occurrence in the early days.

With Lord Marshall in his chair, Cutter and Maxwell went down the stairs to ensure a clear route, free of obstructions to the back garden. Margaret fetched a blanket to place around her father's legs but stopped herself just before tucking it in. "The day is so hot," she said with a weighted laugh. "I don't think you will be needing this."

A knock sounded from the front door. With curiosity, Margaret slipped from her father's room and stopped when she reached the second-floor landing. She stood in the shadows and listened as Maxwell allowed Blair Thornton entry.

"I've come to call on Lady Margaret," he said, somewhat formally. "Is she receiving visitors?"

Before Maxwell was able to give the standard regrets in Margaret's place, Aunt Louisa's voice billowed into the foyer and reverberated up to where Margaret eavesdropped.

"Mr. Thornton! What a wonderful surprise! Margaret was just speaking to me about you this morning at breakfast." Aunt Louisa's voice grew louder as she drew closer to the front door, and Margaret's stomach hardened at her words. She had not spoken with Aunt Louisa at all that day, nor would she ever converse about her troubled relationship with the man who had recently saved her life.

"Was she?" Blair's voice betrayed his surprise.

"I know she has been wishing to speak to you and so it is very serendipitous that you should come to call today."

Margaret inched forward and peered around the corner. Blair Thornton was a very striking man, with a tall physique and broad shoulders. They had known each other as children, each growing up on their abutting country properties near Tunbridge Wells, and had become reacquainted recently. It was apparent, given his numerous enquiries and letters, that he meant for them to remain in contact. Margaret had never meant to lead him on, at least not this far. Her intention was to lay bare her relationship with Jonas Davies long before Blair developed an attachment.

"I heard of the unfortunate events down the street and thought I should come to make sure everything was all right." Blair looked up and Margaret sprung back, praying he had not seen her. "Do you think Margaret will see me?"

"Oh absolutely, Mr. Thornton."

Margaret imagined her aunt turning to Maxwell as her tone changed. "Where is my niece?"

"She is preparing to escort Lord Marshall for a turn in the garden, ma'am," Maxwell answered.

"Excellent. You should join her then, Mr. Thornton."

Margaret's eyes closed as her heart sank. She had been successfully avoiding contact with him for the last few weeks and now there was no way around it.

"What are you waiting for then?" Aunt Louisa said, her commanding tone returning. "Go fetch my brother and niece. They have company."

Moments later the sound of Maxwell's shoes could be heard heading up the stairs. Margaret stepped back into her father's room before they reached the landing.

Panic struck almost instantly as Margaret reached for the bubbly, purple scar at her collar and realized she was not wearing her scarf to hide it as she used to. The weather had been so hot and so seldom did she leave her father's room that she had become used to removing it, and often ended up leaving it in various places. Crossing the room, she plucked it from the back of her reading chair.

When she turned she saw her father's eyes upon her from his chair. He really did look like such a pitiful creature with his lip trembling and his hand shaking. For all the curt words he had ever said to her, all the snide remarks and harsh rebukes, the only thing that she wished to see in his eyes was the love he had for her; love in place of a thousand apologies.

She received neither.

"I'm so sorry, Father," she said, tucking the ends of her scarf into the collar of her bodice. "We won't be walking alone today. Aunt Louisa has made a decree."

The rear garden at Marshall House was not expansive, but it was filled with enough foliage and a high canopy of trees, so that it gave an illusion of seclusion. An area at the centre of the yard was allotted for a small iron table and two chairs, ornately sculpted with filigree leaves and other organic accents. A path circled around the shaded space, meandering through flower beds and a finely manicured lawn. There remained a few stone sculptures that Margaret's mother had once chosen as a young bride and which had since grown green with fine moss and intruding ivy. She tried not to look at them, afraid of the memories of her mother enveloping her yet again.

As Margaret took a turn around the yard, Blair inched along slightly behind her.

Thrice Blair tried to begin a conversation and each time the topics introduced petered out. Margaret was not purposely trying to make their meeting uncomfortable but, circumstances being as they were, theirs was an uncomfortable relationship.

"Your father is doing well, I see," Blair said, gesturing to Lord Marshall in the wheeled chair ahead of them, pushed by Cutter along the path. "All things considering."

Margaret smiled. It was a perfectly ludicrous thing to say. Her father had not been doing well and he showed only slight improvement. She had turned away enough inquisitive busybodies who only came to spy and later gossip about her father's misfortune. She was in no mood to accept such rude behaviour from Blair as well.

Blair drew a breath. "I only mean...well, that my regard for him and your family has not diminished in any way since...well...you understand."

Indeed, Margaret did understand. A cripple, even an exceedingly rich one, was still a cripple. "How is your mother, the Duchess?" Margaret asked, purposely changing the subject. "She must still be in the depths of mourning."

"I have no doubt you have heard," Blair said, his jaw tightening somewhat. "London society is famous for its tittle-tattle."

Margaret stopped and turned. "I have not heard anything beyond these walls," she said, meeting his gaze squarely. "Not that I would care to hear about any trite, slanderous gossip. I would never keep company with anyone who speaks ill of the Duchess. She is like a mother to me. When I ask, 'how is Lady Thornton?', it is exactly what I mean."

She saw his eyes dart to her scarf before forcibly

bringing them back to her face. He had seen her with if off once and Margaret had been very careful to not let that happen again. She began to walk and realized her throat had gone dry. No longer did she have patience for any of this. She wished he would go and that others like him would not think to ring their bell again.

"Forgive me," Blair said. "In no way did I mean you had participated in such gossip. You must understand how difficult the last few weeks have been on my family."

Margaret suddenly felt ashamed. The Thorntons had lost a son, Blair's brother, with whom he was very close. She stopped. "I did not mean..." Margaret floundered, angered by her narrow view of the world. She had spoken of her own suffering, forgetting the suffering of others. Besides, this wasn't precisely the gratitude she should be showing to the man who saved her life.

She took a breath and made an effort to smile. "I'm glad you came to visit," she said, restarting their conversation. "What brings you to London?" Without thought, she slipped her arm into the crook of his elbow and together they walked side by side through the garden.

Chapter 4

At the end of the day, Ainsley left the hospital, foregoing a farewell to his supervisor and instead heading straight to 4 Whitehall Place. He wasn't expecting fanfare or even a lukewarm welcome. He knew he had squandered any remaining goodwill between himself and Inspector Simms by deceiving his constable, but something about where the remains were found troubled him. This wasn't a standard murder, one done in the heat of the moment in a back alley in Whitechapel. The way the body was displayed indicated the murderer wanted his victim to be found immediately and was somehow using it as a message.

The heavy oak desk in the foyer of Scotland Yard created a partition, separating the good men of the Yard from the public they served. A desk sergeant stood on guard, a heap of books, ledgers, and paperwork indicating the mountain of work waiting for him in addition to the many people who streamed in and out of the building. Sergeant Fisher looked to Ainsley without raising his chin from the ledger in front of him. "Not today, Peter. He isn't in the mood."

"Can you summon him down?" Ainsley pleaded. "I may have some information regarding the Belgravia body."

Fisher smirked and slapped the ledger closed. "Dr. Muller is already on that case."

"The drunk? I wouldn't trust a dead dog to that man." Surprised such a doctor remained on the Yard's payroll, Ainsley's voice bellowed louder than he intended.

Fisher glanced left and right before leaning over the wide desk. "I ain't ever heard Simms say as many negative things about Dr. Muller as I heard him say about you. This morning he came here in a right furious rage. Nearly decked my constable here, who tried to go near him. I ain't ever seen him so irate."

Ainsley winced at the thought of it.

"If I were in them shiny shoes of yours I'd run back to

St. Thomas before he found out I darkened those doors." Fisher raised his eyebrows to emphasize his words.

"He's ordered you not to send me up?" Ainsley asked.

Fisher pursed his lips and shook his head as he straightened his stance. "No, sir, hasn't gone so far as that," he explained. "But I ain't the sort of police officer who'd knowingly send a man to certain death, no sir. Won't have that on my conscience."

Ainsley shook his head. "Why don't you let me deal with Simms on my own?"

"I can't, sir."

"Why ever not?"

"Because he's not here." Fisher offered a shrug and a wink.

Ainsley smiled. "I'll leave a note then."

Fisher presented him with a blank sheet of paper and a fountain pen from. After quickly scribbling off a message for Simms to contact him at home as soon as possible, Ainsley folded the page and presented it to Fisher with thanks.

"Well, if it isn't *Mr. Specialist.*"

Ainsley cringed at the sound of a familiar voice. He needn't have turned around to know Theodore Fenton, of the Daily Telegraph and Courier, stood behind him. He was the journalist who held the secret of Ainsley's double life—and he was also the one person with such knowledge who held no loyalty to Ainsley whatsoever.

When Ainsley turned he walked forward, tipping his hat as he passed. "Good day, Mr. Fenton."

"I just spent the entire afternoon canvassing your neighbourhood, Dr. Ainsley," Fenton called out after him.

Ainsley could feel the newspaperman following him as he exited the building and into the street.

"Or should I address you as Mr. Marshall? This life of yours always seems to have me confused."

"You wouldn't be so confused if you just left me and my family alone," Ainsley reminded him as he raised his hand to hail a hansom.

Fenton smiled. "What would the fun in that be?"

Ainsley turned and stepped into Fenton. "Is that what I am to you? Entertainment?"

Fenton blinked. "In part."

The old Ainsley would have thought nothing of raising his fist to the miscreant. For weeks, Ainsley and his family had been the subject of carefully worded passages in the society pages. Already, Aunt Louisa and Margaret had refused invites and retreated to the house to save themselves from the piteous questions and hateful remarks directed at them from the other society women. Many acted as if Lord Marshall's condition were contagious, easily procured through casual contact. No one continued to see Lord Marshall as a prominent member of London society. His condition had made him an outcast and that meant his children were as well.

Ainsley blamed Fenton for fanning the flames with his superfluous articles, having no doubt Mr. Fenton paid their former chambermaid for the private details. Each passing day brought new worry to Ainsley, who would have preferred to concentrate on his father's recovery, or at the very least, his family's adjustment to the new rhythm of their lives. He was in no place to worry about the papers and what they may reveal about him, but he remained anxious nonetheless.

When Ainsley didn't reply to his obvious baiting, the newspaperman spoke again, "What's the matter, Peter, lost all will to fight? Your newfound calm came too late, didn't it? A certain someone would still be alive today if only you had discovered this side of you earlier."

There was a time, not so long ago, when Ainsley, full of angst, leapt at any chance to right all the world's wrongs with his innate strength. It was a flaw that created the current rift between him and Simms, and also managed to etch profound scars upon his soul. A deep scowl set in to Ainsley's features as he looked over his shoulder at the man he so greatly despised, the man who seemed fixated on broadcasting all his misdeeds or, at the very least, threatening to.

A devilish smile spread over Fenton's face. "There he is! That's the man I remember!" He clapped his hands together in glee. "You can take the man out of the cockfight, but you can't take the cockfight out of the man."

Ainsley turned and pressed a finger into the man's

chest. "Who did you pay for the information about my father? The maid?"

"Peter, Peter, calm yourself." Fenton adjusted his collar. "No maliciousness is intended. My respect for Lord Marshall knows no bounds. I see nothing wrong with showing my appreciation for the time it took to conduct my interview."

"So it was the maid then?"

Fenton smiled. "What did you expect? Loyalty?"

"Decency."

Fenton shrugged.

Disgusted, Ainsley turned away. "Good day, Mr. Fenton."

His search for a cab to ferry him home proved fruitless and so he began to walk. He didn't trust himself to keep his temper in check. He needed to put as much distance between himself and Fenton as possible, or else their encounter wouldn't end well.

"Leaving so soon, *Specialist*?" Fenton kept pace behind Ainsley as he weaved between the rush of pedestrians in the streets. "Did you try this hard to avoid a confrontation with Elliot Holliwell? How about the fight you had with that young boxer, what was his name again?"

Ainsley stopped suddenly, turned, and pushed Fenton into the brick wall behind him. With a clenched fist at Fenton's throat, Ainsley leaned in close. "What are you playing at?" he commanded.

Fear flashed over the newspaperman's features and then vanished, replaced by a self-satisfied smirk. He tried to wriggle away, but Ainsley kept a firm hold. "Watch yourself, Peter, we are right outside the Yard, are we not?"

Begrudgingly, Ainsley released him and watched as the man adjusted his coat. "You leave me alone, do you hear me? Or next time I won't find the will to stop."

"That would be unwise, Mr. Marshall," Fenton said, smiling. "The days when the good officers of the Yard protected you are over. It won't be so easy to avoid the swing of the rope from now on."

Ainsley's jaw clenched the man spoke. He was very much aware that he needed to watch his step. Already that day he had tread a fine line, but Ainsley knew he was capable of far worse acts than just misdirecting a body from a crime scene.

"I haven't any clue what you are speaking of," Ainsley said, working hard to keep his voice steady.

An uneasy silence erupted as their eyes met.

"Oh, I think you do." Fenton adjusted his bowler hat so it sat squarely on his head and stepped forward, crashing into Ainsley's shoulder as he made his exit. "Tread carefully, Peter," he said over his shoulder as he left. "I possess endless amounts of information regarding this town and no one is immune, not even the Marshall family."

Ainsley watched as Fenton retreated down the street, glancing left and right, no doubt collecting further tidbits of information as he sauntered along.

Chapter 5

Even though the hour was late, the evening sun gave off a pink glow throughout the city as Ainsley returned home. No one was at the door to greet him, and the house sat quiet as he strode into the foyer.

"Oh Peter, thank goodness!" Aunt Louisa appeared at the top of the stairs clutching a gloved hand to her breast. She scooped up a fold of her taffeta skirt and began a slow descent to greet him. "Your sister has been run off her feet and now your father is in such a state."

Again.

When Ainsley climbed the stairs to meet her she snatched up his hand and nearly dragged him the second half of the way up.

"Katherine did not show up this morning," Aunt Louisa said over her shoulder as she led him along. "The ner'do well!"

"I was made aware," Ainsley said in an effort to forego any long explanations.

Aunt Louisa stopped and jerked her head toward him. "How is that possible? I sent you no missive."

Ainsley stammered, unable to admit it was Julia who had made an unauthorized stop at his place of work. "I received a note by messenger," he answered quickly. "Margaret sent it."

His aunt nodded, though her expression remained doubtful. "Very well." Once again she pulled him along.

"A replacement is coming in the morning," Ainsley said. "An older woman this time, a nurse of course, who informed me she prefers private work such as this."

Aunt Louisa stopped short of Lord Marshall's room. Then she licked her lips, tugging lightly on them with her teeth while still clutching Ainsley's hand firmly. "Does she understand the extent of her duties? The...difficulties?"

Drawing in a breath, Ainsley pulled back his shoulders and managed to pull his hand away. "She understands as much as can be explained. For the rest, she must see in person."

Ainsley's aunt nodded thoughtfully and gave a half smile. "We can only pray then."

She pushed open the door to Lord Marshall's room. In it, they found Maxwell and Louisa's eldest son, Nathaniel, struggling to return the flailing Lord Marshall to his bed. Moaning loudly and using his good arm to strike his helpers, Lord Marshall wriggled and fought as much as his present condition would allow him, which was enough to unseat his opponents. Margaret had retreated to the window, wanting desperately to turn away from the scene, while clutching their father's carpetbag to her chest.

"Goodness, Peter!" she called out when she saw him. "What do we do?"

Each time Maxwell and Nathaniel succeeded in replacing Lord Marshall in his proper place in bed, the master of the house would twist and squirm as if trying to break free of their grasp.

"How long has he been doing this?" Ainsley asked as he crossed the room to stand by his sister.

Margaret shook her head in bewilderment. "Nearly half an hour. I can't make sense of it."

Exhausted, Maxwell released Lord Marshall's legs and reached for the post nearest him, as if preventing himself from falling over. "He will not settle, sir."

As if on cue, Lord Marshall stopped mid-wriggle, his bedclothes wrapped loosely around his legs. He was unable to kick them off completely. Eyes wild, he glared at Ainsley and Margaret before raising his good arm and pointing an erect finger at the pair of them.

"See? This is what I must deal with all day," Margaret said, tossing the carpetbag to the chair next to the window. She raised a hand to her face to brush the loose strands of hair from her brow.

Lord Marshall kicked up again, working hard this time to roll to one side before Nathaniel placed a forceful hand onto his uncle's shoulder. "Stop, Uncle," he said, eyeing the man squarely. "You had a busy day. You must rest now."

Pulling in a determined breath, Lord Marshall's chest rose and fell as he looked at his nephew. A murmur escaped his lips and for a moment Ainsley thought Nathaniel would relay a message to the family. But as Nathaniel turned, a look of confusion evident on his face, it was clear he couldn't decipher anything Lord Marshall had said.

"Enough of this, Father," Ainsley commanded. "Can't you see we are trying our best? Recovery takes time."

Lord Marshall stopped his writhing almost immediately and looked up to the gaze of his second son, his only true son. Ainsley stepped toward the bed, ignoring the mangled bedclothes and manic look on his father's face. He saw past all the violence and saw a man snarled in an internal struggle, one that made the disarray of the room look minor in comparison. A tear escaped the edge of Lord Marshall's eye and slid down the wrinkles of his cheeks, creases that had seemed to appear overnight. Ainsley had never noticed them before. His father, always hardened and sour, now looked more terrified than terrifying. It was a reality that was very new to Ainsley, who until recently could not stand to be in the man's presence.

Defeat settling over his features, Lord Marshall threw back his head into the pillow and sulked.

"What unsettled him initially?" Ainsley asked, leaning in to straighten the sheets and blankets.

"I thought he was asleep so I began tidying up a little," Margaret explained, gesturing to the rest of the room. "Father began moving around and moaning." She crossed her arms over her chest and shook her head. "I just don't understand." She pushed back a tear that lined her lower eyelid.

"He's just an old fuddy-duddy. Wants to do everything his way," Aunt Louisa said, exasperated. She leaned in toward her brother and shook a finger at him. "You better get used to your children doing things for you or one day they may just get up and leave you to your own detriment."

"Aunt Louisa, don't say that," Margaret said in protest.

Their aunt shrugged. "He never could stand it when things weren't done to his specifications. It's a poetic justice for this to be his fate, relying on the empathy and compassion of others. He never gave much of either while he could."

When Ainsley looked to his father he saw a man abashed by his own misdeeds. His father wasn't perfect. Ainsley himself had come to rue the man and actively avoided any interaction with him, but it seemed unfair that now, beholden to the whim of others and vulnerable for his every care, that he should be shamed so openly.

A self-righteous laugh escaped Aunt Louisa as she hovered over her brother's bed. "Why, I could tell you a story or two—"

"Enough." Ainsley gestured for the door. "I won't have you condemning a man who can't speak in his own defense. He seems to have calmed down now. Why don't we all allow him some time to sleep?"

After pulling the blankets over Lord Marshall, Maxwell asked Margaret if there was anything else she needed. She gave a quick shake of the head and he left the room. Aunt Louisa left without another word but Nathaniel paused at the door and turned to Ainsley.

"I have discovered a place of interest that I would very much like to show you," he said quietly, giving a quick glance to Margaret. "A gentleman's club, if you will."

Ainsley smiled, amused by his cousin's enthusiasm. "I doubt there is a public house in London of which I do not know," he replied, without care for secrecy.

Nathaniel looked dejected and almost sullen as he registered what Ainsley had said.

There was no need to hide the truth of it. Ainsley was well aware of any worthwhile venue for drink and gambling, as well as some places not so worthwhile. If Nathaniel wished to impress him, he'd have to do much better than that. With awkward hesitation, Nathaniel gave a sideways glance to Margaret and then left.

Alone at last, the two siblings looked back to their father and found him inviting sleep. Ainsley turned off the lamp next to the bed and joined Margaret out in the hallway.

"Humour him, Peter," Margaret said, closing the door behind them. Her words had a breathy air, one that betrayed her fatigue. "London seems to have bewitched him."

"After so many years in India I doubt it would take

much," he answered with a laugh.

"I hear India is lovely," she said, beginning a slow walk down the hallway.

"I hear it is hot." He pulled at his collar at the memory of the outdoor heat, which was only somewhat abated now that he was in the shade.

Violetta exited Margaret's room, a few items to be laundered in her arms. The maid bowed her head as she passed Margaret and Ainsley in the hall.

"Violetta, where is Julia?"

The maid, one of the oldest on their staff and their mother's lady's maid while she lived, turned a slip of ribbon through her fingers as she spoke. "I'm not sure, ma'am," Violetta said, the wisp of a smile tickling the edges of her mouth. It was as if the woman delighted in her adversary's unapproved absence. "She did not return from her errand."

Ainsley pulled out his pocket watch. "It's been six hours," he said.

"How do you know?" Margaret asked, surprised.

"She came to visit me—"

Margaret put her hand up to hush him suddenly and Ainsley realized his worry for Julia's well-being had almost allowed him to reveal their secret.

"That is all, Violetta," Margaret said. "When Julia returns, have her come speak to me."

The maid bobbed a stiff curtsey and left, her smile broadening as she did so.

Worry pulled on Ainsley's face, not only for his misstep in words but also because Julia had not returned. "This is not like her," he said, turning in place and running a hand over his face.

The doorbell rang and the familiar sound of Maxwell in the hall came to them in the upper hallway.

"I'm sure she is fine, Peter," Margaret said.

"Good evening, Lord Benedict," Maxwell said from the storey below them. "I'm afraid His Lordship is down for the evening."

Ainsley paused his conversation with Margaret to listen in.

"That's quite all right. Er...Is Louisa about?" Lord Benedict asked.

"Yes, sir. You both may follow me."

Ainsley lifted his eyes to find Margaret's.

"Both?" they whispered in unison.

"Could he have brought Cecilia with him?" Margaret asked. Ceceilia was a friend of Aunt Louisa's and Lord Benedict's soon-to-be wife.

Ainsley shook his head. "She's in the country at present," Ainsley said. "I heard Aunt Louisa saying something about her ill grandmother."

After a few more seconds they heard footsteps making their way down the hall before entering one of the rooms on the main floor.

"Then who could he possibly be introducing us to at this hour?" Margaret asked, raising a hand to her temple.

"Perhaps he wishes to bring another doctor," Ainsley offered.

"Oh, I wish he wouldn't. I mean, I don't see why we can't use our family physician, who's been taking care of Father for nearly two decades."

Ainsley shrugged. "Perhaps he feels responsible in a way. I heard him tell Aunt Louisa he was in the room when Father collapsed. Imagine the guilt he must feel."

Margaret heaved a sigh. "I suppose we are meant to go say hello to this new doctor, though what he can tell us that the two others couldn't is beyond me."

The person accompanying Lord Benedict was not a doctor, or even a man for that matter. As Ainsley and Margaret neared the parlour door Maxwell was exiting with a young, negro girl following behind him.

"Maxwell, who is this?" Ainsley asked.

The servants paused in the hall and Maxwell opened his mouth to answer, but Aunt Louisa beat him to it. "This is Vivian," she said, in a markedly sweet tone. "Lord Benedict has asked if our home was open and I had already told them yes." Aunt Louisa suddenly looked alarmed. "Oh, forgive me, Peter. I did not think. I am so used to running the household."

Ainsley shook his head. "I do not object," he said.

Margaret reached out a hand in greeting. "Hello, Vivian. I am Lady Margaret."

Vivian could scarcely see them under the wide brim of her travelling bonnet. "Good evening."

Ainsley knew by her accent that the girl, who could have been no more than fifteen, was from Barbados. Her travelling attire, which included a light blue hoop skirt with white pinstriping and lace gloves, hinted at comfortable living though not extravagantly so.

Before either Margaret or Ainsley could say another word, Maxwell gestured for the girl to follow him down the hall.

"Aunt Louisa, how long is Vivian expected to stay at Marshall House?" Margaret asked.

Aunt Louisa looked to Lord Benedict.

"I can't rightly say," he said.

Leaning into his walking cane, Lord Benedict lowered his head slightly as Ainsley, Margaret, and Louisa entered the parlour.

In his early thirties, Lord Benedict was from a long line of English nobles. He had spent the majority of his youth travelling abroad and, it was rumoured, gambling his inheritance. Short and not attractive by any measure, Benedict had been on the prowl for a wife for some time. He had once hinted to Margaret his interest in her but the idea was quickly squashed by Lord Marshall, who openly confessed a grander plan for Margaret's marital prospects. His future bride, Cecilia, brought a modest income, bequeathed to her by a fiancé who died the previous year from fever.

Ainsley went straight for the sideboard. "Care for a brandy?" he asked, peeking over his shoulder at their visitor.

"Yes, thank you."

Ainsley presented him with crystal glass.

"Will you not have one as well?" Lord Benedict asked.

"Peter has cut down his drinking considerably," Aunt Louisa said, walking toward them. She reached past Ainsley for the decanter. "It's rather commendable, but I don't see why the rest of us have to suffer." She poured herself a glass, filing it with twice as much alcohol as normal, and downed much of it in the first gulp.

Lord Benedict raised his glass, a small salute to

Ainsley's efforts, before taking a sip. "Vivian is a chambermaid at your father's estate in Bridgetown. Her mother passed away recently and she has no one."

"But what is she doing here?" Margaret asked, from the sofa. "Surely Father would have given her a stipend to help her overcome her grief."

Lord Benedict nodded. "He did, and a fine one at that." He tucked his cane under his arm so he could slip his free hand into his pocket. "Truth be told, she just showed up at my door this evening, unannounced." He licked his lips. "As you are aware, I am a soon-to-be-wed bachelor and I wouldn't want to compromise Miss Vivian's good character."

"It would have been far more efficient for her to write," Aunt Louisa said with a chuckle.

"You believe she has come to ask for more money?" Ainsley asked.

"I don't know what she wants," Lord Benedict said. "As far as I knew, the matter was done. Your father was quite generous during his visit."

Margaret swallowed nervously. "Should we tell Father she has arrived in London?"

"Oh, I wouldn't worry him," Lord Benedict said. "I'll make some enquiries with the farm managers back on the island. In the meantime, if you could indulge her a little. I suspect it was the allure of London that brought her this far. She'll return home before long, I have no doubt." He emptied his glass of brandy with one gulp and replaced it on the sideboard. "Let me know if she presents any problems, and I will return, forthwith." He tapped his cane on the floor with a flourish and smiled as he planted a light kiss on Aunt Louisa's cheek. "No need to follow me to the door. I shall see myself out."

The rhythmic tap, tap, tap of his cane on the hallway floor signaled his departure.

Chapter 6

The next morning, Ainsley found Margaret at the dining table enjoying breakfast, a scarce sighting when she so often went to their father first thing in the morning. Ainsley paused behind his chair and rested his hand on the back.

"Father was sleeping still," she explained, putting a forkful of egg into her mouth.

When Cutter entered, carrying a carafe of hot water, she called out to him. "Cutter, can you please tell Julia I wish to see her before our new nurse arrives."

Cutter stopped midstep and gave a quick glance to Maxwell, who stood at attention next to the sideboard. "My apologies, ma'am," he began, "Miss Kemp has not risen yet."

Margaret laid down her fork and snatched up her napkin. She gave a thoughtful look to Ainsley. "She must have come in late," she said, though her tone gave away her worry.

Ainsley, however, was in no mood for guessing. Abandoning convention, he left the dining room and headed for the back stairs, the servants' means of traversing between the levels of the house. Julia shared an attic room with one of the chambermaids, who Ainsley spied at the end of the hall tucking a few curls of hair beneath the bonnet of her uniform.

"Is she ill?" he asked, marching the length of hall.

Startled, the maid jumped and turned toward him, lowering her arms with a jolt. She looked back at the closed door that led to her lodgings. "Sir?"

"Miss Kemp? Is she ill?"

The chambermaid twisted her fingers nervously and stammered as Ainsley passed her and opened the door. The room was empty save for some sparse furnishings. Julia's side of the room in particular looked spotless. "Did Miss Kemp return last night?" Ainsley asked, still trying to harness the panic he felt in his gut.

The maid faltered, her gaze bouncing between her employer and her roommate's side of the room. "Well, sir," she said before tears prevented her from finishing.

Ainsley heard footsteps behind them in the hall and turned to see Margaret approaching. "Peter, you aren't permitted near the female servants' quarters," she said.

The chambermaid swallowed and bowed her head.

"Prudence, to the kitchens." Margaret cocked her head to the side, dismissing the maid, who was clearly at a loss for words. With the chambermaid gone, Ainsley entered the room and went straight for Julia's bedside table.

"Peter!"

He hesitated a moment with his hand on the knob. It wasn't proper for him to rummage through a servant's things and he had never contemplated such an act before. He felt Margaret tugging on his wrist.

"You will regret this," she said.

The man he was before wouldn't have given it another thought. He could always justify any wrongdoing, citing necessity. Recently, though, all his methods had come under scrutiny and he began to question himself more and more. What his sister said was true. He would come to regret rifling through not only a servant's private things but the belongings of the woman whom he cared deeply for. He retracted his hand and turned in place, taking in the sights of the room before stepping back into the hallway.

As he marched back to the main floor he struggled to shake the austerity of his lover's living quarters. He held Julia as dear as he did his own sister, perhaps even more so of late and yet on the nights when they weren't together she was sleeping on such a narrow bed, with either stifling heat suffocating her or penetrating cold nipping at her. As he descended the narrow staircase he realized that to Julia Marshall House must have appeared no better than the orphanage she grew up in.

Ms. Nelson, the housekeeper, came into view at the base of the narrow stairs just as Ainsley began to descend. Clutching the railing, she looked up to him. "My apologies, sir," she said, out of breath after running from kitchens, no doubt. "I had not realized Miss Kemp was not roused."

"I suspect she had not been to bed last night," Ainsley said.

With Margaret following him, Ainsley came down the stairs and the three of them gathered on the tight landing. Ms. Nelson's weathered face soured even further as Ainsley looked at her. "I should have known it would come to this." She shook her head and placed closed fisted hands on her hips.

"What makes you say that?" Ainsley asked.

"Well, she never did fit in with anyone belowstairs. Never did she try neither." Ms. Nelson scoffed at the memory of it.

"I hardly see how that matters in this particular situation," Ainsley answered, pulling out his pocket watch to check the time. Nearly nine o'clock.

"I think it's pretty clear," she answered. "She's skipped out on us. Found a better place. She wouldn't be the first."

"She's been a loyal maid to me for nearly a year," Margaret answered, disbelieving.

"Yes, but with the master and all," Ms. Nelson said, shaking her head, "is it any wonder? She couldn't handle the workload, not like the rest of us." She puffed up her chest then, obviously proud of her conjecture and her longtime tenure with the family.

Ainsley shook his head, refusing to believe Julia would just desert them, but he was too stymied to say anything. His thoughts spun as he tried to recall their most recent conversations. Had there been anything amiss? Did he not recognize signs whilst his mind was occupied by the needs of his father?

"Has she told no one where she intended to go?" Margaret asked. "Perhaps she left a note, downstairs. Or my room, perhaps."

Ainsley nodded, eager to accept any alternative than the one Ms. Nelson presented them. Margaret slipped away to search her chamber while Peter followed Ms. Nelson belowstairs. The servicing rooms of the house were light and airy, due in part to a number of windows along the front and rear of the building, and the narrow courtyards dug into the ground outside of them. There was a door at each end and metal stairs that either led up to the street or the garden. Only the pantry and Maxwell's office was devoid of natural light.

The kitchen staff was in the bustle of morning cleanup and the chambermaids had already disbursed into the farther reaches of the house to polish the silverware, brush the stairs, or dust the portraits. Only Prudence remained, looking nervous and staying close to Ms. Aster, the cook, as if looking for reassurance.

Vivian was seated on a stool at the end of a long counter. In front of her was the kitchen linen, which she pressed out with one of three irons that alternatively warmed on the stove nearby. When her eyes met Ainsley's they darted to her work.

"Like I said," Ms. Nelson said after a quick sweep of the room, "not even a paper to say goodbye."

"With all due respect, Ms. Nelson, I'm not entirely sure we are dealing with someone who has just run off," Ainsley explained, as calmly as he could muster.

"Well, how do you explain it then?" she demanded.

Ainsley inched toward Prudence.

Margaret appeared at the door then, a hand on her stomach as she searched for breath. Maxwell came up behind her but stopped short of entering the room. "There's nothing in my room," she said. "I checked your room as well, Peter."

Ms. Nelson huffed. "Why would she leave anything there?"

Both Ainsley and Margaret were content to leave the housekeeper's questions unanswered. "Perhaps her roommate knows something," Ainsley suggested.

The girl's eyes shot up and then immediately dropped when she saw everyone in the room look at her. She was no more than fourteen and was fairly new to the household.

"Prudence, is it?" Ainsley asked.

The girl glanced to the cook, who had since deserted her chore. "Go on now, tell the master what you know," she said with a quick nod of encouragement.

Prudence gave a quick exhale before lifting her head. "She ain't always been truthful, sir," she said. "Many a morning I've woken to find her bed not slept in."

A gasp escaped Ms. Nelson, but Ainsley and Margaret

only exchanged a quick glance.

"I don't know where she goes, sir, but she's always here in the kitchens or elsewhere in the house, so I never thought it was my place to ask." The girl twisted her fingers in front of her and raised her shoulders in an unsure shrug before biting down into her lower lip.

"And you never thought to tell me, neither!" Ms. Nelson looked livid as she inched for the girl. Ainsley stopped her with one outstretched hand.

"I only thought I had slept in," Prudence answered. "It's a wicked habit, I know, but I am getting better." Prudence gave a pleading glance to Margaret, who no doubt looked to be the most agreeable in the room.

"And so you can't be sure she wasn't there," Ainsley suggested.

"Well, no, not exactly, only that last night I decided to lock the door to our room, on account of the murder, sir. I knew I'd have to get up from bed to unlock it for Miss Kemp, but I figured it would be better to be safe."

"And?" Ainsley grew impatient.

"She never came and when I woke the door was still locked. She hadn't come in, sir. I'm sure of it."

Moments later, Ainsley was ushering his sister into his room and closing the door behind them. Ms. Nelson was content to let Ainsley take any necessary action, as she still believed the woman had simply abandoned her position. Maxwell showed a greater amount of concern, but took Ainsley's direction to reassure the chambermaid that she was not in any danger of losing her place.

"This only proves she didn't return home last night," Ainsley said once he and his sister were alone. "I'm fairly certain I can account for her absence on every other evening Prudence spoke about."

Margaret gave a crooked smile. "Perhaps we should tell the staff to allay their fears."

Ainsley knew she was making a playful jab, but he was in no mood. He was genuinely concerned for Julia. He knew she was concerned too.

"A woman came to see me at the morgue yesterday," Ainsley said as he crossed the room for his bookshelf.

"Did you know this woman?"

Ainsley shook his head. "She told me her daughter had gone missing. That she hadn't returned home from work. She asked me to look amongst the dead."

"That poor woman."

He opened a small, wooden box, a trinket he had bought once on a family excursion to Brighton. He pulled out the lead figurine of Saint Christopher and looked over it once more. Searching for any identifiable mark he turned it over in his palm, debating whether or not to show it to Margaret. "What if Julia came against the same fate? What if both of them were taken against their will?" he asked, examining the figure once more.

"Something tells me Julia is not the sort to fall prey to anyone," Margaret said.

"Anyone can be targeted," Ainsley said, his focus still on the figure.

"What are you looking at?" Margaret asked, stepping closer.

Ainsley snapped the box shut. "Nothing. Just thought, perhaps, she had left a message for me." He turned to his sister. "Did you know Julia was Catholic?" he asked.

"It came up once, I think. I didn't think anything of it at the time. Why do you ask?"

Ainsley shook his head. "She told me yesterday. I had no idea."

"Does it matter?"

"I don't know," he answered. So much information was making its way through his head he really could not tell what was important and what was merely circumstance. "Ms. Nelson sent Julia out on an errand yesterday and she came by the hospital to see me. Why wouldn't she have sent Prudence or one of the other girls?"

Margaret shrugged. "Fear, perhaps. Everyone was in such a state. I imagine Julia was the only one brave enough to leave the house."

Pacing, Ainsley found himself walking toward the window.

"The police were outside the Talbots' all day yesterday," Margaret explained further.

The sun had risen hours ago and Ainsley was most

definitely late for work. "I need you to do something for me, Margaret," Ainsley said, his tone serious. "I need you to call at the Talbots' house. Ask them what they know of the man found outside their door." He turned. "Will you do that?"

"How shall I broach the subject?" Margaret asked. "Excuse me, did anyone here murder the man found next to your steps?"

"Don't be so ridiculous. I'm not in the mood." Ainsley covered his eyes with his hands and tried to steady his breath. "I need to know if he was a servant of theirs, or if there's any connection between him and their house. There must be something."

Margaret's shoulders sank as she exhaled.

Ainsley wondered if it was because she had become accustomed to staying in. "You can't hide away in here forever," he said.

"Why not?"

Chapter 7

Later that day, Margaret found herself standing outside the Talbots' door. A section of the pavement remained quarantined and a uniformed constable stood on guard. A few onlookers remained, milling about and whispering to each other as they looked on.

"They won't answer," one plump man said as he leaned into the iron rail at the bottom of the steps. "They've had greater than thirty souls come for a bit of gossip and ain't no one been granted admittance." He brushed the side of his bulbous, pink nose with his thumb and smiled at Margaret, who looked over her shoulder at him.

"I'm not looking for gossip," she qualified. "Winifred is my friend."

The man chuckled. "Aren't they all when there is a story to be told?"

For the first time, Margaret began to second-guess her decision to come. It had been many months since she had last seen Winifred and that was only in passing at Victoria Station. Prior to that, the last time they had tea was a year before. They parted on good terms, but Margaret always wondered why they never kept in close contact.

Margaret stiffened when the door opened a crack and smiled when she saw the head of the family's butler through the slit he allowed in the door. "Good day, my name is Margaret Marshall. I live a few houses down. I've just come to check on Winifred. To see if she needs anything."

The butler didn't do anything at first. The crack widened slightly as he looked her up and down before pulling the door open all the way.

"Please forgive me, Lady Margaret," he said as she stepped inside the dark entranceway. "Mr. Talbot has given me specific orders not to let anyone in." He closed the door behind her. "I will let Miss Talbot know you are here."

The butler began to walk away when Margaret called

him back. "What made you admit me and not anyone else, may I ask?"

He smiled. "I remember you and your mother."

A few minutes later Margaret was escorted into the sitting room at the back of the house that overlooked the garden, a fairly similar-looking garden to the one at Marshall House. While she waited for Winifred to arrive, Margaret stood at the window and looked out over the green space. Right away, she spotted one noticeable difference to her own garden: a wood and iron gate at the far back corner. Ivy grew up the one brick wall along that eastern boundary and covered more than half the arched entryway.

"Margaret! So good of you to come!"

She turned at the sound of Mrs. Talbot's singsong voice. As she stretched out both arms to embrace her neighbour, Margaret remembered how much her mother, Lady Marshall, had despised Mrs. Talbot. "She is so very contrived, Margaret," the late Lady Marshall had said. "She simply tries too hard to impress. It's quite pathetic, actually."

The countess seemed to take issue with Mrs. Talbot's rise in fortunes after her marriage to Mr. Talbot, who was not a member of the gentry, but was very successful in textiles nonetheless.

Winifred, a pale, redheaded girl, stood unsure beside her stepmother. She was slender to the point of appearing gaunt and painfully jagged.

"Do forgive our somber mood. We've endured such a trial," Mrs. Talbot explained.

"So I've heard. I just wanted to come by and see if there was any assistance I can offer. Perhaps just a familiar face." Margaret gave an empathetic, closed-mouth smile before reaching out and taking Winifred's hand.

The corners of Winifred's mouth curled, but a soured expression overtook her eyes. "Not so familiar of late."

Margaret's ability to remain light and congenial waned as she looked into Winifred's eyes. There was a sadness there, something Margaret had never seen in her friend before.

Moments later they were seated on the sofas while a kitchen maid poured each of them a tea. "I imagine it's been tiring with so many police officers milling about," Margaret said, accepting the teacup and saucer from the maid. "I can imagine the upheaval it has caused."

"It's been terrible," answered Mrs. Talbot, who appeared more than eager to share the story. She touched the curls at her forehead lightly. "It was Jane here who first made the discovery." Mrs. Talbot nodded to the girl who now served Winifred.

"Truly? Oh, it must have been such a fright," Margaret said.

Jane simply looked at Margaret, but said nothing.

"Go on, girl," Mrs. Talbot said. "Tell our neighbour what you saw."

Jane nodded at her mistress's command and knit her hands in front of her as she turned to face Margaret. "I was putting a box of empty bottles on the bottom step—"

"Out front, at the servants' stairs," Mrs. Talbot injected.

Jane gave a nod. "I saw him like a scarecrow, rocking back and forth as if pushed by wind, only there was no wind. I thought it may have been a trick, you know, something the other boys devised to pull each other's legs. But then the light hit it and I saw it was a man." She laughed nervously and turned to her tea trolley.

"What did you do?" Margaret pressed.

"She screamed," Mrs. Talbot said quickly. "Loud enough to wake the dead. Within minutes Mr. Talbot was down the stairs and out the door, thinking some calamity was in progress. Our butler ran out as well. Winifred and I watched from the window." Mrs. Talbot's eyes glazed over slightly as she recalled the memory. "Such a horrid sight." She waved a dismissive hand to Jane, who obediently scurried from the room, pushing the tea trolley as she went.

Margaret wanted to call her back, a long list of questions still formulating in her mind. "Who ran for the watchman?"

"We didn't have to," Mrs. Talbot said with a slight laugh. "Jane's scream did better at summoning him than any other method could. The rest of the morning was a blur. That Yard fellow was here for nearly two hours. I was beginning to fear for my breakfast."

Margaret curled her hand and dug a fingernail into her palm. It would not do to chastise her host's self-centred nature, not when she still had more questions. "So the man was not known to you?" Margaret said, plucking up her teacup and bringing it to her lips. "Not a servant of yours?"

Mrs. Talbot looked aghast. "No, certainly not."

"No one on your staff recognizes him?" Margaret pressed.

"The detective spoke with everyone extensively. The man had no connection to our house. No obvious one, in any case." Mrs. Talbot didn't seem to mind so much inquiry, but Winifred eyed Margaret with a penetrating look.

"You seem overly concerned, Margaret," she said. "Your questions rival those of the inspector."

Margaret looked back and forth between Winifred and Mrs. Talbot, who suddenly looked wary. Margaret gave a lighthearted laugh. "Forgive me," she said. "My curiosity gets the better of me sometimes. Gets me into all sorts of trouble."

Mrs. Talbot laughed and gave some words of reassurance, but Winifred wasn't so easily won over. She remained quiet for the rest of the visit, allowing Margaret and Mrs. Talbot to carry the conversation.

Once her tea was finished, Margaret was obliged to end her call. After saying farewell to Mrs. Talbot, she walked to the front door, where the butler waited with her hat and gloves. She was surprised to find Winifred had followed her.

"Thank you for the tea and conversation," Margaret said, offering her best smile. "You should visit me at Marshall House. It's quite handy now, isn't it?"

Winifred said nothing at first and it suddenly dawned on Margaret why. There was a time in the previous summer when she was sure Ainsley had eyes for Winifred. Margaret could not confirm anything, but she thought perhaps Winifred had more interest in her older brother than she did with her.

Margaret stepped outside and turned to Winifred in the doorway as she slipped on her gloves.

"Would you like me to tell Peter you asked after him?"

Winifred smirked. "Do not bother. He hasn't bothered

with me for some time." She leaned on the doorframe, scowling as she had done nearly the entire visit. "Goodbye, Margaret," she said, pulling the heavy front door. "I hope you achieved a certain degree of entertainment from your little visit, but you needn't call again."

With that, she shut the door, the telltale iron latch catching loudly, leaving Margaret dumbfounded under the portico.

A short time later, Margaret arrived at St. Thomas Hospital and discovered Ainsley in the annex room next to the morgue. There he had constructed his own desk away from the recognized office for the doctors down the hall. He had once told her he preferred it to any of the other corners of the hospital. Margaret peered around the threshold at first, surprised to find him so engrossed in a file opened in front of him.

He held his weary head up at the temples with his knuckles as he leaned into the table, looking haggard and exhausted. When he looked up she saw that he had been crying.

"Has she returned?" he asked, expectantly.

Margaret could only muster a shake of her head. She watched her brother's shoulders slouch further as he returned his attention to the stack of files in front of him. "Did you quarrel, Peter?"

"No," he replied suddenly. "There was nothing amiss in our last conversation."

He sniffled as he shifted on his stool and quickly closed the file he had been looking at. Margaret stepped inside the room and pulled a chair that had been set against the wall closer to Ainsley.

He turned. "Oh, my apologies," he said hopping up to assist her. He placed the chair not far from his own.

"I met with Mrs. Talbot today, as you requested," she said as she took her seat. "And I've made a right fool of myself in the process."

Ainsley did not sit immediately. Instead, he stood over his desk and passively surveyed the papers scattered on its surface. "What did you find out?" he asked hesitantly.

"The body was found by the maid prior to dawn," she

said. "And no one in the house recognized him. Simms has been very thorough in interviewing everyone."

Ainsley smiled. "I have no doubt."

"Perhaps this violence is not related to the Talbots," Margaret suggested.

"The body was put on display," Ainsley said. "It's a message to someone. I can't see the point of it otherwise."

Margaret let out a tiny sigh as she recalled her conversation with Mrs. Talbot and Winifred.

"Why do you say you made a fool of yourself?" Ainsley asked, shifting a small stack of files to the far end of his desk and then plucking up a pen.

"Winifred nearly accused me of preening for salacious details." Margaret choked back her frustration. "It was mortifying."

"Don't take it to heart," Ainsley said, clearly trying his best to console her. "She's always been difficult to please." He shook his head as if shaking off an unpleasant memory.

Margaret popped to the edge of her chair as Ainsley sat down opposite her. "I have a strong suspicion you have done something to her."

"Nothing she did not wish me to do," Ainsley answered, an amused smile tugging at the corners of his mouth. His smile quickly faded when their eyes met. "She was a willing participant, Margaret. Trust me on that."

"Yes, but how did it end?"

Ainsley stared off into the corner of the room before shrugging. "One-sided perhaps." He slapped the pen down on the files and shook his head. "I was a different man back then," he said. "Seems like a lifetime ago."

"This is what I was saying, Peter. You don't know the heartache you've left behind." Margaret sighed. "That's why I had to ask if you quarrelled. I don't think Julia would just run off without at least leaving a note."

A look of pain on his face, Ainsley ran a hand through his hair and looked to his desk.

"What is this about?" Margaret asked, nodding to the files and papers strewn about.

"Do you remember me speaking about a woman who came to see me yesterday, asking if her daughter had been brought here? I've been looking through all our files trying to find other girls her age." He leaned into the top of the desk as Margaret stood and came to his side. "I'm looking for a pattern."

"Do you think this might relate to Julia?"

Ainsley shrugged. "I don't know. I only found two murdered women of the same age and area of the city." He tapped two files in the top corner of his desk. "I'm looking at all the suspected suicides now. Maybe we missed something."

Margaret pulled the two files across the desk and opened the top one. "Female. Sixteen. Throat slit. Pulled from the Thames." She winced slightly at the description and then raised her hand to the scar at her own throat.

"She was later identified as Phyllis Martin, a scullery maid," Ainsley said, pointing further down the page. "She was missing for two weeks before her body was discovered."

Margaret opened the second one. "Mary Stewart," she said, reading the name. "Seventeen. A chambermaid." Her voice shook slightly as she read the details. "Throat slit. Found in Thames at low tide by mudlarks."

"She had been missing eight days."

"They both died in the same manner as the man," Margaret pointed out.

Ainsley nodded. "But they weren't strung up on display like he was. They were both disadvantaged girls with jobs in service. They were both missing for a period of time longer than a day or two. And they were both found within the last three months."

"I don't know, Peter. Feels like a quite a stretch." She gestured to the stack of files at the centre of the desk. "Anything ruled a suicide won't help either. The wounds would be self-inflicted, yes?" After a pause, Margaret spoke again. "And I don't see how this relates to Julia. She's older than these girls and she doesn't work anywhere near the neighbourhoods where these women lived and worked. There's no connection between these women and Belgravia."

"Except our man found yesterday morning."

The connection was small but Ainsley seemed determined to bring them together.

"How do you know the culprit hasn't already been

arrested?"

"I don't," Ainsley answered. "I was just working up my courage to go ask Simms."

Margaret exhaled and looked away. "Oh dear."

Chapter 8

With a handful of files tucked under his arm and more than a little trepidation, Ainsley walked up the steps of 4 Whitehall Place and slid through the heavy wood doors of Scotland Yard. Sergeant Fisher was busy speaking with another officer when Ainsley approached the desk with a look of apprehension on his features. He didn't want any trouble, but he knew his reputation was too well established for anyone to just take his word for it.

The officer and the sergeant turned in unison as he approached. The officer crossed his arms over his chest as Sergeant Fisher leaned over the ledge. "You about-face right now and march out that door and I won't have to tell Simms you disobeyed his order two days in a row," he said so only Ainsley could hear.

Ainsley glanced to the officer beside him. He was a large man, half a foot taller than Ainsley and with a scowl so hardened he wondered if people under arrest handcuffed themselves while in his shadow. From the corner of his eye Ainsley spotted Cooper at a desk not too far from the front lobby. The constable spotted him as well, but averted his eyes immediately, pretending to be engrossed by some paperwork. Even as Ainsley approached, the desk sergeant and mammoth officer at his heels, Cooper did not look up.

"File your complaint with Sergeant Fisher," Cooper mumbled. "I'm sure he cares more than I."

"I'm sorry, Cooper—"

"Sorry?" After a quick glance about the room, Cooper lowered his voice. "You nearly cost me my job," he growled.

Cooper was young and a complete greenhorn in a profession where his height and weight mattered more than his abilities. He'd have to hold his own amongst thieves and murders alike, all the while making a good impression on his superior officers. A major gaffe like the one he had made with Ainsley was enough to put his loyalty into question and cause undue scrutiny. The stress of it was already showing by the way he tapped his pen.

"I didn't intend to make you look incompetent," Ainsley said. "It was selfish of me."

Cooper raised his eyes and swallowed. He opened his mouth to speak and then closed it when his eyes darted over Ainsley's shoulder. "Tell someone who cares," he muttered as he bowed his head toward his papers.

"I'd like to report a missing person," Ainsley said, standing in place and alternating his attention amongst them. "Or is this not part of your job anymore?"

After a few unsure glances between the mammoth officer, Fisher and Cooper, Ainsley was escorted to a small room lined with windows instead of solid walls. There was a single table placed in the middle of the room. Even though the noise of the station grew muffled as Cooper closed the door, Ainsley could still see the manic pace of the place and hoped to God Simms didn't see them before Ainsley could tell them what he had discovered.

"All right," Cooper said, taking a seat opposite Ainsley. He pulled his chair toward the table and positioned a notebook in front of him. "Who is the missing party?"

The murmur from the opposite side of the glass ended abruptly, drawing Ainsley's attention to the desks just beyond the room. Simms stood ten feet from the door, hard-faced and furious. He turned to a nearby officer and said something, but Ainsley could not hear what. With an overwhelming sense of unease, Ainsley stood slowly, using the edge of the table to steady his movements. Both he and Cooper moved deliberately, as one would when encountering a bear, never taking their eye from their adversary and incredibly leery of what they might do.

"What the hell happened between you two?" Cooper asked.

It was no secret the contempt Simms felt for Ainsley, but now it was confirmed—Simms had never told a soul what took place.

"It was the biggest mistake of my life," Ainsley answered.

Simms charged for the door, barrelling in and pushing himself into Ainsley. "You don't belong here!" he bellowed.

Ainsley felt the edge of the table crunch into him as he

tried to back away, wanting desperately to avoid blows. He had no desire to hit Simms. He wanted to repair the damage he had done and despaired at the thought of never being able to heal that wound.

He readied himself for a hit or shove, but Cooper bravely ran to his aid and pushed Simms off him. "He's here regarding a missing person!"

When Simms stepped back, Cooper placed himself firmly between Ainsley and his attacker. Out of breath, Simms stood silent for a few seconds before adjusting his coat. "Who's missing?" he asked.

"Julia Kemp, a maid from our house," Ainsley answered, as Cooper stepped back slowly. Simms's and Ainsley's eyes met, each furious and equally heartbroken.

"Take the report and get him out of here," Simms said.

"There's something else," Ainsley called out as Simms reached the door. He knew his voice sounded desperate and shaky. Simms was the Yard's best man and he needed him to help find Julia. Ainsley gestured to the files sitting in the middle of the table that separated them. "It's about your man from Belgravia."

The tension in the room was palpable, even as Simms closed the door to the rest of the office. He didn't bother looking to the other officers who shared the space. He kept his gaze trained on Ainsley at the other side of the table, studying him and perhaps trying to discern if he spoke the truth.

Moments passed. No one spoke until Simms reached over the desk and grabbed one of the files. "Explain," he said evenly.

"I found evidence of two women, each housemaids, murdered and deposited in the Thames. Their throats slit."

Simms's expression did not waiver as he looked over the morgue reports.

"A woman visited my morgue two days ago enquiring about her daughter, a scullery maid who hasn't returned home from work. I said I would look through our files."

Simms looked up suddenly, his face expressionless, causing Ainsley to falter. Simms said nothing.

Ainsley swallowed. "If my theory is correct, she will be found within the next three days."

"How does this connect to our man in Belgravia?" Simms asked, arching his eyebrow.

"I believe he was killed by the same person," Ainsley explained. "You'll notice in the morgue reports that the wounds sustained by the women were jagged. There were tears in the dermis that resemble more of a rip than a cut."

Cooper went pale as Ainsley spoke.

Ainsley licked his lips and suddenly remembered who he was speaking with. Simms was a seasoned officer but Cooper was yet to be hardened by the streets.

"Continue, Dr. Ainsley," Simms said.

With an inhale, Ainsley proceeded. "I observed a similar pattern on the body found in Belgravia—"

"A body that you were not permitted access to," Simms reminded him.

"Yes."

Thankfully, Simms did not press further as to why Ainsley felt compelled to intercede with the crime scene.

"If our man is related to these maids, why was he not found in the Thames as well?" Cooper asked.

"I believe he was meant as a message, a warning," Ainsley said.

A sudden breath escaped Inspector Simms as he slapped the files back down on the table that separated them. "Here's a warning for you, Peter," he said, using Ainsley's first name for the first time in a long time. "If I ever find you interfering with an official investigation again I won't be as understanding as I have been until now."

"But Miss Kemp?"

"Go home, Peter," Simms said more determinedly. "My holding cells are at capacity, but for you I could always squeeze in one more." The inspector turned his attention to Cooper. "Take the information regarding the maid and make sure he leaves. Sergeant Fisher should know his shadow isn't permitted on our front steps." He turned for the door.

"Wait. You know there's a connection here. I saw it in your face," Ainsley pleaded. "You can't just dismiss me."

"I just did."

The door slammed as Simms left.

Chapter 9

With a stale summer heat pressing down on the city Ainsley opted for a hansom home. As the carriage rolled past the Talbot residence Ainsley peered out the window and saw that all evidence of the earlier crime had been removed. Nothing stirred in the windows of the house and scarcely any light made it past the heavy, drawn curtains. As evening took hold, the streets appeared vacant with only a single boy hurriedly making his way down the pavement.

The carriage pulled up to the kerb on the opposite side of the road from Marshall House and Ainsley disembarked. He tipped his hat to the driver and made his way across the empty street. Once inside he found the foyer vacant. He removed his own hat and jacket and draped them over the bannister at the foot of stairs.

Lamplight blazed from the parlour while a giggle from Aunt Louisa wafted into the hall.

"Peter should be home soon," Ainsley heard Margaret say. "I'm certain he will be glad to see you."

Ainsley found himself smiling. Had Jonas travelled from Edinburgh to pay a visit? Ainsley rounded the corner of the doorframe and stopped suddenly when he saw Blair's recognizable blond head sitting in their father's chair. He was seated looking away from the door but the looks of surprise on Margaret and Nathaniel's faces when Ainsley walked in forced him to look behind him.

"Peter!"

Ainsley forced a smile. "Good to see you, Blair," he said, shaking the man's hand in greeting.

It was then that Ainsley realized how much he had hoped it was Jonas. The entire house had been in deep chaos concerning Lord Marshall, which made a proper farewell nearly impossible. The last time Ainsley had seen Jonas was in the hurried jumble of evening when not even the hired nurse had adopted a working procedure for their invalid patriarch. In the end, the send-off was rushed, lacking in meaning and proper attention. Many days had Ainsley wished an opportunity to recast their goodbyes.

"What have you been up to?" Blair asked. "I have never seen a gentleman so inaccessible as you." He chuckled at his jest and glanced about the room. Aunt Louisa raised her glass and nodded in agreement before downing its entire contents.

"You forget that he has duties beyond the house," Margaret said quickly.

Ainsley found himself annoyed by her subterfuge. Each person in the room was aware of his duties at the hospital. It seemed pointless to dance about the subject in such a way.

"Oh, that's right," Blair said, remembrance dawning on his features. "I guess I just have a hard time imagining you in a surgeon's frock. You could just call yourself doctor, yes? Perhaps you only go there for the women." Again a bright smile erupted.

Ainsley's expression remained blank. He turned to Margaret. "Has any information arrived regarding the package I have been waiting for?"

Margaret's expression fell. "Oh my, I can't remember."

Seconds later she was excusing herself from the conversation, promising a quick return, before walking out into the hall with Ainsley at her heels.

Once out of earshot she turned. Keeping her voice low, she twisted her fingers as she spoke. "I've heard nothing. I spoke with everyone on our staff, hoping someone had some information."

Ainsley drew in a discouraged breath.

"I thought perhaps she had received a note from an old friend or something to such end, but nothing had arrived for her that day or any day in the prior week."

"Have you spoken with Maxwell?"

"Why yes, of course. He knew of her lack of mail." Margaret licked her lips. "Peter, there's nothing here. Nothing that can be done."

"What am I supposed to do, just wait for her to return home?"

Margaret's head titled slightly to the side. "She worked here. This wasn't truly her home," she reminded him.

"This was her home," he answered somewhat forcefully. They both turned and looked back at the parlour door. "She had no reason to leave."

The look on Margaret's face told him she saw a different angle to things.

"What?" he demanded, running a hand through his hair. "What could you possibly understand that I don't?"

After a moment's hesitation she spoke. "Perhaps she wished things to be as they were before matters became so...complicated."

"What is your meaning?"

"Maybe she wished to go a separate way and could not bring herself to tell you."

Ainsley turned and marched for his father's study. He could not fathom any such reasoning. Margaret followed him, and even pushed past the door that he tried to close.

"I knew this would not end well," she said, more forcefully than she could while they spoke in the hall.

Ainsley crossed the floor of the study and went straight for the window that overlooked the dark street.

"Father always said—"

"I know what Father always said!" Ainsley yelled. "Julia and I were different. I don't know how to explain it. It just was."

"How could it be?" Margaret asked. "She is a maid, employed by our father and paid by our riches. How could she turn you away and deny your advances?"

"If you knew Julia as I do you'd know that she'd have no qualms about sending me on my merry way. If my advances were unsatisfactory I have no doubt she would have made it known." The very suggestion that he had taken advantage of her, the woman he now realized he loved, was repugnant and vile. "She would never allow herself to be pushed around. Not by me, or anyone."

A moment of silence passed between them. Nothing in the house stirred, not even the family members and visitor in the next room.

"What did Inspector Simms say?" Margaret said at last.

"He said very little, actually," Ainsley said, rounding their father's desk. "I told them all I knew but even I'm not sure there is a connection now." Ainsley fell back into the leather chair and raised his hands to his face. Exhausted, he wasn't entirely sure he'd be able to stay awake for much longer.

"You are short on sleep," Margaret said. "You should rest. I'll tell Blair you are feeling under the weather this evening."

Ainsley found himself smiling. "Look at you, learning to deceive like a right proper mistress."

Margaret raised an eyebrow. "Between Mother and Aunt Louisa my tutelage has been quite remarkable."

Ainsley's eyes shot open and he sat up in the chair.

"What is it?" Margaret asked, startled.

"Tutelage." Ainsley stood and rushed for the door.

"Peter, where are you going?"

"The Limehouse Foundling Home."

The building stood three storeys high, institutional in its lack of adornments or architectural embellishments. Given the late hour, the place looked devoid of life, but Ainsley knew better than to assume nothing occurred behind the stone bricks and iron-gated windows. The sheer number of orphans housed and cared for by the headmistress, Mrs. Holliwell, ensured any number of misadventures at any given time.

Mrs. Holliwell had been a friend of his late mother, who had become a patron to the charity early on. This foundling home had also been the very place where Julia had been raised. Ainsley and Margaret did not know as much when Julia was first hired on but he had no doubt his father factored in her parentage and background before allowing her to enter the Marshall Home. That was one inconsistency that remained unanswered even after the many months that had passed. Always discerning, even shrewd, Lord Marshall had never missed a chance to turn his nose up at his wife's involvement with the street urchins of the east side. It remained unclear why an exception had been made in Julia's case, who remained the one and only orphan Lord Marshall ever hired.

Ainsley's knock at the heavy, wooden doors echoed back to him and then moments later the door swung in.

Mrs. Holliwell squinted as she peered around the door. She raised a small lantern that she held in her hand and smiled instantly.

"Mr. Marshall!" She opened the door wider and ushered him in. "Come, come," she waved. "I had hoped you and Margaret would come for a visit soon."

With the door to the street closed behind them, Mrs. Holliwell smiled warmly. "My, you are looking well," she said.

Ainsley laughed. "Merely a trick of the light," he said, nodding to her lantern.

She waved off his humility and gestured for him to follow her. They walked down a long hallway and then turned toward the common rooms. The halls above them remained silent save for a weak cough or the squeak of one of the metal beds.

Another adult, complete with dirtied apron and tight-fitted bun, approached them from the other end of the hall.

"The boys have settled, ma'am," she said, shoving her hands into the pockets of her pinafore. "Jack is still crying, but he's not disturbing the others."

Mrs. Holliwell gave an uneasy glance to Ainsley before nodding toward her staff member. "Thank you, Kate. Make sure the kitchen is tidy for the morning."

The woman gave a nod and then left, retracing her steps down the corridor.

"We were forced to give one of our younger boys the strap," Mrs. Holliwell said as she entered the open door beside them. "A lash for each year of the boy's age."

Once inside Ainsley noticed she had led him to her office, where a second lamp sat aglow and radiating a warm luminance into the room.

Ainsley hesitated. "How many would that be then?"

"Five, or so we believe."

Ainsley tried not to physically react at the thought of such punishment. He himself was no stranger to the penalty. His father had been rather fond of the strap whereas their governess preferred the switch, the directive most likely coming directly from his father.

"Please, Mr. Marshall, take a seat." Mrs. Holliwell nodded to the upholstered chair that sat opposite her desk.

"I was just planning meals for the next month," she explained as Ainsley took his seat where directed. Taking her seat she placed her pencil into the page of her ledger where she wrote and closed the book. "I think you should know I have not seen my son for some time," she said with a pained smile. "He does not bother me any longer and no longer comes to see the children."

Her use of the word *'see'* caused Ainsley to internally cringe. The man she spoke of, her son, had been taking too many liberties with the children, the girls especially. Once Ainsley had become aware of this he took extreme measures to ensure Mr. Holliwell never thought to even look at a child, let alone lay a hand on one. Ainsley had told some of the older children to send word if Mr. Holliwell returned. Their silence allowed him to believe the orphans were safe, and now Mrs. Holliwell's words confirmed it.

"You know as well as I that it is for the better that he refrains from contact," Ainsley reminded her gently.

Mrs. Holliwell nodded and raised a wrinkled hand to her cheek, as if recalling the number of bruises it had received at the hand of her son over her lifetime. "Yes, I do, indeed."

Ainsley drew in a quick breath to steady himself and then leaned into the edge of his seat. "That is not why I am here," he said. "You know a woman who has come to work for my family."

"Julia, yes," Mrs. Holliwell volunteered quickly. "Is she all right?"

"The last I spoke with her she was entirely all right. Healthy, content, happy even," Ainsley said. As he spoke he could picture the smile she gave him from the other side of his bed. Many times they had talked for hours into the night, both happy to exchange sleep for those precious hours of solitude.

"Something's happened," Mrs. Holliwell said suddenly, breaking his reverie.

"Yes." Ainsley rubbed a hand over his face. Tears stung at his eyes, but he willed them away. Mrs. Holliwell could not know the extent of their relationship. As far as she could know he was an anxious employer merely concerned for her safety. "She was sent on some errands for our housekeeper, but never returned home. That was two days ago."

He decided not to tell her about the other maids found with their throats slit. Such details would only further distress Mrs. Holliwell, whom he knew Julia regarded as her mother.

"I believed she was happy working at Marshall House—"

"Oh, she was!" Mrs. Holliwell cut in quickly. "She was exceedingly happy."

The look on Ainsley face must have betrayed his surprise because when Mrs. Holliwell looked to him she smiled.

"She begged me not to say anything to you or Margaret, but she would come have tea with me every Sunday afternoon." A grimace spread over Mrs. Holliwell's face as she pulled a handkerchief out of her sleeve at her wrist. "She told me very little, mind you, very little about the workings of the house and such, but she said that she considered Margaret a dear friend."

Ainsley smiled awkwardly, wondering if she ever spoke of him and knew she would not. Their relationship was far too illicit.

"She spoke of you as well."

His heart rose, wondering what she may have said.

"She said you were faring quite well at the hospital and that she was ever so proud to work for a righteous and amiable man."

"Amiable?" Ainsley wasn't sure what he had expected her to say. He imagined her limitations mirrored his. As much as he'd like to claim her publically as his own, his position and status prevented him. Such a declaration meant scandal and while he cared little of his own reputation he knew he could never do such a thing to Julia, whose position relied on her good name.

"Why would she leave?" Ainsley asked.

Mrs. Holliwell shook her head. "I don't know. Marshall House has provided a stability she had never known before. It seems inconceivable that she would simply give it up. Was there no note, no indication where she might have gone? Perhaps one of the other maids—"

TRACY L. WARD

"There was no such note and all the maids have sworn they know nothing."

"Oh my." Mrs. Holliwell rubbed her nose with her handkerchief and sniffled. "I've been so afraid something might happen."

Ainsley watched as the foundling home matron licked her dry and cracked lips, tears pooling on her lower lids. "Why do you say that?" he asked.

Mrs. Holliwell looked up but did not speak.

"What are you afraid will happen?" he pressed.

From her position across the tiny and dimly light room, Mrs. Holliwell shifted slightly, as if turning away, but then shifted back toward him. She opened her mouth to speak twice, but stopped herself before finally choosing her words. "Julia came to me as a young girl on the cusp of womanhood. She had already seen so much it broke my heart that she had not been brought to us sooner."

"Her parents had passed away?"

"Her mother, yes, but at this time her father still held a spell over them."

"Them?"

"Why yes, her brother and her." Mrs. Holliwell wiped her nose. "They never wished to stay here. They kept running away, running back to him. But he could not care for them and she always ended up back on our doorstep begging for food. Often Robert wouldn't be too far behind. Some of my volunteers said I should stop allowing them back, but I couldn't bring myself to do it. Julia was so bright and keen to learn, the complete opposite of her brother, who never did learn to read."

"She must have been here enough for you to consider her a daughter," Ainsley suggested.

"Two years after the first time they were brought here their father died in a knife fight. They were with him at the time, but neither of them ever told me what happened and I thought it best not to pry. Neither one ran away after that." Mrs. Holliwell smiled. "Julia applied herself to her studies and found a position in the service not too long after her fourteenth birthday."

"What happened to her brother?" Ainsley asked.

"Against my advice he became involved in some illegal

82

betting scheme, boxing or some such nonsense. He was a good fighter, strong despite his small size, but I had a feeling he'd get himself into trouble one day. He was good for little else given his disdain for books. I had already let him stay here longer than usual, on account of Julia and he being so close."

"Do you know where Robert lives?" Ainsley asked, inching to the very edge of his seat.

"It's been nearly ten years," Mrs. Holliwell confessed. "I couldn't even tell you *if* he lives."

"But if Julia was close to him she would have said something, yes?" No reply came. "Do you know who he was working for? Maybe Julia mentioned a visit with him."

Mrs. Holliwell shook her head and covered her face with her hand. "I wish I could help," she sobbed.

"There must be something," he pressed. "I fear she may be in trouble." Ainsley leaned into the space that separated them and handed her his own, clean handkerchief from his inside pocket. "Mrs. Holliwell, please."

Apprehension marred her features as she accepted Ainsley's handkerchief. She looked away as more tears filled her eyes. Ainsley reached over and placed his hand over hers, which lay on her skirt.

"I have to find her."

She closed her eyes and winced against the pain it caused her. "How I have wished Julia would break free of that man," she said. "Getting her a position in Belgravia was the best I could do. I thought she would be safe there." She eyed him as she dabbed her cheeks with the soft cloth.

"Safe from her brother?"

"No, not Robert." Mrs. Holliwell looked at Ainsley squarely then, her mouth shaping into a frown before she spoke again. "Thaddeus."

"He recruited Robert in the illegal fighting?"

Mrs. Holliwell nodded. "He is a terrible man. Vindictive and volatile."

"She had a relationship with him?" Ainsley asked, aware how uncomfortable the subject made him feel.

"Yes. I believe he made her feel protected in some way, a way in which her father and brother had failed." She sniffled then and took a breath to steady herself. "You have to understand life in these neighbourhoods for young women like Julia. Society grants them no power over their lives and these men offer them something they could not have otherwise." Mrs. Holliwell paused, her gaze fixated on something on the floor. "She would not tell me what he did but I saw the bruises, as you saw on me. We both fell victim to the men in our lives. I could not help her any more than I could help myself."

Ainsley stood suddenly, the anxiousness he felt for Julia's safety nipping at his heels. He flexed his hands into fists at his side and took a deep breath as he paced. "Where can I find him?"

"I don't know. I know very little. Julia told me nothing. She did not want to place me in jeopardy."

Ainsley went for the door. Mrs. Holliwell trailed him down the hall and back to the front door.

"These are not men you trifle with, Mr. Marshall," she called as she scurried along behind him.

Ainsley turned just short of the door that led outside, softening his tone somewhat but still clearly agitated at the thought of Julia in harm's way. "Do you have an address?"

"No. I have told you what I know."

Ainsley nodded absentmindedly. "Thank you for speaking with me, Mrs. Holliwell," he said, replacing his hat and buttoning up his overcoat. He was out the door and down the steps when Mrs. Holliwell called out. "You will let me know when you find her, yes? You will let me know she is safe."

"Yes, ma'am," Ainsley answered as he tipped his hat and went on into the night.

Chapter 10

When Margaret re-entered the parlour, Aunt Louisa, Nathaniel, and Blair were speaking in hushed tones that ended abruptly when her footfalls sounded the creaks in the floor. Blair and Nathaniel jumped to their feet as Margaret entered.

Aunt Louisa raised her chin and looked beyond Margaret to the hall before speaking. "Where's Peter?"

Margaret gave a halfhearted smile. She hated how circumstances demanded she make excuses for her brother. However, she knew he would never rest until Julia was found and that gave her some comfort. "He was called away," she said, taking her seat next to Aunt Louisa.

Blair held up his coattails as he settled back into his chair. "He's quite a busy man, your brother," he said. "It's a shame to always seem to miss him."

Aunt Louisa waved her hand and clicked her tongue. "You'll never pin Peter down," she said, with a slight laugh. "I have learned as much since our return to England."

"He's quite self-interested, if you ask me," Nathaniel injected, as he finished off the last of his alcohol.

Margaret gave him a disapproving look, but was unable to think of a quick retort.

"I only wished that I could, perhaps, get to know him better," Blair explained, keeping his eyes trained on Margaret. "It's my greatest wish that he should approve of me."

It was then that she noticed everyone in the room was peering at her, as if they expected her to offer words of approval to encourage his interest. Margaret had no desire to give such an impression. Jonas had only been gone a short time and even though she knew she had hurt him greatly she held to the hope that one day they'd be reunited.

When Margaret said nothing Aunt Louisa cleared her throat. "A lovely gesture, isn't it, Margaret?" she coaxed.

Forced to nod in agreement, Margaret offered a closed-mouth smile.

A quarter of an hour later and the four of them were saying farewell at the parlour door. Before his departure, Blair pulled Margaret's hand to his lips and graced the top of her fingers. "Shall we take a stroll in Hyde Park tomorrow?" he asked, while he held on to her hand.

Before Margaret could answer Aunt Louisa was at her side. "Sounds lovely." The high tone and light air she took while in Blair's presence was enough for Margaret to question who was courting who.

With great relief he was gone and Margaret found it much easier to breathe. Nathaniel followed Blair to the front door.

"Goodness, child," Aunt Louisa said, suddenly abandoning the charade. "You'd think you'd be a little more...encouraging." She retraced her steps back into the parlour to grab her reading spectacles, which she had left on one of the side tables.

"I do not understand your meaning."

"I doubt that, my dear." Aunt Louisa slipped her glasses onto her nose and then plucked a stack of small cards from the table. "You are as smart as a whip. No one is fooled by your pretty face." She smiled over the card she read. "You know very well that Blair is here to court you. His entire family mourns in the country, yet he remains in London. You heard him yourself. He intends to call each day, I imagine, until he has won you over."

"I wish he wouldn't bother," Margaret said, crossing her arms over her chest. "I cannot be *won* over."

Aunt Louisa regarded her for a moment before pulling off her spectacles and stepping forward. "If this is about that Dr. Davies, I'm sorry to say it, but you are wasting your time." Aunt Louisa grimaced as her gaze trailed about the room. "It would be foolish to believe you have all the time in the world to wait for a man to make up his mind. The reality is you don't. Beauty fades, hope dies, and potential beaus get snatched up one by one. You could spend a lifetime waiting for that one love to love you back."

"Aunt Louisa—"

"Don't argue. It's far too late in the evening and I

haven't had enough to drink. Just think about what I said." She gave Margaret a gentle pat on the cheek before leaving the room.

Margaret didn't want to think about a life without Jonas. In fact, for much of the last few weeks Margaret had been doing everything and anything to keep herself from thinking about him. Her late-night vigils with her father, the great care she took with organizing the household, and the interest she had in Ainsley's work were all a means to ignore the heartache that burned away inside her. Her future with Jonas remained unclear. She hadn't been able to speak with him but imagined he was cross with her. If he wasn't already he certainly would be once he found out Blair had been calling at the house with marked frequency. He had accused her before of changing her mind, a charge she emphatically denied.

In a perfect world, Margaret and Jonas would have been wed already, eloped at some chapel in Scotland. Had everything gone as planned she'd be fumbling her way around a town home, one befitting the income of a doctor, unable to cook a proper breakfast or iron a shirt. Jonas would laugh at her, perhaps even tease her for her lack of womanly skills, but he'd love her. Boy, would that man love her.

Margaret felt a thump form in her throat as she thought of him.

Nothing could be done for it now. What was done was done. He was gone and she was at Marshall House, where duty demanded.

She lingered in the parlour for a few moments, soaking in the quiet of the room, when the door opened and Vivian appeared with an empty tray to collect the dishes left by the family. She immediately bowed her head.

"My apologies, miss," she said softly, her Barbadian accent colouring her whisper. The girl began to back away.

"Stay a moment," Margaret said, taking a step toward her. "I wanted to ask how the others are treating you. Belowstairs, I mean."

There was no delicate way to put forward her concern. Vivian was visibly different with her brown skin, crimped hair, and slave heritage. Margaret had no doubt their

English servants would see their negro colleague as someone completely beneath them.

"As well as can be expected, miss."

Margaret noticed a silver, oval locket around the girl's neck, etched with a filigree pattern and dotted with a very tiny green gem. "That's a lovely piece," Margaret said, genuinely attracted to its beauty.

With a quick, jerky movement, Vivian raised her hand as if to protect it.

"Does it carry a picture?" Margaret asked. She had seen similar necklaces in the shops, and around the necks of a few friends, but had never owned one herself.

Slowly, Vivian released the front of the locket and showed Margaret a tiny photograph of a coloured woman. A gold cross had been secured to the opposite side.

"A mourning locket." Margaret nearly cried at the sweetness of the tribute. "My mother passed away recently as well. You must miss your mother and your home country terribly."

"Yes, miss."

"Has your father passed as well?" Margaret asked with hesitation.

No reply came immediately. Vivian avoided Margaret's gaze as if trying to find the right words to explain her precarious position. "My father lives," she said as she raised her brown eyes.

Margaret felt a sweeping recognition. Vivian's complexion was much lighter than the woman in the image and there was something in her features that resonated as British.

An interesting dynamic existed in Barbados. Slave labour once dominated the tobacco and sugarcane plantations in the Caribbean and was only abolished twenty-odd years before in all parts of the Empire. Even though the population between negro workers and British transplants was equally divided, there remained obvious disparities between the wealthy and the poor. That dynamic made it easy for noblemen to take advantage of many of the vulnerable females. It was possible Vivian's mother had been a victim of the British hierarchy.

The thought was disturbing enough but in that

moment, looking into the deep brown eyes of the fifteen-year-old, Margaret wondered if her father could have had an affair with a woman who worked at their estate in Barbados. Could Vivian be related to them, as an illegitimate child of Lord Marshall? It would explain his sudden departure to the island. It would explain the girl's sudden appearance at their home in London. Did Lord Benedict know?

Margaret started at the thought, but she maintained her composure. "Well, then you shall stay with us until the two of you can be reunited." She forced a light smile and hoped the girl didn't see the trembling in her hands.

"Yes, miss." The girl nodded and then skirted around her to return to her task.

Margaret watched for a few moments as Vivian went to each of the tables systematically to collect what had been easily discarded by the family and their guest. Margaret looked for anything that would signal to her that Vivian was her sister. Perhaps there was a mannerism, a stance that would confirm Margaret's suspicion, but there was nothing so obvious.

Chapter 11

The number of fighting venues, the types of underground cesspits where illegal betting and underhand dealings flourished, was countless. Ainsley knew of a mere handful. In London, he trusted only one.

Ainsley hadn't walked through the doors in many months, not since that night when the world crashed down around him. That night he entered the ring with boyish humiliation on his mind and a desire to see his greatest adversary brought to his knees. The fight ended with a split-second decision, one that he couldn't retract. The bang and then the silence that followed haunted him still. Ainsley shuttered internally at the memory brought on by the smell of whiskey, cigar smoke, and sweat that greeted him as he entered. How he wished Jonas was with him, as he had been that night, to add more muscle to his side should anything about his visit go downhill.

The room, a wide-open basement complete with low ceilings and large brick columns, was filled with men transfixed by the fight taking place at the centre of the throng. There was no doubt they all had wagers placed on the outcome. Only a few women were present, ladies of the night willing to help any successful gamblers part with their winnings. One, most likely lured by his fine tailored suit and young features, approached him.

"Hello, darling," she said, inching her voluptuous chest to his.

"Where's Jerry?" he asked sharply.

Her pasted smile faded as she looked him over. "Who's asking?"

Ainsley pulled off his hat and ran a hand through his hair.

Recognition flooded over her as she watched. "Well now," she said happily, "Peter!" She turned to the men closest to her. "Hey everyone, it's Pe—"

Ainsley snatched her wrist as she was raising it up to

call everyone over and pulled her into him. "Just tell me where Jerry is."

Startled, she nodded and he let her go. "He's down the hall, farthest door on the left." She cocked her head to the side, indicating a narrow passage opening to the right of the bar.

He left her, unsure whether she would continue to tell everyone about his return or not. It was partly due to the support from the crowd, those who knew him, that he was able to escape the gallows that night. Ainsley was one of them. He had trained and fought in the ring at the centre of the room, and they weren't about to turn him into the Yard for doing what they all wished was in themselves to do. No one held sympathy for the child killer. Many felt he got his due and were glad enough they were there to witness his death. Little did they know the price Ainsley paid for the deed and the internal anguish that would never leave him.

Ainsley inched down the corridor, aware of the walls brushing his shoulders on both sides as he moved forward. The rooms he passed appeared to be storage rooms, with dark ominous shadows piled high with any number of discarded goods. The door at the end was closed, but beams of light escaped into the corridor around its misshapen fit.

"I told you, I don't want any more tonight!" came Jerry's raspy voice from inside the room.

Ainsley pushed the door open with his knee and leaned into the eroding red brick that served as the doorframe. "Hello, Jerry."

"Holy Mother of God, where the hell have you been?" Jerry stood, the volume of his voice indicating his surprise. "Jesus Christ, Peter! I had guys looking all over the city for you." Jerry walked toward him with his arms stretched out, a fat cigar pinched between two fingers. "How the fuck have you been? Doing well, I see!" He tugged on Ainsley's lapel and slapped his stomach.

It was then Ainsley realized how overdressed he was for a visit. In the past he would have never worn his finer clothes as a way to fit in and protect his identity.

"Shit, man, what have you got yourself into? You my competition now then?" Jerry asked, hinting that Ainsley had gone into the bookman business. "Come in. Sit down." Jerry waved his arm at a chair opposite his, where a large weathered desk sat between them. Jerry circled the desk, but stopped short of sitting down when he realized Ainsley had only taken one step into the room. "I thought you got pinched," he said, his tone suddenly nervous.

"I'm looking for someone," Ainsley said.

Jerry shrugged. "Maybe I can help."

"Goes by the name Thaddeus."

Jerry's face grew sullen. "Why would you be looking for a man such as that?"

"I need to ask him a few questions."

Jerry licked his lips, circled the desk, and went straight for the door. After checking the corridor, he returned to the room and closed the door behind him. "I never heard of him and neither have you." Jerry pointed a finger at Ainsley as he went back to his chair. His jovial tone had come to an abrupt end and a nervous demeanor took its place.

From across the room Ainsley could see Jerry's hand trembling as he picked up the bottle of ale on his desk and took a large gulp.

"I heard you and he are cut from the same cloth," Ainsley said stoically.

Jerry looked shaken at the accusation. "Peter, after all we have been through together?"

Tilting his head to the side, Ainsley raised his eyebrows. "*Because* of all we've been through."

A light tap sounded at the door.

"Yes?" Jerry called, clearly agitated.

The door creaked open and a large gentleman appeared. "Molly said you had a visitor," the man said gruffly.

Jerry waved him away. "Yes, yes. It's all right. Leave us. And keep away from the door."

The man eyed Ainsley suspiciously, but relented under his employer's command.

"You expected trouble, Jerry?" Ainsley asked after the man left.

"You can never be too careful." Jerry admitted. "Please, Peter. Sit."

Finally yielding to Jerry's requests, Ainsley slipped into the chair, but only after Jerry had sat in his. His elbows propped up on the chair arms, he knit his fingers together. For a moment it looked as if Jerry was unsure what they had been talking about.

"Thaddeus," Ainsley said sharply. "Tell me about Thaddeus."

Jerry closed his eyes and shook his head slightly, as if second-guessing what he was about to do. "He runs a club in Southwark. Promise me you'll never go there." He used the fingers with the cigar to point at him.

"Why?"

"That man and anyone who works for him is up to no good," he said, lifting his glass for a drink. "Cheats and swindlers. They take wagers from men that don't have money and when they lose he takes his payment by...other means." Jerry looked visibly shaken as he spoke. "Take it from me, his fights are never fair."

"He pays fighters to take a fall," Ainsley said matter-of-factly.

"He owns much of Southwark and some of Vauxhall too. He's got all manner of butcher, baker, and candlestick maker in his books."

"Gambling?"

"Debts," Jerry said. "Debts and secrets. Makes the world go 'round." He took a long gulp of his ale before slapping it back on his desk. "If you have a deal with him, honor it and then leave town. Don't return until he's forgotten all about you."

"I have never met the man," Ainsley confessed.

"Keep it that way!" Jerry slammed his palm down on the desk.

"Where is he?" Ainsley asked, ignoring his friend's warning.

Jerry laughed. "You really are thick, aren't you?"

Ainsley shook his head. "No. There's just a woman I am trying to find."

The smile slid from Jerry's face. "Forget about her. If she's gone with him, there ain't no getting her back."

Ainsley pressed out a fold in his trousers. "I just need an address."

For a time it looked as if Jerry wouldn't oblige. He sneered at Ainsley, studying him in earnest; as if unsure he wanted to be responsible for such a meeting. With sudden clarity, Jerry put his cigar between his teeth before ripping a page from his book and quickly scribbling something on the paper. He stood and thrust the paper at Ainsley. "If anyone asks, you did not get this from me, you hear?"

A frantic knock came at the door.

"Not now!"

Molly burst in, blood trickling from her nostril. "All hell's broken loose," she gasped, pulling her shawl over her bare shoulder. A roar of noise, yelling and shouting, wafted in from down the hall. "It's Wendell again."

Jerry jumped up and ran out the door. "Jesus Christ, Wendell!"

And with that he was gone. Ainsley left the room, Molly's inviting gaze examining him as he walked by. The noise of the ruckus swelled as he moved toward the main room.

The bout in the ring had been forgotten as the fighting spilled out into the rest of the club. Men, old and young, swung widely and furiously as the brawl spread. The few women in the room cowered behind the bar counter even as glasses and bottles were thrown about all around them. Jerry was already in the middle of the fray, pushing the combatants away from each other, his fat cigar still clenched between his teeth.

Slipping the piece of paper in the breast pocket of his jacket, Ainsley skirted the edges of the tussle and smiled as he slipped up the stairs to street level. Had Jonas been there he would have begged him to come back, but that night Ainsley had little strength to fight. All he cared about was finding Julia.

Chapter 12

Even as dawn teased the eastern skyline, Ainsley had no desire to head home. The heartache and strain he would find there was unconquerable, whereas each step on London's cobblestones made him feel active, if not successful. Thaddeus and his present-day connection to Julia remained unclear, but Ainsley possessed a dark foreboding about the entire thing. Apprehensive steps brought him to Blackfriars Bridge with Southwark and the address Jerry had given him waiting on the other side of the Thames.

If Thaddeus was as vindictive as Mrs. Holliwell said then Ainsley doubted Julia would go back to him willingly. If Mrs. Holliwell had helped Julia get her position at Marshall House to keep her safe, then there remained the possibility that Julia hadn't wanted to be free of him, just as she didn't want to be free of her father. She had a history of remaining with men who could neither care properly for her nor commit to her.

Ainsley was all too aware of what this meant for their relationship. It was entirely possible she had made a similar mistake with him; wishing to be free of him, yet unable to break the ties. The thought pained Ainsley to his core, causing him to pause at the midsection of the bridge and use the railing to hold himself vertical.

"*Tell him. Tell him,*" voices urged from behind him.

Ainsley whirled about just as a dark carriage rolled by on the bridge. The driver kept his eyes on him as he guided his team further down the bridge. The young doctor swallowed back the fear that resonated from his gut.

"*Not him. He's too scared,*" the voice came again. They came as whispers, harsh and desperate.

"*I'm scared too.*"

"*It has to be him.*"

"*Look, look.*"

The world spun relentlessly and he could feel his head

lolling to one side. The words began repeating themselves, overlapping and then rising in volume.

Tell him. Not him. He's too scared. Look, look.

Ainsley caught hold of the railing. He leaned over to face the water, readying himself to hurl should his body retch. Beneath him, the water flowed black with the ripples and dips, catching the glint of the midnight moon. This too made him nauseous.

He would have retched had it not been for the body floating face down in the rippling tidewaters just beneath him. It took a moment for the sight to set in and for him to realize it was truly real and not another conjured image of his tormented soul.

"Help." His voice was horse and muffled against the sounds of the water. "A body!"

No one was on the bridge with him and he was too far from the shore to clamour down. A rowboat shifted into view, manned by a weary young boy barely able to maneuver the bulky, wooden vessel. "Boy, stop!"

The lad looked up, holding his hat to keep it from slipping from his head.

Ainsley pointed, extending the entire length of his arm toward the dark and murky water. The woman, with brown tresses and a light-coloured frock, bobbed with the gentle waves of the Thames, unmoving and clearly deceased. "Take hold of that body!" Ainsley called.

Following where Ainsley pointed, the boy looked and nearly fell back from his seat on the boat at the sight of it only a few feet from port side.

"Catch hold of her!" Ainsley yelled, watching as the tidal waters drew her away.

The boy shook his head rapidly and looked to slink away from the discovery.

Again Ainsley scanned the bridge, this time seeing an older man walking toward him. "Sir, sir!" Ainsley caught the man's attention. "Summon the watchman! There is a body."

The man gave one quick glance and gave Ainsley a nod before running toward the closest shore. When Ainsley looked back he saw the body floating further still, the gap between the boy and the corpse growing with each roll of the water.

Without further thought, Ainsley pulled at the sleeves of his jacket, tugged off his shoes, and stepped up on to the railing.

"You stay there," Ainsley commanded to the boy before saying a silent prayer and hurling himself from the safety of the bridge.

Ainsley was indeed thankful for the heat wave that had hit London in recent weeks. Even still, the cool tidal water snapped over him like an animal trap, sharp and unforgiving. The world was black even after Ainsley's head broke the surface.

"Here, here."

The voice of the boy was so much closer. Ainsley realized he had brought the boat close to his side and was reaching out one of the oars to him. A well-enough swimmer, Ainsley didn't need assistance, at least not until he retrieved the body.

"Follow me," Ainsley said.

With the boy directing him, Ainsley was able to find the body, which felt twice as heavy as it looked. Just as he turned back to the boat light encircled them. On top of the bridge a watchman stood, his lantern pointed directly at them.

"Stop!" he boomed. "Police!"

The boy stood in the centre of his boat, squinting against the light that showered down around them. "She drowned, sir," he said in his tiny voice.

"I'll be the judge of that!" the officer yelled.

Ainsley was too out of breath to argue. The swim to find her and the effort needed to pull her back to the mudflats was all he could focus on. The boy trailed alongside him, helping as much as he could but affecting little. At shore, Ainsley was able to pull her body from the water and lay it out over the weatherworn planks of a slender dock.

"Do you know her?" the boy asked, suddenly no longer afraid and more riveted by the sight of the dead body. He scrambled up the ladder and knelt down alongside Ainsley.

"No," Ainsley answered, carefully positioning her body so she lay flat. He pushed the wet strands of hair from her face and thanked God it was not Julia. The victim's eye was swollen purple and there was a slim pink slit etched deeply into the flesh of her throat.

"Step away from the girl," a deep voice boomed from behind them. Ainsley turned and again found himself blinded by the light from the watchman's lantern.

"It's all right. I'm a doctor," Ainsley said, assured that would set the man's vehemence to rest.

"I said step away." The man raised his billy club as if to strike Ainsley and perhaps even the boy at his side. Instinctually, Ainsley positioned himself between the watchman and the boy, who recoiled in fear.

"Get a hold of yourself man!" Ainsley yelled.

He wanted to face the man, challenge him and the unnecessary force he was threatening to use against him but he was too late. A Yard constable appeared, one Ainsley did not recognize. "What is the problem here? There's enough ruckus to raise the dead." He saw the body and immediately scowled.

"I saw him, sir," the watchman said quickly. "He was holding the body under the water."

"Certainly not!" Ainsley yelled. He stepped forward, meaning to close the distance between them, but the constable raised his billy club and pushed Ainsley back.

"You are coming with me," the constable said, readying his handcuffs.

"Keep your hands off me!" Ainsley yelled, ripping his arm away as the constable reached for him.

"Sir," he said with a sigh, "don't make us convince you."

Simultaneously, the officers snapped the butts of the billy clubs in their opposite palms with a sharp snapping sound and Ainsley realized he was not in a position to argue. With his hand restrained at the wrists, he was escorted to the police carriage that waited at street level and was surprised when he saw the boy lifted up behind him.

"You as well?" Ainsley asked.

Their eyes met as the boy sat down beside him. "Should've kept rowing down the river."

The amused smile on Simms's face was unmistakable as Ainsley watched him saunter down the basement steps at the Yard. From his seat, Ainsley glanced to the boy, who had been occupying himself for the last few hours reading the names and dates etched into the foundation stone of the Yard's holding cells. The boy was named Louis, Ainsley had found out, and was taking lessons at St. Mary's Church in the afternoons. Listening to him try to read was painful, but Ainsley did his best to help when he was especially stuck.

Simms stopped in front of their shared cell and slid his hands into the pockets of his trousers. The arresting constable stood behind him, Ainsley's jacket and shoes in his hands.

"It seems there's been a misunderstanding," Simms said, looking over his shoulder at the constable.

The constable's head bowed.

Ainsley didn't move. The hours of relative solitude granted to him in that tiny cell was just what he needed to turn over all the information he had learned in the last few days. He knew that the girl he had pulled from the river that morning was another victim, dispatched in the same way as the others. He knew they all were related to the man found in Belgravia. He also knew that when he had told Simms all he had found during his last visit that Simms had made light of his claims, not because Ainsley was wrong but because he didn't want to admit Ainsley was right.

"Open the cell, constable," Simms demanded.

Fumbling, the young man pulled a sizable key ring from his pocket and unlatched the iron door. Louis only glanced over as the heavy iron door groaned open. He looked to Ainsley, who remained in his seat.

"You are free to go to," Simms said after a moment.

"Not until you tell me all you know about the girls from the river," Ainsley said, raising his gaze enough to look Simms in the eyes. "And Thaddeus."

A long breath escaped Simms, as if preparing himself for an undesirable task. Finally, he cocked his head toward the stairs that would lead them up to the main floor. "We should talk in my office," he said.

One look to Louis confirmed he was reluctant to go. Ainsley accepted his jacket and shoes from the constable and turned to Louis. Pulling a fistful of coins from his pocket, those that remained after his morning plunge, Ainsley handed them to him.

"For your troubles," Ainsley said.

The boy's small hands could barely hold the bounty and his excitement morphed into worry. "No, sir," he said, "my mum will not like it. I did not properly earn it." He reached out his hand to give it back.

"But of course you have," Ainsley said, slipping on his shoes. "You have kept me in good company all these hours."

"Tell your mum if she has a problem with it she should come speak to me," Simms said before turning to the constable. "Make sure this boy gets back to his skiff."

The constable nodded sheepishly.

Simms turned to Ainsley. "Sign the paperwork with Fisher and meet me in my office. We have a lot to discuss."

Sergeant Fisher gave a look of utter delight as Ainsley approached. When he had first arrived Ainsley shivered with the water of the Thames dripping from the fibers of his clothing. He was denied both his shoes and his jacket, which he had left at the crest of the bridge and was left to dry unaided.

He knew he must look a fright; his fine tailored shirt and trousers wrinkled and tainted by the murky waters. He could feel a thin layer of filth on his skin, but banished all nagging thoughts of what it might be. His desire to clean himself was superseded by his need for answers. This was the first time since his return to London that Simms was willing to talk to him. The prospect of a meeting at last filled him with apprehension and relief as he stood at the chest-high desk.

"Bought your way into his good graces again, I see," Fisher muttered as he shuffled papers.

"I beg your pardon?" Ainsley repeated the man's words in his head. "I don't believe I catch your meaning."

The desk sergeant smiled out one side of his mouth, but pretended he had not heard Ainsley's remark.

"He means you enticed him with the Queen's likeness."

Ainsley turned to his left, where a handsome young woman leaned against the desk, her arm and a delicate gloved hand on the glossy wood. Her white braided hat sat slightly askew on her ginger hair, which cascaded in tight curls around her plump face. She smiled when Ainsley looked at her. "Don't look so shocked. My mother says there ain't a watchman nor inspector who doesn't respond in your favour when there was a little inducement to be hand."

"Sounds like your mother has experience in such matters," Ainsley said.

The desk sergeant presented a slip of paper and handed Ainsley a pen. "Sign there," he said, pointing sharply.

"She most certainly does," the woman said, pushing her tongue into her upper lip.

Ainsley signed the paper in front of him and handed it back to the sergeant, who looked as if he had already moved on to his next task.

The woman offered her hand in greeting as she stepped toward Ainsley. Another inch and they'd be pressed into each other's chests.

"Delilah," she said, a teasing smile producing a single dimple on her right cheek.

Reluctantly, Ainsley took her hand and squeezed gently. "Dr. Peter Ainsley."

Her smile grew broad. "That's not what that paper said," she answered, stealing a peek over the counter. "I can be whatever you want me to be, but I've never been able to master gullible." Delilah took a gloved hand and slowly trailed it up Ainsley's arm to his shoulder. She lifted her gaze revealing round, green eyes. She moved her hand to touch his face, but he caught her wrist.

"That's enough," he said, sternly. "Away with you."

She shrugged and pulled back her hand. "Very well." She took one step back, but kept her eyes on him until Constable Cooper came into view. "Goodness David, you do cut a fine figure in that uniform."

Cooper approached with a wide, exuberant smile. He stopped short of scooping her into his arms. Ainsley could tell how much he wanted to.

"Good morning, Miss Delilah," he said, desperately

trying to remain proper as Ainsley watched. He bowed awkwardly.

Delilah slapped at his shoulder playfully. "David."

Ainsley turned back to Fisher and leaned in. "Is that all, Sergeant?" he asked.

The man nodded and finally Ainsley was free to go.

Simms's office was just as Ainsley remembered. So tidy it was almost sparse save for the tiny framed picture of a young boy whom Ainsley still did not know the name of.

Simms motioned for Ainsley to take a seat. He himself remained standing, choosing to lean into the low shelf that lined the bottom of his window. Clearly with much on his mind, he crossed his arms over his chest and looked down on Ainsley.

"You are a stubborn ass," he said sternly.

Justifiably chastised, Ainsley nodded. He opened his mouth to speak but Simms continued, cutting him off.

"You are arrogant, boastful, and a drunk."

"Yes," Ainsley said quickly. "I admit I am all those things. I—"

"You"—Simms pointed a finger directly at Ainsley— "believe you are above the law," he bellowed, clearly annoyed. Simms exhaled steadily as he looked over the papers on his desk.

"No, I do not," Ainsley said quickly before Simms could continue his admonishment. "I will admit to many faults, but what happened that night was not purposely done."

"You expect me to believe that? You didn't bait him? You didn't beckon him into the ring with you?"

Ainsley's conviction waned. Nothing hurt more than the realization that he had lost Simms's respect. His soul had paid the price for his misdeed and it appeared no amends could be made, not while Simms looked at him with such resentment.

"The case consumed me. I wasn't behaving like myself. I would never—"

"If you think your actions should be applauded—"

"Not applauded. Understood." Ainsley licked his lips and looked down. "You remember what he did."

"We have a rule of law—"

Ainsley stood suddenly. "I only did what you and everyone else in that room lacked the conviction to do! I did not face him for my own gain. He needed to be stopped."

Simms's eyes burned into him, narrow and harsh. "The only reason why I have not arrested you is because I agree with you."

Afraid of falling over, Ainsley sat. "You agree with me?" he asked after a moment to collect himself.

Simms nodded reluctantly. "No one in that place would collaborate. No one spoke against you. Not one single person."

"How did you know it was me?"

"I knew." Simms stretched his neck side to side as if finally relieved of a great burden. He pulled out the chair to his desk and sat down. "You are wrong about one thing, though. I did want him dead. I even wondered what I might do if given the chance. Would the strength of my conviction overrule my sense of righteousness? I hate what you did, but I don't hate you for doing it."

The floor beneath Ainsley felt as if it would collapse at any second. The room spun as he sat there, blood rushing to his feet. The validation Simms offered was more than he ever hoped for. He raised a hand to his forehead and realized he was shaking. The words Simms spoke, while harsh, were just what he needed to hear.

"You want to know what I have on Thaddeus?"

Ainsley was brought back to attention when Simms slapped a slim file on the desk in front of him.

"Almost nothing, at least not officially." He knit his fingers together over the file and leaned into the table. "He arrived in London ten years ago with his family, or so I think. A brother, sister, mother, and uncle. He began as a boxer." Simms scrunched up his nose and shrugged. "He was moderately successful until he decided it was time to determine who won from outside the ring. An informant told us of a man in Southwark enticing young men to rig bout results. The idea was to help rich socialites like yourself depart with their money. He started paying his fall guys for their troubles at first and then Thaddeus began collecting favours and secrets. What started off as small potatoes grew into blackmail and money laundering.

Anyone found stepping out of line gets beaten or worse."

"Why doesn't the Yard just arrest him? Have him charged?"

Simms sighed and looked as if he wanted to hang his head. "Every time we get close a witness suddenly disappears. Their bodies are usually found floating face down in the Thames." Simms pulled a crude map of London from the side of his desk and laid it over the file. "He has a compound here. It consists of a public house, a few warehouses, a few tenements that he rents to his workers and a house that he shares with his family." He made a circle with his finger over a section of Southwark. "He controls most of this area here and is using his influence to grow into other territories." He looked up to Ainsley. "You have to understand, in these communities they hail him as a hero. He protects them, keeps the other scoundrels out. No one steps out of line because they all know what he's capable of."

"He intimidates them."

"And it's working."

Ainsley placed his elbow on the arm of his chair and raised a finger to his mouth.

"There's something else I think you should know." Simms hesitated.

"What? What is it?"

After moving the map aside, Simms opened the top of the dossier and pointed to the middle of a handwritten page to the line that said: *married Julia Crandall.*

"I recognized her at your home. Your maid."

"No." Ainsley fell back into his chair, his jaw clenched in an effort to settle the anxiousness that overtook him. "There must be a mistake." Ainsley rubbed a shaky hand over his forehead and willed himself to stay seated when every cell in his body beckoned him to run from the room.

Simms's expression softened when their gaze met. "Julia Kemp is Julia Crandall, former ward of the Limehouse District Foundling Home. Estranged wife of Thaddeus Calvin. Suspect in the murder of Edgar Calvin."

Seconds passed as Ainsley digested what Simms was saying to him. "Edgar Calvin?"

"Thaddeus' brother."

Chapter 13

Margaret had spent most of the morning in her father's room helping their new nurse, Edith, get acquainted with Lord Marshall's needs. "He likes two pillows," she said, bringing a recently starched pillow to the head of the bed and gingerly placing it behind her father's head and shoulders. She purposely looked at him while she hovered over him, but he didn't even dart his eyes to her. Instead, he stared blankly at the opposite wall, focused on nothing in particular. She turned to Edith, who was standing on the other side of the room, cleaning up the water and toiletries they had used to give Lord Marshall his daily bath.

"He needs to be moved quite frequently," Margaret reminded her.

"Of course, m' lady."

Edith was an older woman, who had started as a laundress at Guy's Hospital as a young woman before becoming a nurse in her thirties. Nearing sixty now, she looked frail and tired, not the sort of person Margaret and Ainsley needed to assist their father, but Margaret was in no position to send her away.

"Sometimes he drools out the right side."

"Yes, m'lady," she said, walking toward Margaret.

"And sometimes he can get a little—"

A rap came at the door behind her. Aunt Louisa entered the room, a small card in her hand, and the open envelope it arrived in tucked behind it. "Seems we will have a visitor this afternoon," she said, with a smile.

Margaret turned. "Yes?"

"Lord Benedict would like to come for a spell. He said he is most interested in sitting with Abraham for a while."

Margaret could do little to hide her surprise. Lord Benedict had been there two days prior and had shown little interest in meeting with her father. "That's interesting,"

Out of the corner of her eye, Margaret saw her father arch his back before hurling himself from the bed. A sound escaped him as he rolled, similar to the cry of a wounded animal.

"Father!" Margaret rushed to the opposite side of the bed just as Lord Marshall hit the floor with a pronounced thud. Even as Margaret held on to his shoulders, a feeble effort to calm him, he writhed and wriggled.

"Fetch Maxwell and Cutter! Hurry!"

Aunt Louisa fled the room as Edith and Margaret attempted to stop his outburst. Margaret focused on the protection of his head, which was dangerously close to being knocked against the wooden bedside table that held his lamp and books.

"Father, stop it! Just stop it!"

He kicked and bucked, trying to throw the women from him. Then all at once Edith was pulling at his arms, trying to lift him back into the bed on her own.

"What are you doing?" Margaret asked, trying to pull her father's limbs away from her grasp.

"Be not alarmed," the nurse said. "I've needed to do this many times before." The woman's words were stunted by the exertion of trying to calm Lord Marshall's flailing and fighting against Margaret's efforts to stop her. "I've dealt with many drunk men 'afore."

"He's not drunk," Margaret said.

Cutter and Maxwell appeared one after the other and went straight to work. Knowing how the scene had played out before, Lord Marshall did not fight them as they took his arms and legs in hand and hoisted him back into the middle of the bed.

Margaret pulled herself up from the floor, and pushed a loose strand of hair from her eyes just as Aunt Louisa returned. The newfound silence of the room was in deep contrast to the chaos moments prior.

"Perhaps we should tell Lord Benedict your father is indisposed," Aunt Louisa said from the doorway.

Margaret nodded, but was too out of breath to reply.

Half an hour passed and complete calm was restored. Lord Marshall was tucked tightly in his bed while Edith sat in the chair, a pair of knitting needles and yarn in her hands.

Margaret hesitated on the opposite side. She had been staring at her father for some minutes, almost daring him to look at her, wondering if he would apologize in some way for his outburst. He didn't turn his head toward her and returned his gaze to the opposite wall.

"It's all right, Miss Marshall," Edith said, "I can see to him now."

Margaret gave a hesitant nod before pressing down the folds of her skirt and leaving the room.

George and Hubert skirted by her on the stairs, leaving a rattled governess lumbering after them. "Boys! Boys!" Clutching the bannister firmly, the governess swung her free arm widely as she tried to catch up to them.

"Pardon me, miss," she said as she bounded by.

From her place halfway down the staircase, Margaret saw them nearly plough into Maxwell, who had been making his way to answer the front door. Just shy of the door, Maxwell turned to face them. "For goodness' sake," he bellowed as he placed his hands on his hips.

The two young boys stopped suddenly and looked up at the rather tall butler.

"This isn't a county fair. If that's the way it is then get outside with ye."

With wide swinging hand motions, he shooed the boys toward the back of the foyer and down the hall, their governess more than happy to escort them the rest of the way.

Margaret watched as Maxwell pulled down his jacket and adjusted his tie. "They keep us on our toes, yes?" she asked.

"Yes, they certainly do," he said, ill-amused.

A second later Maxwell snapped open the door and revealed Winifred standing on the other side. She started at the abrupt opening. "Oh, I was beginning to think no one was coming."

"Can I assist you?" Maxwell asked.

Before Winifred could reply Margaret was at his side. "Winifred, I'm delighted that you should stop by."

Winifred suddenly looked regretful for having called.

"Is everything all right?" Margaret asked, pushing past the butler.

"Yes, of course." Winifred glanced down toward her house and pressed her lips together.

"Thank you, Maxwell. I'll take it from here."

Maxwell bowed slightly and left them both standing on the portico.

"Has something happened?" Margaret asked.

"It's Mother. She's in such a state. She bid me come for you," Winifred explained. "I wouldn't have come otherwise." The woman spoke so quickly Margaret could feel the panic radiating from her words.

Margaret purposely took a breath to coax Winifred to do the same. "Tell me what it is," Margaret said.

"We found something and we don't know what it means. We didn't realize it was there until just this morning. Please don't think awful of us, Margaret. We had nothing to do with that man's death."

"Of course not," Margaret said, softly. She pulled at Winifred's hand and led her down the few steps to the pavement. "Come now. Let us see what can be done."

Margaret was led through the dark hall of the house and into the back garden. Just outside the back door, Mrs. Talbot stood dabbing her nose with a lace handkerchief. A female servant stood close at hand consoling her.

"It's just over here," Winifred said.

"Oh, don't look, Margaret," Mrs. Talbot pleaded between sobs. "It's too ghastly. I've already summoned the police. They should be here shortly." She raised her handkerchief again and hid her face.

Margaret turned to Winifred, who looked cautiously at her mother before pulling Margaret toward the back of the garden. They circled an ancient yew tree that shaded much of the yard and stopped at the ivy-covered gate that led into a rear alley. The iron hinges groaned as Winifred pulled the gate toward them, standing carefully to one side so Margaret could see.

Behind the gate on the cobbles was a rather large pool of blood, congealed and solidified. As the gate swung further in Margaret could see blood had also trickled over the wood panels that made up the gate.

"Merciful heavens," Margaret said in a near whisper.

"We did not see it until this morning," Winifred said, almost apologetically. "I nearly stepped in it myself."

Margaret inched closer. She could see faint footprints in the blood and then immediately around the area. She hiked up her skirt to walk around the discovery and made her way into the alley. It was a narrow passageway that ran parallel to the houses on both sides. Other gateways were visible all along the block. There were a few more footprints in the passageway that led out to where the lane connected with the street.

"Do you think this has to do with that man?" Winifred asked from the other side of the gate.

Margaret's heart sank at the thought of it. "I'm afraid so." She pulled out a plain white handkerchief she had under the hem of her bodice and unfolded it. Winifred stepped closer as Margaret laid the fabric on one of the bloody footprints with the crispest outline.

"What are you doing?" Winifred asked.

Gingerly, Margaret pressed the cloth into the blood, taking extra care not to shift it side to side. When she plied the handkerchief from the ground a marking had transferred to the cloth, faint but clear enough to see with the naked eye.

"What do you plan to do with it?" Winifred asked.

"If this is where the man met his end, then it's likely this is the killer's footprint," Margaret said, holding the handkerchief flat on her upturned palm.

"Don't show Mother," Winifred cautioned.

Margaret took great care to fold the clean edges around the print in such a way as to preserve the marking. She held the squared handkerchief in her hand as they made their way back into the Talbot's garden.

Mrs. Talbot still stood at the back door, sobbing into her handkerchief.

"Do you wish you had heeded my advice?" she asked, looking at the pair of young women as one would look at chastised children.

Margaret and Winifred exchanged glances before nodding in unison. In cases such as these it was much better to agree than force an argument.

"I think I may faint," Mrs. Talbot said suddenly, placing a hand on her stomach. "Fetch some tea," she said to the maid beside her. Mrs. Talbot showed Margaret into the drawing room. Each took a seat, but they all looked expectantly out the large window, none of them able to take their eyes from the back gate.

"How was the discovery made?" Margaret asked.

"Winifred heard some cats in the back lane," Mrs. Talbot said.

"They made such an awful racket this morning. I could hear it from the window in my room," Winifred explained. "I wanted to make sure neither of them was badly hurt."

Mrs. Talbot huffed then, rolling her eyes at her stepdaughter's concern. "I can't stand the beasts," she said.

"Mother doesn't care for cats," Winifred said, lowering her voice.

"Filthy creatures." Mrs. Talbot crinkled her nose and shook her head.

The maid entered the room and placed a tray on the table in front of them. One by one, she prepared a cup of tea for each of the women before Mrs. Talbot dismissed her.

"Do you think the blood is from that man?" Winifred pointed to the front of the house.

"Yes," Margaret said slowly. "It most certainly is human, as I believe there is too much to be feline."

Winifred blanched at this remark. Mrs. Talbot merely closed her eyes. "I do not understand how you can speak of these things so casually," she said.

Margaret faltered. She couldn't confess that these types of things were a regular occurrence for her and her brother. "I've been reading a lot of newspaper serials lately," she said, "and a book on Florence Nightingale."

The mother-daughter pair seemed assured by this explanation.

"I knew there was a reason I told Winifred to fetch you," Mrs. Talbot said, offering a comforting smile. "You are so bright, my dear."

Chapter 14

The two-room flat Mary and Robert called home grew stifling hot by midday and never cooled enough at night to make any time spent there bearable. The adjacent buildings blocked any breeze from entering their two windows, no matter how far Julia was able to prop up the sash. Mary and Julia were forced to fan themselves with whatever they could find, Mary a tin pie plate and Julia a leaflet paper on the virtues of regular prayer, while they sat at the table. With only a nappy to cover her bottom, Lucy slept in a wooden box lined with blankets between them.

"It's been too long," Mary said fretfully. "'E's been gone too long."

By the time Julia arrived, two days prior, Robert had already gone in search of his friend, Jeremiah, who hadn't been seen since he made the journey on foot to Belgravia. Julia knew now Jeremiah was the man discovered tied to the lamppost, but she said nothing for fear of distressing Mary even further.

"Something's 'appened to 'im," Mary said. She looked to Julia imploringly. "What do we do?"

"We wait," Julia said, trying hard to keep her voice even and calm. By the time Julia arrived, Mary had been driven to near-hysterics, worrying and fretting for her husband's safety. She couldn't just leave her niece in the care of a woman who could barely care for herself, so Julia stayed. She did her best to care for the child and Mary, who seemed less concerned with the running of the house and more concerned with perpetuating her worry. No matter how much Julia tried to coax her from her listless state, Mary became despondent and preferred to sit at the table staring at the opposite wall.

"T'is yer fault," Mary said, somewhat casually. "'E was going to take us far away from 'ere, but 'e insisted on taking ye wit' us." A fresh set of tears glistened in Mary's eyes. "We would 'ave been 'alfway across the Atlantic by now."

Julia shook her head at the woman's careless words and her lack of geographic knowledge. "Hardly halfway," she said under her breath.

Mary turned at the sound of Julia's voice, and gave a look of disgust. "'Ow can you know?" she asked, wrinkling her nose.

Julia ignored Mary's protest and craned her neck to look out the window. They couldn't see much of anything save a small sliver of the alley below. Julia had spent much of the night before watching for signs of both Robert and Thaddeus. If anyone had seen her walking into Robert and Mary's place, he'd know before long.

"Ye know, I ain't ever seen anyone put on so much airs as ye. Ye'd think ye were a princess the way ye prance around here in yer fine dresses and shiny hair."

"Please, Mary, let's not get at odds here." Julia looked down to Lucy, who stirred in her makeshift cot.

"Ye spend one 'ear with the toffers in Belgravia and that makes ye better 'an the rest of us?"

Julia closed her eyes and turned her head as her sister-in-law raised her voice. It had come to her attention there were two types of people when it involved the hardships of life: those who use adversity to spur action and those who use it to wallow in misery. She highly suspected Mary was the latter.

"I am not your enemy, Mary," she said. "My only wish is to help you and Lucy until Robert returns and even then perhaps I can help with your passage to Boston."

Mary snorted in disgust. "We don't want yer help, not from the likes of ye. Ye forget, Princess. I know who ye really are." Mary stood and leaned over the table to point a finger at Julia. "I know what ye've done, Julia Calvin."

Julia snatched Mary's wrist and pushed her hand hard into the table. "Pipe down," Julia hissed. "Or you are going to get us all killed!"

Lucy let out a deep-throated wail at this and Mary simply collapsed back into her chair, holding to her injured hand. She cried openly as Julia bent down to pick up the baby.

"He's dead," Mary said, crying into her hands. "I know he's dead. And 'ere I am left with a babe and no way to feed her. I'll be in the workhouse 'fore long."

"Don't speak like that," Julia said, cradling Lucy against her chest and shoulder. "He will be home. We just need to wait." Julia bobbed Lucy up and down gently. "Quietly," she added.

Chapter 15

It seemed repugnant to think Julia was capable of such a thing as murder. She had always been soft-spoken, kind, and patient. All the things Ainsley was not. There were hints of strength, situations that revealed a formidable force behind her amiable exterior. It was that strength that drew Ainsley to her. He knew there were pieces to her past that she preferred to stay hidden. Out of respect for her he didn't pry. In the end, he was just happy to spend time with her, knowing she was as equally enthralled with him as he was with her.

"There must have been a mistake," Ainsley said at last. "It's just not possible."

Simms said nothing and only tilted his head to the side, his expression sympathetic.

"You don't really think she killed someone."

"I know she did. And I'm willing to bet Thaddeus knows she did too."

Ainsley felt like throwing up.

"I don't know what your relationship with Mrs. Calvin is—"

"Kemp. Her name is Miss Kemp."

Simms ignored Ainsley's correction and continued. "The only reason why I haven't arrested her is the same reason why I haven't arrested you. No one will collaborate and Mr. Edgar Calvin isn't the type of person the Yard likes to waste manpower on, if you understand my meaning. Are you going to be all right, Peter? You don't look well."

Ainsley pulled his hand away from his forehead and sat up. He nodded, but his gesture lacked conviction. "He must have her then. He found her. What if he's already instituted his own justice for his brother's death?"

Simms slowly placed his palms onto the top of his desk in an effort to calm Ainsley down. "We don't know that."

"What else could it possibly be?" He laughed nervously

and then looked down, aware that he could break out into tears at any moment. "What did Thaddeus and his family do before they came to London?"

Simms looked confused at first, almost flustered at such a query. He flipped through a few pages before finding his answer. "Worked with horses on the canals. Why do you ask?"

"He's responsible for the women found in the Thames," Ainsley pressed, the muscles in his face tightening as he spoke.

Simms blanched. "How do you know this?"

Ainsley hesitated. "I saw something as I pulled the woman from the water earlier."

"What did you see?"

This was his chance, an opportunity to assist the Yard again and perhaps find out what happened to Julia. He may not like what he found and he'd certainly be heartbroken if he discovered Julia had gone back to her husband, or worse that she had been killed by his hand, but he knew he'd never sleep again until he knew for certain. "Let me examine the body properly," he said sternly, "and all the others. I want notes and files."

Disturbed at the thought, Simms shook his head. "Peter—"

"I want back in, Simms. London has a disease and the symptom is murder. Let me right the wrong I did."

"You want redemption?"

"I want peace"—Ainsley pointed to his chest, slightly to the left—"here."

For a moment it looked as if Simms could not be won over. His face remained hardened and, while his tone had softened, his expression was marred by disbelief. After a long pause, Simms pulled the papers in front of him into a neat pile. "I'll have Cooper bring her to St. Thomas," he said as he stood up. His words sounded like a grunt, something done against his better judgement.

Ainsley pushed down a smile.

"But from now on there will be rules and you *will* follow them," he said with a pointed finger.

Ainsley nodded. "Yes, Inspector."

"I hope I don't end up regretting this," Simms said

sternly.

"I'm a different man now," Ainsley said in earnest.

"Aren't we all?"

Ainsley left the offices of the Yard with a dejected feeling in the pit of his stomach. His dishevelled appearance betrayed his dishevelled heart. Julia was married? It seemed impossible and yet he knew Simms to be an honest man, exceedingly so. There would be no reason for the detective to lie to him. Ainsley didn't want to think Julia had left them to return to her husband, not willingly at least.

His steps were slow as he made his way back to Belgravia. Not surprisingly, the people approaching him on the pavement parted rather anxiously as he came toward him. With his coat draped over his arm, he approached Marshall House and saw that Margaret stood at the top of the steps with Miss Winifred Talbot standing opposite her.

"Goodness gracious, Peter!" Margaret's eyes widened as she took in the sight of him, ashen and filthy from his romp in the Thames. Although mostly dry, his fine clothes were ruined, their once bright, clean colours dulled by the grungy din of the river water. She stepped forward as if to come to him, but then suddenly recoiled and raised her hand to block her nostrils. The look on Miss Talbot's face wasn't any more favourable.

"Forgive me," Ainsley said as he slipped by them. "I am in no position to receive company." At the door he stopped and gave a quick bow to Miss Talbot. "Lovely to see you again, Miss Winifred."

Judging by the look on her face, he had no doubt a quick departure would be appreciated. He heard the women giggling as he closed the door behind him.

Once in his room he summoned Maxwell, ordered a bath and began the long process of washing the Thames from his skin and hair.

An hour later he was presentable again. Dressed in freshly pressed trousers and a crisp linen shirt, Ainsley was putting on a cufflink when Margaret appeared at his door. The look on her face, fatigue mixed with apprehension, saddened him.

"Any trace of Julia or where she may have gone?" she asked, entering the room.

"Simms and I are following a lead," he said.

"Simms? So he has forgiven you?"

Ainsley smiled, amused by her enthusiasm. "Not exactly." With his cufflinks in place he pulled at the edge of his sleeve to adjust his shirt on his shoulders.

"Why was Winifred here?" he asked.

"I believe we found where that man was dispatched," she said. "There's a large pool of blood in the laneway behind the Talbot's house."

"The Yard didn't discover it earlier?"

"It doesn't seem like it." Margaret pulled a bit of folded cloth from the inside of her sleeve. "I was able to get this." She opened the layers slowly and deliberately until the cloth revealed a faint, pink impression. "I pressed my handkerchief into one of the footprints. I thought perhaps it could help in some way."

Ainsley accepted the offering and carefully transported it to the small table near the window, where he could enjoy better light.

"It may well be the impression of the killer?" Margaret looked to him expectantly, but it took a while for Ainsley to gather his thoughts.

"I'd have to rule out the possibility that it belongs to our corpse," he said.

"Naturally."

Ainsley smiled slightly. "Thank you, Margaret." He began to fold the fabric in on itself again.

"There's more. Earlier this morning Lord Benedict sent word that he'd like to call upon us later," she said.

Ainsley nodded, but he remained confused. "Why is this upsetting to you?" he asked, knowing very well that it was a visit she was not looking forward to. He had seen that look on her face a hundred times.

"Because Father went into one of his fits again." She let out a deep breath. "Really, Peter, I don't know what's gotten into him."

She walked the length of the room and paused at his desk, where a number of medical texts were piled. He hadn't been able to continue his research in recent days but they remained alongside his copious notes as if he had just been working on them yesterday.

Margaret fingered one of the books, an ancient text by modern medical standards. So far it was the only one that gave a detailed description of apoplexy.

"I'm trying to find something to explain it all," Ainsley said.

Margaret nodded absentmindedly as she turned her attention to another, more recent medical journal. Quietly she read, running her finger down the tiny typeset.

Ainsley walked toward her and pulled one of the other books from the top of the pile. "Father's outbursts seemed to be atypical of this type of affliction."

"What's this?" Margaret asked suddenly. She turned the opened pages toward him and pointed to an illustration.

"That's an experimental treatment. A surgeon in America believes that accessing the vein at the base of the neck and encouraging blood flow to the brain reduces the long-term effects of the episode." Ainsley smiled slightly then. "Father has a scar just like it, which leads me to believe his doctor in Barbados was aware of this new procedure."

"Doesn't Lord Benedict know what procedures were performed?"

"Lord Benedict seems very confused about the extent of his medical care while on the island. He isn't much help to me in that regard. I've been meaning to write to the doctors to find out precisely what was done for him. I'm grateful for Lord Benedict's assistance, but he leaves too many questions unanswered."

Margaret closed the book sharply and tossed it back on the desk with a thud. She nodded as she turned away, a far-off look in her eye. She stopped a few paces away and then turned to face Ainsley. "Do you think he could be hiding something from us?"

"Such as?"

Margaret shrugged. "Something about Vivian."

Ainsley eyed her suspiciously and didn't immediately reply.

"Don't tell me it hasn't crossed your mind. That Vivian could very well be Father's child. She has the Marshall cheekbones."

He had indeed pondered the possibility when the girl first arrived but said nothing at the time. "I'll admit, it's a perplexing situation," he conceded.

"I've thought it over," Margaret said, walking to the door to close it. "Why else would she come all this way? Lord Benedict brought her here because she is our responsibility now that her mother has passed."

"Have you spoken with the girl? Has she mentioned a father?"

"Only to say that he lives." Margaret licked her lips. "Peter, if she is our sister then she shouldn't be a servant to us. It's not proper."

Ainsley raised his hand, coaxing Margaret to stop, or at the very least lower her voice. "I agree. I agree. We'll just keep this between us for now, understand?"

Margaret gave a reluctant nod.

"Does Father know she is here?"

"I'm fairly certain that Mrs. Nelson has kept her below stairs."

Ainsley ran a hand through his hair. "Good. I'm not sure he's ready for further surprises." Ainsley paused as he rubbed the back of his neck. "I don't think any of us are."

Chapter 16

When Ainsley arrived at work midmorning he was surprised to find the body from the river on his examination table. Accompanying the corpse was a note from Simms. *You have until 1 p.m.* Without hesitation, Ainsley set to work. He summoned an available porter and together they scrubbed the body. As they worked, Ainsley gave a preliminary exam at the same time.

"There was something that caught my eye earlier," Ainsley muttered, more to himself than his assistant. Adjusting the light, Ainsley pulled the woman's hair back and examined the skin just behind her ear.

The porter paused his task and watched as Ainsley snatched his magnifying glass from the arrangement of tools behind him. The mark was oval in shape but the main line did not complete the circle. The inside of the shape was pink but not raised.

"Looks like a scar," the porter said, as Ainsley ran his hand over the raised, pink skin. "A burn, perhaps?"

"Just what I thought." Ainsley let his magnifying glass bump the edge of the table as he bowed his head.

"What is it?" the porter asked, leaning in for a closer look.

"She's been branded."

Simms arrived shortly after noon. He made his way down the centre aisle of the morgue, his hands shoved into his pockets and a dispassionate look on his face. Whatever his reasons for allowing Ainsley a look at the body, it was clear he wasn't entirely happy about it.

"I understood that I have until one," Ainsley said, when he glanced up from his work. The dissection was nearly complete. The woman's organs had all been removed and examined. Ainsley was able to take some tissue samples and planned to run a few tests before his deadline.

"Curiosity got the better of me," Simms answered

unapologetically. He stopped just short of the examination table and looked at the corpse uneasily. "Your findings?"

Ainsley nearly laughed at Simms's insistent behaviour. "Am I not permitted to finish?"

"No." Simms circled the examination table and went for the heart and lungs that sat in enamel dishes on Ainsley's work bench.

Ainsley pulled his attention from the body and went to the trough sink to wash his hands. "There was some liver damage, which I didn't expect from someone so young," he said over the splashing of the water. "And an interesting heart condition that clearly went undetected."

Ainsley pointed to the aorta and then pulled the two halves of the dissected heart apart to show the detective the difference between the two valves. "She probably only had another year or two before that took her life."

"Is this related to her current cause of death?" Simms asked with a clear impatience.

Ainsley swallowed. "No." He turned back toward the body. "She didn't drown," he said. "I knew that as soon as I saw her throat." Ainsley pointed to the woman's neck. The wound, deep and most certainly the cause of death, was pink after the Thames had washed most of the blood away. "Again, done with a dull blade." He snatched his magnifying glass from his tools and positioned it so Simms could see the tearing of the skin.

"She wasn't pregnant and aside from the damage to her eye and a few healed bruises there's no obvious sign of trauma. She was more or less well fed. Certainly not starving," Ainsley explained.

Simms kept his eyes on the woman and didn't look at Ainsley as he spoke.

"Do we know if she's been reported missing?" Ainsley asked.

"No."

"Have you looked at archived reports?"

Simms let out a quick breath and gestured to the body. "Can we just get this over with?"

It was then that Ainsley knew their relationship had a long way to go before it could be repaired. Previously they could converse openly, sharing information and offering observances—but no more. Simms seemed determined to keep Ainsley at arm's length and pushed back anytime Ainsley tried to inch closer.

"I found a curious mark." Ainsley went to the head and pulled back the woman's hair. He handed the magnifying glass to Simms.

The detective put the brass-rimmed glass in front of him and leaned in.

"It's a letter," Ainsley said before Simms could say anything. "I think it's the letter C."

Immediately Simms replaced the magnifying glass on the counter and turned from the body.

"It's a branding. A hot iron implement is warmed in coals—"

"A horseshoe."

Ainsley froze. "Pardon?"

"It's a horseshoe, not a C."

Ainsley leaned in for a closer look as Simms spoke.

"If she were standing, the curve would be directed down and the opening of the horseshoe would be up. An upside down horseshoe allows all the luck to fall out." Simms waited quietly as Ainsley looked.

"Is it Thaddeus then?"

"Let's not jump to conclusions," Simms said, returning his hands to his pockets. "Thank you very much, Dr. Ainsley. I'll have her removed by one."

"That's all?" Ainsley called out as Simms marched the aisle to the double doors.

"Yes, that is all," Simms said, turning to touch the brim of his hat. "Thank you, doctor."

The door to the morgue swung back into place before Ainsley could say another word.

Simms's behaviour seemed odd and left Ainsley dumbfounded as he stood next to the body. Why allow him to examine it if he didn't wish to converse with him about the case?

He looked at the mark again, knowing it must be a mark of ownership, like the gangs in Whitechapel and Spitalfields. They all had their own mark identifying men in their ranks and those indebted to them. He imagined Thaddeus was no different. Ainsley had never seen any such mark on Julia, though that didn't mean he hadn't marked her in other ways. He wouldn't have cause to mark her if she was willing to be with him, if they didn't believe she would run away.

Ainsley closed his eyes, abolishing the thought that Julia had willingly become his wife.

It was then that Ainsley realized he still had the files Crawford had given him of the other women brought to the morgue in previous months. He couldn't recall if any of the autopsies reported a similar mark, but he had only been looking at the main identifying features and hadn't delved too deep into the reports themselves. They were safely stowed in his cabinet in the annex room and he would retrieve them later. For now, he needed to finish up, replace the woman's organs, and stitch her together again.

At precisely one o'clock Cooper arrived, stone-faced and mission-bound. Another constable followed him as he marched down the centre aisle to the examination table. One gesture from Cooper sent the other constable to the woman's feet while Cooper took position at her head.

"I just finished," Ainsley said, as Cooper pulled the stained sheet up over the woman's body. "She told me some pretty interesting things."

The other constable went pale as he waited for Cooper's signal to lift his end of the stretcher.

"Do the dead always give up their secrets, Dr. Ainsley?" Cooper asked, ill-amused.

"They cannot help themselves."

The other constable laughed, but Cooper hardly flinched.

Ainsley watched as Cooper tucked the ends of the sheet between the body and the base of the stretcher, as one would tuck a sheet under a mattress. In just a few more seconds the body would be gone and so would Ainsley's last connection with the case. It wasn't enough to examine the bodies and pass on the information to Simms. Ainsley needed to piece the puzzle together. He needed to see how they all connected.

"Did Simms ask you to bring me anything?" Ainsley asked cautiously.

"Like what?"

"Some case files. I offered to look through the medical examiner notes."

Cooper shrugged and walked past Ainsley back to his position at the head. "He never said anything to me."

"I could really use them," Ainsley pressed, even as the pair of officers signalled to each other to lift the stretcher up. "I can compare them to our files and let Simms know if I find connections."

"You'll have to speak directly with Simms," Cooper said as they walked for the aisle. "I'm making a point to only take my orders from him from now on." The constable raised a hardened gaze to Ainsley, in challenge, before pressing his body into the door and guiding the stretcher out of the morgue.

Ainsley followed them hurriedly down the hall to the double doors at the back of the hospital. "Cooper, I'm just trying to help."

The police wagon had been waiting, the horses out front stomping on the cobbles and rocking the box compartment at the back. After balancing the stretcher bars on the back of the wagon, the assisting constable hopped up and was able to pull the body into the opening. Cooper slammed the back door shut after the constable jumped down.

"I just don't understand—why would Simms let me perform the dissection if he didn't intend for me to help?"

Cooper turned suddenly and pressed a finger into Ainsley's chest. "Because he's using you, old chap, to get what he needs and nothing more."

Ainsley watched as the two men climbed up into the bench at the front of the wagon, snapping the reins slightly and clicking their tongues to urge the horses forward.

If what Cooper had said was true Ainsley was ashamed that he had fallen for it. He truly thought he was a contributing member of the pair again, as he and Simms had been before that horrid night. He felt his throat go dry at the memory and tried to banish it from his mind. The face of the man he killed remained burned in his retina, every once in a while flashing into his vision. It taunted him and teased him. He wasn't sure how he would ever redeem his soul after what he'd done, but finding justice for these missing maids was a good enough start.

Shoving his hands into his pockets, Ainsley turned to head back to the morgue but stopped suddenly when he saw Delilah standing next to the double doors. She smiled out one side of her mouth and held a very small pistol, a derringer, in her gloved hands.

Ainsley froze, and reactively raised his palms up.

"Hello, doctor," she said, twirling a rather long silver necklace in her free hand. "My brother would like a word with you." She jerked her head to the side, where a closed carriage waited under the shade of a large oak tree. The side door was popped open by a single leather gloved hand that quickly retreated into the darkness inside.

There was too much distance between them for him to charge her. She'd have more than enough opportunity to pull the trigger, and would probably do it gleefully, judging by the cheerful look on her face.

"Let me grab my coat," he said, trying to walk past her and back into the building.

"Ah, ah, ah." She stepped into the doorway to block his entry and pressed the end of the gun into his rib. Her slight frame pressed into him provocatively as the metal dug even further into his torso. "You are very handsome," she said with a smile. "I would hate to make this an ugly encounter."

He could feel the short barrel pressing deeper into his gut.

He nodded his willingness to go with her and allowed her to steer him toward the carriage. With her close behind him, he climbed the steps and noticed a man seated on the one bench. He wore a bowler hat and a dark green overcoat and matching vest over his white shirt. He flexed his gloved hands, pushing the seams into the tight spaces between his fingers as Ainsley climbed in and sat opposite him.

"Are you the brother?" Ainsley asked.

The man suppressed a smile, but his intimidating gaze didn't falter.

When Delilah entered, she sat down with a jubilant bounce that rocked the carriage. "I told you I could do it on my own, Stanley," she said, slipping the small firearm into her reticule. When she looked up from her bag, her happy demeanor soured. "You don't look scared," she said, glancing to Stanley on her right.

"Should I be?" Ainsley asked as Stanley pulled a pistol from an inside pocket and laid it on his knee, pointing the barrel at Ainsley. It took a great deal of effort for Ainsley to supress his fear. He carefully calculated each of his movements, knowing fear was the desired outcome. Fear is what controls a man.

While Delilah sulked, Stanley raised a fist to the ceiling and banged on the red velvet twice to alert the driver they were ready.

They made no effort to conceal where they were headed. Through the window Ainsley could plainly see the carriage was being led through the south London streets, past Waterloo Station and Blackfriars' Bridge before turning down a narrow passage and into a wider courtyard. Ainsley could smell the thick sour yeast of the nearby brewery, churning out a fermented exhaust that permeated the already heavy air. The substantial gate at the courtyard entrance, caked with green paint and cracked intermittently, was already closed by the time the carriage came to a stop.

Delilah was the first to exit while Stanley motioned with the pistol for Ainsley to go before him.

Outside the carriage, Ainsley was granted a better view. The building was a large, three-storey red brick warehouse with black-framed windows, some boarded up with arched wooden panels. Dormer windows dotted the attic storey, matching the pattern of the windows below them. Delilah stood at the entrance of a breezeway, a passage that led from the courtyard to the main road.

"Come now," Delilah beckoned him. "My brother has no patience."

With one hand on her hip, she held the pendant of her silver necklace with her free hand as Ainsley passed.

Ainsley walked the length of the breezeway, noticing Chubb locks on each warehouse door they passed and then one door left wide open. Inside he could see a public house not yet opened for the evening's business. A tall man stood at the counter hunched over a wide-paged book. When his gaze caught Ainsley's he straightened his stance and hardened his expression.

Delilah stood halfway in the door. "Where is he?" she asked the barkeep.

"His usual place."

Ainsley saw a smirk on the man's face before he turned away. Delilah retraced her steps back into the courtyard. Stanley nudged Ainsley from behind. "Get on then," he said.

Ainsley obliged. He wasn't bound or restrained in any way. If he truly wanted to run he could, and could probably have made it to the other side of the yard before Stanley would think to raise his gun. There was something else to their method of security, something unseen. Out in the sunlight again, Ainsley scanned the yard but saw nothing except a young man tending the horses that had just brought them by carriage. Ainsley kept an eye on Delilah, who was already twenty paces ahead, while he scanned the windows. They were all devoid of life.

Delilah stopped at a set of stairs that led down and placed a hand on the top of the iron railing. "This is where our boys train," she said, almost boastfully.

Tell him. Tell him. The whispers echoed and reverberated as they swirled around him. *You can't leave us.*

And then movement caught Ainsley's eye, forcing him to look up. By the time his vision focused the image was gone but Ainsley already recognized what he had seen. A girl hiding behind one of the dormer windows. He didn't get a good enough look to formulate a description and for a second or two he thought perhaps his mind was playing tricks on him again.

"Is there a problem, doctor?" Delilah asked.

Ainsley shook his head. "No."

She gestured to the stairs, inviting him to head down. At the bottom a set of double doors were propped open but he could see nothing beyond.

"After you, ma'am," he said.

Delilah gave a half smile and a quick glance to Stanley behind him before hiking up her skirt and marching down the steps. On one of the stairs Ainsley thought he saw a pool of blood, caked on and melted into the stone of the steps.

Beyond the doors came the familiar sounds of the boxing ring, only instead of two fighters sparing in a centre ring there were countless shirtless men paired off and running training exercises. The familiar smell of sweat, old and new, met them at the door as they walked in. Ainsley scanned the dimly lit room, trying to pinpoint who exactly was Thaddeus. Eventually, he spotted a man in a white dress shirt with his sleeves rolled up and cigar in his hand. He was no older than Ainsley but he carried himself with as much authority and charm as any man Ainsley had seen in the House of Lords.

Delilah crossed the room, enjoying the stares and whistles she drew from the room full of men, perhaps even inviting the attention with a wider swing of her hips, and went straight for her brother. Ainsley held back at the door as she spoke.

"This is Dr. Ainsley, the man I was telling you about," she said, turning to look Ainsley in the eye.

Thaddeus raised his cigar to his mouth as he looked Ainsley over.

"See? I told you I could get him here." Delilah chuckled at her own cleverness. She reached into Thaddeus's inside breast pocket and pulled out a palm-sized silver box. With a slim cigar in her slender fingers she slapped the metal case into her brother's hand and turned from him. "He needed very little persuading."

Ainsley watched as Thaddeus leaned into her and whispered something in her ear. Delilah shrugged as he pulled away and said nothing by way of a reply.

Thaddeus took a few steps, shortening the gap between them before he spoke. "Welcome," he said, switching his cigar from one hand to the other. "I am honoured to meet the great Dr. Peter Ainsley. My name is Thaddeus. Thaddeus Calvin."

The man's smile looked natural enough, but Ainsley knew how men like him enjoyed putting on the show, as much as the fear they caused.

A man from the right fell into Ainsley, pulling them both to the ground. The man had a black eye and contusion to his cheekbone. He looked Ainsley in the face as he landed on top of him. "Tell Julia," he said, in an almost inaudible whisper, "to pray for me."

The man was pulled off him by Stanley, who swung him back toward his sparring partner. "I'm sorry, sir," the boxer said. "Terribly sorry."

Thaddeus appeared over Ainsley and offered an outstretched hand to help him to his feet. "I do apologize. It can be a madhouse in here, sometimes. Perhaps we should go talk in my office."

As Ainsley was brought to his feet he looked to the man who had just tackled him, but was afraid to draw too much attention to the incident. It was clear he had been handed a message, but from who?

Moments later, Ainsley was being shown upstairs to a sizable room above the public house. Thaddeus led the way and gestured to a blue velvet conversation set, two armchairs and a sofa circling an oval table as he walked past.

"Please, have a seat."

He headed straight for the table just beyond the sofa, where an assortment of liquor decanters was displayed on a glass tray. Beyond the sitting area was a platform only six inches above the rest of the room where a large, empty desk was placed.

"Care for a drink?" he asked.

Ainsley didn't move from his spot behind the chair. Delilah came in the room, twirling her silver pendant in her hand. She perched herself on the arm of the opposite chair, a vantage point that allowed her to look at both Ainsley and her brother.

Thaddeus poured two drinks and walked toward Ainsley with one in each hand. He handed over one of the glasses. "This conversation would go much smoother if you would humour me and sit."

Ainsley allowed him to slide the glass into his hand and only sat when Thaddeus himself returned to his seat at the sofa. Ainsley eyed the amber liquid in his glass as he swirled the vessel from side to side. It had been nearly a month since he had had a drink and now was not the time to cave in to the call.

"Well, go on," Delilah pressed, puffing on her cigar and blowing the smoke into the air above her. "Ask him."

Sucking on the inside of his cheek, Thaddeus raised his gaze to Stanley, who stood just inside the door. Stanley gave a nod but didn't move from his post.

"That will be all, Delilah," Thaddeus said with a sigh. Delilah's face hardened as she stood tall, clearly startled by her brother's dismissal. She looked to Stanley and, perhaps seeing his resolve, decided not to press the issue. Thaddeus and Ainsley sat quietly as Delilah crossed the room, her footsteps punching her frustration down into the floorboards.

Thaddeus nodded to Stanley, who promptly closed the door as they left.

"Forgive her," Thaddeus said. "My sister is easily excitable. She doesn't know when to hold her tongue." He leaned further back into the cushions of the sofa, crossing one leg over his knee. He took extra care to make himself comfortable while Ainsley sat near the edge of his seat, eyeing the enticing liquid in the crystal glass.

"So, Dr. Ainsley, what kind of doctor are you?" Thaddeus asked.

"A surgeon."

He raised his eyebrow. "Is that so? I often am in need of a good surgeon."

"I'm not looking for employment."

"Then what are you looking for?" Thaddeus asked. His features were stern, as if steeling himself against anything Ainsley might say. His gaze did not unlock from Ainsley's. For a long while, they sat refusing to break the stare, like two stags held in a standoff.

Eventually, Thaddeus reached into his pocket. Ainsley watched as he unfolded a piece of paper and tossed it onto the table between them. From his place across the table Ainsley could see the scribble of Jerry's hand and the address Ainsley had begged him for the night before. It was then that Ainsley realized Delilah must have picked his pocket at the Yard that very morning and in front of a dozen officers no less. He worked hard to suppress a smile of amusement.

"You a boxer?" Thaddeus asked.

"At times."

"Looking for some side action? A bout or two?"

Ainsley shook his head.

Thaddeus smiled and pulled the cigar from his mouth. "Then tell me why you would have a piece of paper with my address written on it in your breast pocket." He licked his lips. "A breast pocket is reserved for items of great importance, are they not?" Thaddeus slid back into the comfort of the chair, and crossed his ankle over his opposite knee. He looked so comfortable and unaffected by Ainsley's presence. This was a man who was used to his own authority. "Why is my place of business so important to you?"

Ainsley placed his glass, the alcohol untouched, onto the table in front of him before he spoke. "I pulled a body of a young woman out of the river this morning—"

"Tragic."

"—she bore a branded mark on the back of her neck," Ainsley said, touching the spot with his finger.

"Is that so? You believe I am connected to a random woman found in the Thames?"

"I am looking into the deaths of a number of women. I was wondering if you knew anything about them."

"I should say not. I like my women livelier than that." Thaddeus smiled coyly and drew a long breath from his cigar.

Realizing the man was well-versed in the art of deception, Ainsley nodded. This was the man he had been desperate to track down, the one everyone warned him about. Despite the gun they pointed at him and the strongman who waited just beyond that door, it was clear Thaddeus was attempting to disarm him with charm, his preferred weapon.

"Is that all—?"

"What about a young woman named Julia?" Ainsley asked, raising his gaze to meet Thaddeus' squarely. "Perhaps you know something about her."

Thaddeus' jaw tightened at the mention of his estranged wife. "I haven't seen Julia for some time," he said, his hardened demeanor softening somewhat. "I had thought she left London altogether."

"She was reported missing two days ago. My investigation brought me to you."

"You're a surgeon with the Yard then?"

"Not directly."

Thaddeus nodded his understanding before giving a nonchalant shrug. "Like I said, I haven't seen her."

After a long, self-reflective pause, Thaddeus lifted his glass and downed its contents in a single gulp. He stood suddenly and began walking to his desk.

"Did you know I used to work the canals in Skipley with my uncle?" He glanced over his shoulder and shrugged when Ainsley shook his head. "Our job was to lead the horses back and forth on the towpaths, bringing limestone from one point to the next." Thaddeus stopped and looked to Ainsley. "Have you ever seen those horses?"

Ainsley thought it best not to answer.

"I was seven years old and they were *enormous*. Great beasts. Legs wider than my entire body. They absolutely terrified me." He stopped at a hutch behind his desk and unlocked the middle cupboard.

Still uneasy, Ainsley watched intently, wondering what the man was up to.

Thaddeus pulled out a bottle of liquor and then locked the cupboard again. He smiled when he turned and found Ainsley looking at him. "I save my best for conversations such as this," he said as he poured some in his glass. He walked toward Ainsley with the bottle in front of him. "Sherry?"

Ainsley shook his head and raised his hand to stop Thaddeus from giving him any.

He shrugged and returned to his seat. "You see, while the horses scared me as a young boy, it didn't take me long to realize they were more scared of me than I was of them. Each Friday my uncle would stop the barge and buy a pie for our lunch at the bridge. He'd tie the horse to the tiniest wooden chair set against the tunnel wall." He took a sip of his sherry and smiled at either the memory or the taste.

"Now that horse was so strong from leading heavy limestone barges all day that he could have easily ripped that leather strap free within seconds and trampled us both, but he didn't." He held his glass up and used his index finger to point to his temple. "The tether is in here, doctor," he said with a smile. "We choose to be broken, or we choose to be free."

Ainsley felt beads of sweat formulate on his forehead as Thaddeus spoke, waving his hands about, accentuating his points.

"My mother, my sister Delilah, shit, even Stanley out there, chose to be tethered," he said, with a laugh. "But Julia"—the expression on his face soured as he raised his eyebrows—"she could never be broken no matter how hard I tried."

Bile rose up into Ainsley's throat as images of Thaddeus trying to break Julia took over his imagination. The thought of that man touching her with a loving hand had been harsh enough. Ainsley downed the contents of his glass while his free hand curled into a fist.

Thaddeus laughed and licked his lips. "You say little but that right there told me many things that I desired to know."

"Where is she?" Ainsley's words came out as a growl that he could not subdue.

His adversary seemed surprised by Ainsley's question. "I told the truth when I said I haven't seen her in almost a year," he said raising his eyebrows. "I told you, she could not be tamed." He leaned over the table to pour himself another drink and then raised the bottle toward Ainsley. "Another?"

Ainsley stood, agitated by Thaddeus' couth attitude but also his own frantic state.

"Did she not tell you she was married?" Thaddeus teased. "I'm not surprised. She is a woman, after all. Cunning, and somewhat deluded." Thaddeus stood then, choking the neck of the bottle of sherry as he walked back to the locked cupboard. "I had a feeling this might happen one day, that her mess would be mine to clean up." He locked the cupboard and turned to face Ainsley. "Do you know what I do, doctor? I clean up other people's messes. I get rid of bodies found in backyards. I don't ask how they got there. I just clean up the mess. I find uses for useless people. I protect people from themselves—"

"You extort them."

Thaddeus shrugged. "Semantics." He reached down and opened the top drawer of his desk. "We all have secrets. Every single one of us." He placed a pistol on the desktop, pulling his hand away and slipping it into his pocket.

Ainsley recognized it instantly as the G. & J. Deane pistol he himself had possessed months earlier, the very one he had on him the night he lost his mind. The room spun and then tilted on a diagonal, forcing Ainsley to close his eyes.

"I knew this would be difficult for you to see," Thaddeus said. "You see, that night, I cleaned—"

"You're lying," Ainsley growled.

"Excuse me?"

"You cleaned up nothing. The club...my friends, protected me."

Thaddeus clicked his tongue and shook his head. "No, no, my friend, it was me and my little army of soldiers. I couldn't abide by a child killer any more than you could. I applaud your actions and only wished I had done it myself."

"But you didn't have to."

"You're right. I didn't. There will always be others willing to do the dirty work."

Ainsley felt bile itching up his throat.

"You owe me, Peter," Thaddeus said, using Ainsley's first name for the first time.

"I owe you nothing," Ainsley snarled as he turned his head. He could not fathom being blackmailed into such a partnership, not when he suspected the man capable of murder.

Thaddeus wagged his finger at Ainsley as he rounded the desk. "I beg to differ," he said, chuckling to himself. "I would think nothing of presenting this lovely piece to your dear Inspector Simms. I wonder how his conscience will force him to respond."

Thaddeus sauntered toward Ainsley, unfastening the buttons at his sleeve and folding them up inch by inch. Before he could reach Ainsley's chair, Ainsley stood up and met him eye to eye.

"Will he look the other way, you think?" Thaddeus asked, his face hardened and eyes focused. "Will Julia?"

Ainsley snatched him up by the collar and pulled him

close. "What have you done to her?" he yelled.

"She's dead, as far as I'm concerned, and I hope to God she stays that way, or I'll kill her myself." Thaddeus pushed up on Ainsley's wrists before delivering a powerful uppercut to Ainsley's stomach. Ainsley landed one hit to Thaddeus's face before the office door swung open, bouncing off the wall from the force. Stanley charged in, another man close at his heels. They easily pulled Ainsley away from their employer and forced him to his knees in front of Thaddeus.

"I've given you fair warning, doctor," Thaddeus said as he adjusted his jacket and collar. Then he appeared to reposition his gold ring, ensuring the widest part of the metal was faced outward, before ramming his fist into Ainsley's jaw.

Ainsley fell to the floor and could hear the men shuffling their feet over the ringing in his ears. Blood welled up in his mouth so Ainsley spat it toward Thaddeus, catching his shoe and the hem of his trousers.

"Fuck! Get him out of here!"

The two men pulled Ainsley to his feet and guided him from the room. In the hall Delilah was walking toward the door when Ainsley was pushed to the stairs.

"What the devil?" she called as Stanley pushed her away.

Ainsley barely had enough time to get to his feet before Stanley struck him in the stomach. The force sent him backward, head over heels down the stairs. When Ainsley opened his eyes he realized they had taken him outside to the courtyard. As one man held Ainsley's arms behind him, Stanley removed his jacket and began rolling up his shirtsleeves. Ainsley glanced up to the window and saw Thaddeus and Delilah standing at the glass, watching silently.

The first punch rocked him left, the second sent him right, and the third was delivered right to his gut.

Of all the hits Ainsley had endured through his life these were the easiest to bear. It was clear he had failed Julia. He had failed to gain enough trust so that she could tell him who was after her. And he had failed at protecting her from the monster of her nightmares. Ainsley welcomed the pain of each hit and hoped he'd black out soon so he'd never have to know when it was all over.

Chapter 17

"Release him!" An older woman appeared beside them.

Ainsley's vision was streaked with blood, but he could see her white form rushing toward them.

"For God's sake, I said release him!"

The ground rose to hit Ainsley on the side of the face. The impact sent a ricochet of tremors through his body. He couldn't recall how many times he had been hit. Somewhere inside him he had begged for it not to stop. If Julia was dead by the hands of that man, or soon would be, they would do well to kill him.

He could feel himself being shuffled into a carriage, his body discarded on the bench. Seconds later, he felt the conveyance begin to roll from one side to the next as the carriage left the courtyard. When he opened his eyes he saw the older woman seated opposite him. He recognized her but could not recall from where. Her eyes were fixated on something beyond the window. With blurred vision he saw her twirling something in her hand.

"You only have yourself to blame, doctor," she said, without bothering to look at him. "He would have killed you."

Ainsley tried to say something, the words clear in his mind, but the sounds that escaped his mouth were incoherent.

The woman didn't seem to notice. Her attention was trained on the scenes that played out just beyond the window. "My son nearly died as a baby," she said, swallowing hard and fighting back tears. "We had so little back then there was scarcely enough for any of us to eat and he was already so tiny." She closed her eyes. "I suppose my guilt made me overindulge him and made him into something callous." Her chin trembled and Ainsley could hear her crying. "But he was still my son."

With only one good eye, Ainsley saw the woman pull a handkerchief from her sleeve and use it to dab her eyes.

She finally looked over at him and leaned in close, as if looking over his wounds.

"You are very fortunate," she said, pulling back some of his hair, which had fallen over his face. "Like I said, he would have killed you."

"Why are you doing this?" he asked, aware that his voice was muffled by the velvet cushions of the bench.

She turned her head to look at him. "Because you were nice to me."

The next time Ainsley opened his eyes he was face down on his morgue floor, the cold stone soothing the pain in his jaw.

"Wait," he called out, trying to move. "Wait, what's your name?"

But he was alone and the woman was long gone. The drumming in his head grew louder as he tried to pull himself to his feet. Another minute of rest, he told himself. You need just one more minute.

Ainsley started awake when he realized he was on his back, in one of the hospital's metal cots.

"Finally!" came a familiar voice beside his bed. "I was just about to give up on you." Simms looked completely unimpressed by Ainsley's current state. "It's been two hours since Sam found you out cold."

Ainsley pushed himself higher on the bed, clenching against the soreness that resonated through his body. His head in particular felt heavy and swollen.

"Do you mind telling me what happened? I don't believe it was one of your patients."

"There was a woman," Ainsley said, wincing at the hollow echo his voice made in his head. He looked about, perhaps expecting to see her nearby. Simms was seated in a standard hospital chair, with one leg crossed and his pocket-sized notebook opened to a middle page. The space around them had a curtain partition that blocked the bed and a small radius from the rest of the hospital ward. Beyond, Ainsley could hear moaning from some of the other patients, as well as shuffling beneath the starched bed sheets. A gaslight overhead gave a small ring of light over them, but did little to give their surroundings definition.

"What woman?" Simms asked, poised to take notes.

138

"A woman saved me," Ainsley said, still somewhat confused. "Sam found me?"

"Yes. Now who was the woman?" he pressed.

Ainsley shook his head. "I don't know. I never got her name. She looked familiar, but I couldn't keep my eyes open long enough to get a good look." He pulled on his jaw to force his ear to clear and then wished he hadn't.

"The doctor said you are very lucky your jaw isn't broken." Simms leaned in to take in Ainsley's wounds.

Ainsley raised his hand and felt a large lump on the left side of his face. The skin there felt rough, almost scaly, but the heat that radiated surprised him the most. He could have lied. Part of him feared telling Simms the truth about his current state. He could have easily told him he'd taken on a bet in the boxing ring and lost miserably. However, that kind of behaviour would only reinforce Simms's distrust.

"Thaddeus."

Simms sat up straighter. "Why on earth would you pursue him? On your own?"

Ainsley shook his head. "I didn't. They came for me. They forced me in their carriage and took me to his office."

Simms looked wholly unimpressed.

"She had a gun."

"Who?"

"Delilah. I don't even know if that's her real name. She's his sister." Ainsley raised a hand to his jaw and felt around for stitches.

"The woman Cooper has been taking out to tea nearly every afternoon?" Simms set down his pencil and ran a hand through his hair.

"Do you think he knows who she is?" Ainsley asked.

"I don't know."

"You could have warned me," Ainsley said, feeling himself becoming more awake as the seconds passed.

"If you will recall, I did warn you. Thaddeus is a man I wanted you to have no contact with."

"You ask me to examine your dead lady, but won't tell me anything more about the investigation. You meet me in your office to relay salacious details about the woman I love, but refuse to involve me in the search for her. I apologize for any confusion."

Simms sighed and folded his notebook over his pen. "I thought telling you about her marriage would help you forget about her. I had no idea it would do the exact opposite." Simms leaned in closer and lowered his voice slightly. "Meeting you in my office was the best way to ensure we wouldn't be overheard." Simms suddenly looked abashed. He slid the notebook into his inside breast pocket. "I've long suspected someone in the unit was feeding Thaddeus information. I just never suspected it would be Cooper."

"Something is not right about this," Ainsley said, raising a hand to his temple and allowing his head to sink back into the pillow.

"We know the man in Belgravia is related to the women in the Thames," Simms said. "All had their throats slit."

"But the man was put on display and the women were discarded," Ainsley pointed out. "Unless the man was a message, like I said before."

"For who?"

Ainsley lifted his head from the pillow. "Julia," he said, closing his eyes. "I spoke with Mrs. Holliwell. She told me Julia needed a place to hide and Belgravia was the best she could do."

"Seems odd for your father to take on an orphaned woman. I doubt she possessed any references save for Mrs. Holliwell. And as a lady's maid, no less."

"She confessed to me once that Father wanted her to keep an eye on mother and report back to him," Ainsley said reluctantly.

Simms raised an eyebrow. "An interloper?"

"I don't doubt my father has a few," Ainsley admitted. "That's just the type of man he was...I mean, is." The correction was painful to make but necessary unless Ainsley wanted to admit the father he remembered was his father no longer. Thankfully, Simms didn't mark Ainsley's amendment.

"So can we assume Thaddeus has been looking for Miss Kemp these past eight months?" Simms asked.

Ainsley found himself nodding. Had he known she was

a target he would have whisked her away to Kent or even encouraged her to go to Edinburgh with Jonas, anything to get her as far from the city as possible, even if it meant infrequent contact. He'd have done anything to keep her safe. Absolutely anything. If only he had known.

"Thaddeus wanted her to know she had been found," Ainsley said, tears burning behind his eyelids. "That's why he made sure the body was put in a place for all to see."

"But how would she have known it wasn't completely random?"

"Saint Christopher."

"Pardon me?"

Ainsley couldn't bring himself to look at Simms and raised his hands over his face. "Our last conversation was about the miniature of Saint Christopher I found on the body in Belgravia. She had seen me place it in my pocket at the scene."

Simms's face hardened at the mention of Ainsley's mistake. "Withholding evidence and tampering with a crime scene is a criminal offence, you do know this?"

Ainsley nodded. "I knew you'd never agree to accept my help."

"So you just do it anyway?" Simms's voice rose, causing a nurse from beyond the curtain partition to hush him.

"I'm sorry," Ainsley whispered harshly. "I don't know what I was thinking."

"Why did you not tell me this before?"

"Truthfully, I forgot. You were so angry with me for confiscating the body, I never had the chance. I did mean to tell you," Ainsley said. "I wanted to work this case. The man was found three houses from my front door, for God's sake!"

A nurse pulled apart the partition curtain and poked her head into the confined space. "Dr. Ainsley, please!"

Ainsley recognized her instantly as the head nurse, a matronly woman known for whipping the hands of her subordinates with a metal rod she kept in her apron pocket. The hospital board recently forbid her from administering such punishments, but Ainsley had no doubt the desire still existed inside her.

"Sorry, ma'am," Ainsley and Simms said in near unison.

The head nurse left. A shared look between Ainsley and Simms sealed a mutual agreement to quiet down.

"So Miss Kemp sees the Saint Christopher figure, knows it's a warning from Thaddeus, and leaves London?" After a moment of thought, Simms spoke again. "Or she doesn't make the connection and is snatched in the same manner as you were."

Ainsley shook his head. "She would have made the connection. You don't escape a man like that and stop looking over your shoulder. Besides, Thaddeus said he hadn't seen her since last year."

"So where would she run and who would she seek?"

"She has a brother. The matron at the orphanage told me they were close. If he still lives in London, she may have gone to him."

"Thaddeus would certainly look for her there. That would be heading straight for the viper's nest."

"But Julia would do it. I have no doubt." Ainsley smiled in admiration of Julia's strength. He pulled the covers off of himself and swung his legs to the side of the cot. "I have to go find her."

Simms pressed a firm hand into Ainsley's chest, preventing him from getting up. "No you don't. You rest. I'll go see what I can find out."

"Mrs. Holliwell said she didn't know where Robert Crandall lives. He could be anywhere."

Simms smiled. "All the more reason to rest your head and let me do the groundwork." Simms stood just as Margaret popped her head into the partition.

"Peter Benjamin Marshall, what sort of trouble have you found yourself in now?" She slipped inside the cramped quarters and stood at the end of the hospital bed.

Ainsley licked his dry, swollen lips and turned away from his sister's disapproving stare.

Margaret pulled a folded handkerchief from her reticule and handed it to Simms. "I was able to get this impression from the Talbot's garden," she said, as Simms unfolded the fabric.

He took in an audible breath when he saw the

bloodstained boot impression.

"I had given it to Peter to give to you but he forgot it in his room this morning." She placed a hand on her hip and gave her brother a disapproving look.

"My apologies, Margaret. I forgot."

Simms nodded as he carefully refolded the image back in on itself. "Thank you, Lady Margaret. This may become useful." He turned to Ainsley as he backed away to the opening between the screens. "I'll let you know what I find," Simms said with a smile. He bowed his head and tipped his hat as he walked past Margaret. "Lady Margaret."

Once Simms had left, Margaret took his place on the metal chair and leaned in close to Ainsley's bed. "Inspector Simms sent a message to the house. Aunt Louisa is beside herself with worry. I knew it must be something like this. What on earth happened to you?" She inspected his face with the movements of a mama bird, jerking his head from side to side to see the extent of his injuries.

"Margaret, please stop fussing," he said, snatching her wrist as she reached out to touch his swollen face.

She pulled her hand away, realization coming over her. "Have you found Julia?" she asked suddenly. "Do you know where she is?"

Ainsley shook his head. "And I'm not the only one looking for her either." He shifted in the bed, and turned to get out the other side.

"What do you mean?" she called after him. "Peter, what's happening?"

He grabbed his jacket from a hook on the wall and gingerly slipped his arms into the sleeves. "I don't know," he said, "but lying around in a hospital bed is not helping anyone."

In the carriage on the way home, Margaret looked unsettled. She kept looking to Ainsley on the opposite bench. "It will heal," Ainsley said, ignoring the warmth that radiated from his face.

Margaret shook off his words of comfort. "I know," she said. "It always seems to."

"Then what is it?"

For a moment it looked as if she wouldn't say. "I sent

a message to Lord Benedict just after you left for the hospital this morning, inquiring about Vivian."

"And?"

Margaret exhaled and closed her eyes. "He confirmed it. Vivian is our sister." Her voice was even, as if resigned. The realization that their father had had an affair, even while knowing the pain such activities caused, was heart-wrenching. "He came to the house just as I was leaving and pulled me aside. I haven't had the chance to ask him for more details."

"What sort of details do you expect him to give?" Ainsley asked.

Margaret shrugged. "I don't know. It just all seems...so out of character for Father. So seldom did he visit the island. Why, I could probably count the number of Atlantic crossings on one hand."

Ainsley nodded. It did seem odd. The man was devastated by his wife's affair, even as the years passed. Ainsley doubted Lord Marshall would have even considered such an act, unless it was retaliatory.

"Should we tell Aunt Louisa?" Margaret's eyes shot to him. "What about Daniel?"

"No," Ainsley answered, shaking his head. "We wait. There's no point in alarming them when I haven't spoken with the girl."

"You will speak with her then?"

"Yes, though perhaps not tonight," Ainsley said. "I'm not as easy on the eyes as I was yesterday."

Chapter 18

Julia pushed up the sash of Mary's bedroom window, propping it up with a somewhat sturdy piece of wood, scavenged from a broken crate in the other room. Drops of rain peppered the outside of the window as Julia stood there, looking down on the alley below. She stretched out her hand, catching a few droplets in her palm, and then brought them to her mouth. It was a tradition she and her brother had done as children, slurping rain from their hands, the tastiest water to be had. Julia smiled at the memory and reached out her hand again but pulled it back sharply.

Even in the darkness she could see a shadow cross the alley below. As she watched, another darted past her line of sight. She could see nothing but the outlines, dark forms making their way from Old Nelson road to the narrow passageway that led to Mary and Robert's front door.

Mary was in the other room. Lucy was sleeping just across the bedroom.

"Mary," Julia said calmly, "can you come to the bedroom please?"

She inched toward Lucy, who was only just waking up. She did not cry in the usual way of babies. She only lay there peering up at Julia, expectantly.

Julia could hear her sister-in-law groan at her request. Mary was exhausted. Neither of them had been granted much sleep in the last few days. Their worry for Robert's safety had grown steadily as they waited, but Julia knew their troubles were about to get much worse.

Julia pulled Lucy up from her laundry basket bed and cradled her gently to her chest. She bobbed up and down slowly as she walked for the window.

A narrow ledge was just outside. It wasn't much but it could give them enough stability to make their way to an adjoining roof and freedom beyond. Julia had been eyeing it for days, praying they never would have need to use it.

"Mary, there's something we need to talk about," Julia pleaded, circling the room in search of a blanket for Lucy to protect her from the rain.

Mary appeared at the bedroom door, weary and despondent. Her eyes were swollen from crying and her hair a tangled mess from her constantly pulling at it.

A powerful knock rattled the entry door. Mary started and whirled around in terror. "Oh my God, what do we do?"

Julia walked toward her slowly. "We need to take Lucy and go."

"But Robert, he's coming back."

Even with her child directly in front of her, Mary made no movement to take her from Julia. In the last few days Julia could not coax her to nurse her child or rock her to sleep. Since Robert's disappearance it was as if little Lucy didn't exist anymore.

"We have to think of Lucy now," Julia said, not wanting to admit her brother might have been killed like Jeremiah had.

Another hard knock sounded. "Mary Crandall?" came a gruff voice from the other side.

Mary shook her head fearfully as Julia pulled Mary's cloak from the end of the bed. "I cannot leave him."

"You must. For Lucy's sake," Julia hissed, trying to hand her the cloak.

The rain pelleted down in sheets, bouncing off the still sun-hot bricks and parched pavement. Steam rose from the stones.

The knocks on the door ended and a determined pounding began, rocking the thin wood of the door and inching the small table barricade farther into the room.

"We have to go now," Julia said. She reached for Mary's sleeve but missed by a fraction of an inch.

Mary was already walking into the main room when the door finally gave way and three men burst in.

Julia recoiled back to the window. Good God, if only Mary had come when Julia first called for her. With Lucy snug beneath her blanket and Mary's cloak, Julia slipped through the window, and perched herself on the ledge, making herself as slim as possible. She listened as the men went about the rooms. She waited for Mary to appear, all the while inching toward the adjoining roof.

Above the rain, Julia could hear them turning over tables and chairs, moving the bed and smashing knickknacks. And then Mary screamed sharply and Julia stopped. Lucy began to stir beneath her layers of protection and Julia closed her eyes, willing her to settle down.

"We only want the bitch," one of the men said, as Mary moaned in agony. "Where is she?"

Mary let out another yelp.

Julia's heart lurched at the thought of leaving Robert's wife behind. If she stayed on the ledge they'd find her before long. If she left both she and Lucy had a better chance of survival.

"My baby," Mary said from somewhere in the room. "Please don't hurt my baby."

"No one checked outside the window!"

Mary had betrayed her.

Chapter 19

When Margaret and Ainsley walked through the front door of Marshall House a heavy mood greeted them. Cutter was on hand to help them shed their outer clothes, which has been soaked by the torrential rains that pelleted them as they ran from the carriage to the door.

"Where is everyone?" Margaret asked as Cutter took her hat.

"Lord Benedict hasn't left, Lady Margaret," he said. "They are with His Lordship."

The brother and sister pair exchanged glances. In the upper hallway of the house, a series of shouts, muffled by the maze of rooms and doorways, rang out.

"Was that Father?" Ainsley asked.

They went for the stairs, Ainsley charging ahead and racing down the hall to their father's room. Inside, Aunt Louisa and Lord Benedict stood around Lord Marshall's bed, as the invalid wriggled on the floor, clutching his hands over his chest. Ainsley went to him immediately. "What is God's name?" he asked, kneeling on the floor beside his father.

"That creature bit me!" Lord Benedict bellowed.

When Ainsley looked up again, Margaret was rounding the threshold. He also saw Lord Benedict clutching his right hand, a small amount of blood trailing between his fingers. With a determined look, Lord Marshall raised his face to Ainsley, blood staining the edge of his mouth.

"The creature you speak of is my father," Ainsley yelled from his place on the floor. "And he's still Lord Marshall, Earl of Montcliff, member of the House of Lords. I demand you treat him as such."

Turning his attention back to his father, Ainsley saw the leather valise held tightly to his torso with his one useable arm. Margaret appeared at his side, kneeling as well.

"This cannot be normal," she said quietly so only Peter

could hear.

"Our deepest apologies, Lord Benedict," Aunt Louisa began behind them. "My brother has not been himself, as you well know."

"Aunt Louisa, call for Maxwell, please," Ainsley ordered.

Begrudgingly, she crossed the floor to the mantel and pulled on the cord that hung from the ceiling. "I fear he may be losing his mind, Peter," she said, folding her hands in front of her. "Perhaps it's time to face facts."

Ainsley placed his open hand on the side of his father's face, a gesture meant to coax him from his agitated state. "It's all right, Father," he said softly, pulling the valise from Lord Marshall's grasp.

The old man had very little strength in his good arm and that is why he had rolled onto the bag. There was something in it, Ainsley reasoned, that his father did not want Lord Benedict getting a hold of.

"What is it?" Ainsley asked, gently pulling the mouth of the bag open.

"It was empty when I checked," Margaret insisted. "Father would not let us remove it from the room."

The bottom of the valise was empty, the black satin lining shimmering in the lamp light. There had to be something else, Ainsley told himself. He reached in and began feeling for anything out of the ordinary.

"He's a fool. A right, damned fool," Lord Benedict insisted, while Aunt Louisa fussed.

"Peter, please, come take a look at Lord Benedict's hand. I'm afraid he may need a stitch or two." Aunt Louisa presented a handkerchief, which Lord Benedict applied to his wound.

Ainsley ignored the pleas from his aunt and ran his hand along the smooth lining. He stopped when his fingers felt something hard beneath the fabric. His face must have changed because Margaret's face alighted.

"What is it, Peter?" she asked, moving closer.

Lord Marshall became instantly relaxed as Ainsley ripped into the inner seam of the valise. He pulled out a frayed envelope with papers folded inside. There were three letters, each addressed to Lord Abraham Marshall of

Belgravia.

Ainsley noted the return address.

Maxwell appeared at the door. "Sir."

"Maxwell, help me return His Lordship to his bed," Ainsley said soberly.

Without any fuss, Lord Marshall allowed the butler to move him, but he never took his eyes from Ainsley.

"What are those?" Aunt Louisa asked, inching forward, prepared to take them from him.

Ainsley turned, using his body to stop her from seizing them. There was a special reason their father would hide them. At first, he wasn't sure if he should open them, but Lord Marshall gave a nod and then his eyes welled up with tears.

He opened the first letter and saw that it had been written the prior winter. "They're letters to Father," he explained. "From Lord Benedict."

Margaret inched closer and read over her brother's shoulders. After scanning the first letter Ainsley handed it to Margaret so he could read the next. A few tense moments passed before Ainsley could read no longer. The anger he felt began to overshadow his sense of reason. He felt his hands curling into fists at his side and he was forced to look away. He walked to the window that overlooked the back garden, unsure how to proceed.

"What is it?" Aunt Louisa asked, coming toward them to read the letters herself. "What's the matter?"

"Lord Benedict begged Father to come to the plantation in Barbados," Margaret said, allowing Aunt Louisa to take the letters.

"A matter of dire urgency," Ainsley said airily from the window.

"It must be about Vivian's mother," Aunt Louisa said. "She was sick for some time, yes?" She turned to look at Lord Benedict, but he refused to make eye contact as he inched toward the mantel.

"Vivian is not our sibling," Ainsley said, finally able to look at the others in the room. "She is the result of an affair Lord Benedict had with a maid at Father's estate near Bridgetown. Father had been seeing to the child's care and education these fourteen years."

Ainsley did the math. Lord Benedict would have been eighteen when Vivian was born.

All eyes turned to Lord Benedict, who bowed his head in defeat.

"It's true," he said quietly, after a few moments. "I wasn't in a place to claim her as my own. Not as a child myself. My father was sick and I was soon to be the heir to a dwindling fortune." He licked his lips and clenched the handkerchief to his wound tighter. A few times he opened his mouth to speak and then stopped himself. "Why should I have to pay the rest of my life for a careless mistake?" He searched the room for allies. "We are all friends here, and I would appreciate it if we all could keep this knowledge amongst the four of us. For Cecilia's sake."

"You allowed me to believe she was our sister," Margaret said. "I asked you without reservation."

"Now, Margaret, what was I supposed to say? My fiancée—"

"Is a dear friend of mine," Aunt Louisa said suddenly. "And she will know the truth of it, whatever the outcome."

"It wasn't just a short affair," Ainsley said, walking toward Lord Benedict. "You said in the letter the woman was content to see you once a year, but that she'd grown demanding."

Lord Benedict's expression fell. "She asked for more money. She was always asking for more money. What was I supposed to do?"

"You asked Father to help you find a solution," Margaret said, flipping to the next page of the letters. "What exactly were you asking Father to do?" she pressed.

Moments passed by but no reply came. The room fell silent as everyone looked to Lord Benedict for answers. It was unfortunate that Lord Marshall could not speak for himself and Ainsley feared they would only achieve one side of the story.

Then a tiny voice came from the door. "He asked him to say I was his. He said if his fiancée found out her family would take her dowry and he'd be left penniless." Vivian stood, tears streaming down her cheeks.

"Now hold on, just a minute!" Lord Benedict walked forward, but Ainsley prevented him from getting to the girl.

"It's true!" Vivian yelled from the door. "I heard you fighting in His Lordship's room after mother finally passed. You said if he didn't claim me, you'd tell everyone that his son"—her eyes went to the floor—"that his firstborn son was from another man."

Aunt Louisa gasped.

"Daniel." Margaret closed her eyes. "He doesn't know."

Lord Benedict chuckled quietly and shrugged when Ainsley looked to him. "Better to have an illegitimate negro girl than an illegitimate male heir, yes? A lesser scandal as scandals go."

"How dare you!" Aunt Louisa slapped Lord Benedict across the face and when she tried to hit him a second time he grabbed her wrist and pushed her away. She fell to the floor, her dress billowing out around her. Margaret cried out and Ainsley stepped forward, placing himself between Lord Benedict and everyone else in the room.

Lord Benedict recoiled at the sight of him, unable to take his eye from Ainsley's swollen jaw and black eye.

"Is that what you did to my father?" Ainsley asked, pushing his hands into Lord Benedict chest to drive him away from the women. If things came to blows he wanted the scuffle away from those who were most vulnerable. He had no doubt his face looked a fright after the beating Thaddeus had given him. Benedict was clearly terrified.

"Peter, what are you saying?" Margaret asked, as she helped Aunt Louisa stand.

"Father doesn't have apoplexy," Ainsley said without taking his eyes from Lord Benedict. "He has a brain injury, most likely sustained from blunt trauma to the head. He refused to be blackmailed and you pushed him, didn't you? You pushed him and he fell, yes?"

Lord Benedict shook his head rapidly. "No, no," he said as he backed away. "He tried to go for the door but tripped. Honest."

Out of the corner of his eye Ainsley spotted Benedict's walking cane leaning against the chair next to the fireplace. Ainsley snatched it up to examine the brass clutch. "Is this what you used to hit him as he walked away?"

"What? No?" Lord Benedict's eyes darted to the side as he lied.

Ainsley stepped closer and raised the cane to strike. Lord Benedict cowered and cried out before Ainsley even touched him.

"Don't hurt me. I've been a friend to your family for years!"

"Peter, don't!" Margaret rushed to him and held his arm. "We'll call the Yard. They will see to it."

Knowing his father suffered daily because of the cowardly actions of such a man sickened Ainsley. A man's life has been changed irrevocably and here Benedict begged for mercy.

"Coward." Ainsley nearly spat as he spoke. "I'm not going to hurt a sad, pathetic imbecile like you." He dropped the walking cane to the rug. "I'm going to alert the authorities in Barbados and direct them to do a thorough investigation into that poor maid's death. This night, I am putting you on the very next boat to sail the Atlantic and I will ensure you make the voyage in chains!"

A half hour later, Lord Benedict was led away by Det. Inspector Wright, who seemed very pleased at the prospect of a voyage to a tropical locale. Ainsley returned to his father's room and found Aunt Louisa seated in the chair next to Lord Marshall's bed, a book in her lap ready for her evening routine of reading.

Margaret and Vivian were standing at the foot of the bed.

"Why have you not said anything until this night?" Margaret asked.

"I did not know I could trust you, miss." The girl's eyes went from Margaret to Aunt Louisa and back again. "I had wanted to tell you both so many times."

"Have no fear, child," Aunt Louisa said. "You are amongst friends now."

Lord Marshall began murmuring and raised his good arm to Ainsley. Ainsley walked to the bedside, grabbed his father's hand, and squeezed it. "I told Inspector Wright to interview all the doctors who saw to your wound," he said. "We'll have some answers before long."

Aunt Louisa sighed. "Not that it matters now," she said. "What's done is done."

"Even still," Ainsley said. "It's better to know what we are facing."

Margaret pushed aside a tear. "We should see to getting this young lady a better room on the family floor."

"Oh no, miss," Vivian said. "I couldn't."

"You can and you will," Ainsley said in a lighthearted tone. "You are the daughter of a noble, yes?"

Vivian's eyes grew bright at the prospect. She pressed her lips together as she looked up to Margaret. "Thank you."

Margaret followed Ainsley down the hall as he walked toward his room. "Do you think Daniel will loosen the purse strings for our new ward?" she asked as they crossed beneath the door.

"He'd better," Ainsley replied, pulling at the buttons of his collar. "I'll make him."

"Don't you think we should tell him? About his father?"

Ainsley shook his head, wishing he weren't the custodian of such a secret.

"He deserves to know. Once the secret is out no one will be able to use it against us," Margaret pleaded.

"And what will that mean for you? Do you think Blair, the eldest son of a duke, will be so understanding? Our family is riddled with scandal. Whichever way we turn there is another reason for society to shun us."

"I thought you cared little for society," Margaret said.

"My only care is for you. Much longer and you'll..." His voice trailed off as he took in the look on her face.

"I found the one for me," she said, tears pooling on her lower eyelids. "But I can't be with him. Father needs me. I've accepted my fate and I really wish you would as well."

"Margaret—"

But by the time he spoke, she had already left the room.

After the confrontation with Lord Benedict the house fell into a predictable quiet as family members took to their rooms and the servants scattered into the bowels of the house to prepare for the following day. As midnight ticked past, Ainsley sat wide awake in his chair, which he had set by the window, his mind plotting Thaddeus's downfall. The man couldn't be reasoned with through any logical means. According to Simms, he was untouchable, always able to skirt the law and never being called to task for his misdeeds. Too many men depended on the work he gave them. None would think to turn on him. He's like a god, Ainsley realized. Or a king.

And how does one dethrone a king?

A murmur of agitated voices found its way to Ainsley's room from downstairs. Ainsley could tell there was someone at the door, but who it was he could not say.

"If you'll just let me see him," said a female voice, the drumming of the pouring rain outside nearly drowning out her words.

"You must use the servants' entrance," Violetta commanded, her hand firmly on the door.

When Ainsley came to the top of the stairs all he could see was their maid at the front door and a silhouette of a woman opposite her.

"Please, I haven't any time. I must speak with him!"

Shaking her head, Violetta began to push the door closed.

"Violetta, who is it?" Ainsley demanded halfway down the stairs. "Let them in."

After a moment's pause, Violetta pulled the door open and stepped aside. On the other side of the threshold, hunched against the relentless rain, Julia stood, a tattered cloak pulled over her shoulders. Ainsley stopped at the bottom of the stairs, his hand clasped tightly on the bannister, the only thing keeping him from falling to a heap on the floor. He closed his eyes for a second, wondering if it was just a dream, and when he opened them he saw that she had stepped in the door and was walking toward him.

Relief, sadness, overwhelming joy, and grief enveloped him. His limbs trembled at the sight of her, safe and within arm's reach. He finally let go of the bannister and went to her, rushing to scoop her into his arms and whisk her away.

She was alive. Oh, thank God, she was alive!

"Peter, who's at the door?" Margaret appeared at the top of the stairs with Aunt Louisa close behind her "Julia!"

Ignoring them, Ainsley wrapped his arms around Julia and kissed her, madly, passionately, not caring who witnessed it or what they might think. He touched the side of her face and relished the overpowering delight in feeling her skin against his. How dare Violetta banish her to the servants' door? As far as Ainsley saw it, she would never use the servants' entrance ever again. He felt her one arm wrap around him as he embraced her and he could feel the smile on her lips as she kissed him back.

And then something moved between them. A tiny flicker and then a squeak of a cough. Ainsley pulled away and saw that the cloak had fallen away in their embrace. A helpless infant no more than three months old was cradled in Julia's arm, held tightly to her body.

"Who is this?" Ainsley asked, smiling at the cooing baby.

"This is Lucy, my brother's daughter."

Aunt Louisa and Margaret made their way down the stairs. "Where is your brother then and the child's mother?" Aunt Louisa asked cautiously.

"There is so much I must tell you," she said, adjusting the baby in her arms. Their happy homecoming was marred by fear in her eyes and a terrified jitter to her voice.

"Where have you been all this time?" Margaret asked. "We've been searching everywhere."

"My deepest apologies, Miss Margaret," Julia began. She looked back to Ainsley, still clutching his arm as if he would fall away from her. "I went to find my brother. I think he is dead and his wife as well."

Chapter 20

"Come to the library," Aunt Louisa urged, waving her arms for Julia, Ainsley, and Margaret to follow her. "Violetta, I'm sure you have other duties to perform before bed."

Chagrined, Violetta nodded and headed for the servants' stairs.

Ainsley kept a hand on Julia's back as they walked side by side to the library. Aunt Louisa stood at the door until everyone had entered and then closed it. "Well, now we can have this conversation without prying eyes and ears," she said, somewhat pleased at her own cleverness. "I'm going to pretend I didn't see that display of affection at the door."

"You have been gone for days," Ainsley said.

"I know. My—"

"Have you been with your brother this entire time?" Margaret asked.

"Yes, I mean, no. He wasn't there when I arrived. Mary, my brother's wife, was in such a state. I couldn't just leave Lucy with no one to care for her." The baby started to squirm and wriggle in Julia's arms.

Aunt Louisa reached out her hands to the baby. "Come now," she said. "The wee thing needs to sit with me." She took the baby to one of the armchairs, sat down, and began entertaining her with funny faces.

Slowly, Margaret and Julia took seats on the sofa while Ainsley pulled an armchair closer before sitting down. Julia turned to look at him. "I hadn't meant to be gone this long, honestly. I just needed to make sure he was all right."

"What made you believe he wasn't all right?" Margaret asked.

"It was the man killed in front of the Talbots," Ainsley explained. "And the miniature of Saint Christopher."

"Yes." Julia swallowed nervously. "I knew once I saw it he had sent it for me. The man was Jeremiah Locke, my brother's neighbour. They were trying to warn me."

"About what?" Margaret's voice cracked. "You haven't an enemy in all of Christendom."

Julia looked abashed and averted her gaze. "There are things of which neither of you know about."

Margaret huffed. "I'm sure it's not as bad as that." Her face fell as Ainsley and Julia grew quiet. "Is it?"

"My husband is a very dangerous man," Julia said.

"Husband?" Margaret nearly popped up from her chair.

"It's all right," Ainsley said, reaching over and placing a hand on top of Julia's. "I won't ever let that man near you again."

"No, you don't understand. Mary is dead. I heard them do it as I ran away with Lucy. I have to go back and make sure she is given a Christian burial."

"Did Thaddeus do it?" Ainsley asked, feeling his jaw tighten and his fist clench.

"I don't know. I couldn't see. It all happened so fast. They kicked in the door and Mary was screaming. I ducked out the window and held Lucy tight to my chest so she wouldn't make a sound. I was so terrified I would smother her, but if they heard us I knew they would kill us." A tear spilled over her lower eyelid. "She told them where I was and begged them to not hurt her baby. I couldn't stay. I had to run."

"Who was it, Julia? What did they want?" Ainsley inched to the edge of his seat, ready to hunt down Thaddeus as soon as she gave the word.

"They wanted me. Nothing else. Just me." Her silent tears gave way to sobs as the memory of the previous hours enveloped her. "She's always hated me, and the relationship I had with my brother."

Unable to hear anymore, Ainsley stood. "I have to find Simms," he said.

Julia and Margaret left their chairs and followed him out into the hall. "Peter, wait!" cried Margaret.

"They will come here next, Margaret. Believe me, they will come here and no one will be safe." Ainsley was at the front door and pulling on the handle when Julia appeared beside him.

"I'm coming with you."

"No. Absolutely not. You stay with Lucy and Margaret. I can't have you out there alone again." He laid a gentle hand on the side of her face and pulled at the tear streaks on her cheeks with his thumb. He opened the door and stepped outside into the portico.

The hammering rain pounded the pavement ruthlessly, drowning out the noise of the city. A second later the door opened again and Julia popped outside beside him. She handed him his coat and an umbrella.

"I wasn't asking," she said without inflection.

It would take too long to hitch the horses to the carriage and there were no carriages for hire in sight, so Ainsley and Julia ran the streets to Great Scotland Yard, aware that their clothes were soaked within the first block, and holding hands the entire time.

Scotland Yard was overrun with officers and civilians alike. A pool of rainwater sat stagnant at the front door, its near-constant opening and closing sending the rain into the building. The usual hum of the office had been replaced by angry shouts and whistles as officers called over the melee to their partners. The desk sergeant looked inundated and overrun and was barely able to look up when Ainsley approached him.

"Where's Simms?" he asked, holding fast to Julia's hand as she stood slightly behind him. He would have rather put his arm around her to keep her from being pulled into the scrum but holding hands was much more discreet than that.

Sergeant Fisher huffed. "Haven't seen hide nor hair of him," he said. A crash came from the right side and the sergeant was forced to look up. "You two, sit down!" he bellowed, pointing a sharp finger at two boys in handcuffs along the wall. They couldn't have been more than ten years old and already bore the look of the other hardened criminals in the building. When the sergeant turned back to Ainsley he looked even less pleased than before. "You're welcome to wait for him here," he said, but Ainsley was already scribbling a note.

"Just tell him we've gone here," he said, handing it

over. "But be cautious."

The sergeant barely looked at it and tossed it somewhere in the mess of his desk. Another handful of loose papers were thrust at him even as Ainsley turned to lead Julia from the throng.

"You don't look so good, yeah?" one of the boys on the bench said, a smile revealing a mouth with only half his original teeth. "You were that toff my man took a liking too, yeah?"

Sneering, Ainsley stopped to look them over. The boy next to him on the bench smiled, but he looked far less assured than the one who spoke. "Yeah, it was you," he said, laughing openly. "Didn't recognize you, what, with all t'at...damage, yeah?"

Ainsley could feel nothing but pity for them, commissioned into the ranks of the likes of Thaddeus before they even had a chance in the world. Choosing a criminal life, protected by even a temperamental leader, was better than what awaited them on the cobblestones of London.

Recognition dawned on the other boy's face as they stood there. He sat up straighter suddenly, interested in the woman standing behind Ainsley. "I know you," he said, unease sweeping over him. "They be looking for you." His voice cracked as he spoke.

The other boy looked much less alarmed but extremely pleased. "Won't Thaddy be happy to hear it were me who saw her wit' the toff."

Ainsley could feel Julia inch behind him, as if asking him to protect her. "Let's leave," she whispered.

"'Ey, 'ey!" the boy yelled as Ainsley turned her toward the door. "Watch out! E's coming for ye. E'll be coming for bot' of ye!"

Outside, Ainsley scanned the street, suddenly paranoid. The rain had left a slick sheen on all surfaces, making Northumberland Avenue shine black. He could feel Julia closely behind him, both hands clutching his. "We'll take a cab," he said, seeing one a few paces away.

It wasn't long before they were in Spitalfields. They paid their fare to the driver at Bethnal Green Road and approached Old Nelson Street on foot.

At first Ainsley led, but after they walked one block Julia tugged at his arm from behind.

"It's this way," she said, nudging her head to the right.

She let go of his hand as they moved through the alley, the second floor of the building closing in around them the farther they went. A rat scurried past, bounding over mounds of refuge left along the crumbling brick wall. Ainsley felt something stick to his boot but he kept going, not willing to have Julia alone in such a place. He banished all thoughts of her running for her life through the pouring rain with little Lucy clutched in her arms.

The covered alley opened up to a wider courtyard where muddied linen dangled from loose clotheslines and piles of garbage littered the space. With purpose, Julia walked past a group of people arguing amongst themselves and headed for another narrow passage between the buildings. The group stopped to watch, enthralled, as Ainsley followed her.

"How long has your brother, Robert, lived here?" Ainsley asked as she approached a rickety wooden staircase. A steady stream of stormwater slid down the side of the building, eroding the brick as many other storms had previously.

"A few months," she said. "Their flat before this one burnt down in a fire. Mary was lucky to escape with her life."

At the top of the stairs they slid through a doorway and down a hall. Julia slowed her steps as she neared an open door. A shadow was cast on the hallway wall from inside the flat and they could hear rummaging.

"This is it?" Ainsley mouthed as they approach.

She nodded.

He bent down and picked a metal pipe that had been laying along the floor. It felt heavy and awkward in his grasp, but it was that or a rotten piece of wood that would surely crumble on impact. He motioned for Julia to get behind him as he inched for the door.

Ainsley's heart raced as he stood with his back against the hallway wall. The shadow had grown dim as whoever was inside went farther into the room. He held his hand out to Julia, telling her to wait there, before tightening his grip around the pipe and jumping around the doorframe.

"What are you doing here?" he yelled as he charged for the figure in the far room, the pipe ready to swing.

The figure turned around, a stick in his own grasp ready to strike at Ainsley.

"Simms?"

Ainsley lowered his weapon and Simms heaved a sigh of relief. Ainsley eyed him thankfully as his heart rate returned to normal. "I thought you were one of Thaddeus's men," Ainsley said apologetically.

"I had the same thought."

Julia crept in the room and Ainsley noticed the front door hadn't been opened but rather smashed in, the frame barely hanging on to the wall. What little furniture the couple had owned had been tossed about and smashed. The table was overturned and much of their personal belongings lay discarded and trampled on. Taking it in, Ainsley realized he was very lucky not to have walked in farther or he would have tripped over a body that lay in the rubble.

"She's dead," Simms said, even as Ainsley knelt to take her pulse.

"Mary," Julia said, somberly. Even in the dim light, Ainsley could see she was holding back her tears.

Dressed in a modest frock of muslin, hand-sewn and paper-thin, Mary's body lay on her side, her arms raised as if to protect her head. Ainsley moved her arm away from her face and saw a series of small gashes on her cheeks, chin, and neck. He pulled a handkerchief out of his pocket and used it to clear away some of the blood that had gathered at her throat.

"They aren't deep enough to kill her," Ainsley said, knowing Simms was waiting for preliminary findings. Ainsley looked over the torso and then rolled the body onto her front. That's when he noticed the large collection of blood that had seeped into the raw wood floors. Two puncture wounds entered the lower back on either side of the spine. "They attacked her kidneys," Ainsley said, closing his eyes momentarily. "It's a brutal way to die."

"Was it instant?" Julia asked from behind him.

Ainsley shook his head but couldn't bring himself to

say the words.

"I should have stayed. I could have helped her."

Ainsley stood and faced her. "No, you did the right thing for you and Lucy."

"Why the smaller cuts then if they didn't do much damage?" Simms asked.

"They are painful and no one wants scars to their face." Ainsley looked down with empathy. "They tortured her. They probably wanted information about Julia's whereabouts."

Julia knelt down and took Mary's hand into her own. She lowered her head and kissed Mary's knuckles. "Hail Mary, full of grace...pray for us sinners, now and at the hour of our death. Amen." Julia sniffled and planted another kiss on Mary's hand before laying her arm down gently.

Ainsley and Simms exchanged glances.

"She never did like me," Julia said, rising to stand.

Ainsley stopped himself from reaching out to her. Their eyes met and held each other for many seconds.

"You were here for all of this?" Simms asked, breaking the reverie.

"I was in the other room when they broke in. I took the baby out the window with me. I didn't know what they intended to do but I knew it wasn't good."

Ainsley looked into the adjoining room, where a cracked window led out onto a narrow ledge that hovered over a twenty-foot drop. A mound of discarded, broken wood and garbage that had been thrown out and left to rot waited at the bottom. He could just make out a space where Julia could have hid with the baby. "How did you get down?" he asked. He turned to find Julia had followed him.

"There's a stairwell on the other side of that building," she said, gesturing toward an adjoining structure.

"You scaled the roof? In that rain?" Simms asked from behind her.

Julia nodded. "I ran for help but saw no one. Everyone was in from the rain so I just kept running."

"Do you know where Robert is?" Simms asked.

Julia shook her head. "I came here straight after I spoke with Mr. Marshall at the hospital, but he was already gone. Mary was in such a state and Lucy wouldn't stop crying. I couldn't just leave her so I sat and waited with them, hoping that each set of footsteps outside the door was Robert who had come back."

Ainsley pulled a silver-plated picture frame from a ledge. The grainy picture was of a young man and girl in orphanage uniforms standing in front of a brick wall. Ainsley recognized the wall instantly as the foundling home where Julia and Robert grew up. The girl, with a solemn expression, stared blankly ahead while the boy, nearly a foot taller, glanced off to the side with a look of disdain.

"Mrs. Holliwell had these done," she said. "She did it for everyone. Her friend was only learning."

It was then that recognition dawned on him. "I know where Robert is," he said. "He's in Southwark with Thaddeus."

"How do you know?" Julia asked.

"Thaddeus has a network of buildings all over the city. He could be in any of them," Simms said.

Ainsley shook his head. "I saw him at the club below Thaddeus's office. They have him."

"If they were willing to dispatch Mrs. Crandall so easily, why would they hold on to him?" Simms said.

"He's fighting for them again," Ainsley said. "They're using him."

"They'll kill him. We have to get him out of there." A look of sheer panic spread over Julia's face.

"That is exactly the reaction they are expecting you to have," Simms said.

Julia shook her head and tried to push past them for the door. "I waited here like a coward when I could have saved him. I could have saved both of them."

Ainsley held fast to her shoulders. "Julia, by no means are you a coward. I can't have you running off again. Not without me."

Julia searched his face. "I can't just let him die," she said, before burying her face in Ainsley's chest. Her shaking hands clutched mercilessly to the lapel of his jacket. "He's the only family I have."

Mary's body was sent to St. Thomas and Julia was

given a few minutes to collect what she could for Lucy's care, though it was apparent the Crandalls owned very little. "I'll send some men to guard your house," Simms said as they left the apartment, "as a precaution."

Ainsley nodded, but the added security did not allay his fears.

"Do not to anything stupid, Peter. This is Thaddeus, a career criminal, not some boy frustrated with his university studies," Simms warned, referring to the last case they had worked on.

In his heart, Ainsley knew Simms was right. So much could go wrong. In this case, they needed to proceed cautiously.

The carriage ride home to Marshall House was silent, filled with more contemplation than communication. Ainsley's thoughts in particular bounced between wanting revenge for what was done to Julia and her kin and protection for both her and Lucy. The sinking feeling that Robert was dead, or would be soon, nagged at him.

"I'm sorry I did not tell you," Julia said, without lifting her gaze from her knitted hands. She sat beside Ainsley, far enough away that they did not touch but close enough for Ainsley to feel the warmth in the air around her.

"Trust is built over time," Ainsley said, recognizing the fact that their relationship was still young despite the intense feelings that he harboured for her.

"I trust you implicitly," she said. "There is no other with whom I hold such high regard." She lifted her gaze then, revealing a stream of tears that trailed down her face. It broke Ainsley's heart to see her so shattered and to know there was so little that could be done for it. "I should have told you about Thaddeus a long time ago. I was just..." She looked about the carriage as if searching for the word.

"Scared?" Ainsley offered.

"Yes. I've spent most of my life being scared. It's hard to believe anyone could make me feel safe and protected, as you have." Her voice faltered somewhat but she continued. "I thought that by marrying Thaddeus I would find that protection. I saw his harsh demeanor as strength and his control as love. I didn't see what he really was, not until later. I watched him cut a man's tongue out and feed it to his dog. I've overheard terrible fights where his enemies were left far worse than you." She reached over and touched Ainsley's swollen and blackened cheek. "No one is safe around him. No one."

Ainsley grabbed her wrist gently and pulled her hand away so he could look her squarely in the eye. "You never have to return to him. I'll find you a place, a place for you, your brother, and Lucy, where you never have to worry about him again. I will see to that myself, which is the least I would do for a friend, if nothing more."

"What if I want more?"

Ainsley gave a small smile. "You need time," he said, disbelieving his own words. "I'll not be the next domineering man in your life. I am the son of your employer. I don't want you to think that our relationship is another duty to perform. I'll take care of you and protect you from anyone who wishes you harm, but I couldn't live with myself if I thought you were only with me because of your fear of Thaddeus."

The carriage stopped and Ainsley realized they were already home. "I'll get the door and help you down the steps," he said. He slipped past her and was halfway down the carriage steps when she snatched his hand and pulled him back.

"Please don't say that!" she cried openly, and looked as if at any moment her trailing tears would give way to sobs. "It's never been like that. I love you, Peter, with all my heart. Your knowledge, your arrogance, your sense of honor, I love all of it. Don't demean what exists between us as a feeling of duty on my part. It was not duty that drew us together and it is not duty that brought me back to you. I love you as I have never loved before nor will again. It is because of you that I have come so far. It is because of you that I felt strong enough to go to my brother and save my niece. I can bear your rejection, but I cannot bear any misunderstandings. I beg you not to leave this carriage without the knowledge that these words are spoken with the strongest feelings of love and not one ounce of fear."

Tears scrolled down the crests of her cheeks, spilling onto her bodice. She made no move to brush them away as Ainsley pulled her from the darkness of the carriage and out onto the pavement. He held her cheek in his hand and used his thumb to brush the tears aside.

"Your strength is not contingent upon my love. You are stronger than any material known to science and you prove that to me again and again. Just now you confessed an undying love for a man who has made you no promises or commitments because he's been so blinded by his own selfish needs. I am so unworthy of your love or admiration because you, Julia Kemp, are the most loyal, caring, determined woman I have ever met. Whoever does not see how special you are is a damned fool and I will not stand for it." Ainsley felt a sting in his own eyes as he looked down at her. "When this is all over, and I know you are safe, I would like to marry you."

Julia's eyes grew wide.

"If you'll have me," he added.

"What about Thaddeus? I'm still married."

Ainsley shook his head. "I've never been known to follow the rules."

Julia chuckled and gathered his hands into her own. "In that case," she said, "I'd love to."

He leaned toward her, circled his arm around the small of her back, and pulled her close. The kiss they shared, in plain view of everyone on the street that day, was the envy of all kisses shared before it.

Chapter 21

Arms crossed over her chest, Margaret stood at her father's office window, which offered an unobstructed view of the street. She felt a tightening in her chest as her brother scooped up Julia into his arms. Suddenly, she was aware of Aunt Louisa beside her, straining her neck to get a better view of the display on the pavement.

"Well now," Aunt Louisa said, slowly, "isn't this an interesting development?" A smile teased her lips as she ogled the couple below. "Your brother isn't the staunch academic I mistook him for."

Margaret chuckled to herself. "Hardly."

Aunt Louisa backed away from the window and glanced about the room. Lord Marshall's office had sat neglected for nearly the entire time he was away, though Margaret had caught Daniel seated behind the desk once or twice, perhaps getting a feel for the power over the family that would soon be his. "I came in here to speak to you about the staff."

"What's wrong with our staff?" Margaret turned and crossed her arms over her chest.

Aunt Louisa slapped a new edition of the paper on Lord Marshall's wide, mahogany desk. "Someone's talking to the press about Vivian, and about Peter's attachment to a certain lady's maid."

"Oh good grief." Margaret reached out and pulled the paper from the table. She truly didn't want to know what they said but curiosity overcame her better judgement. "Nothing about Father this time," she noted.

"No, not this time."

"So it wasn't Lisle who was selling our secrets," Margaret said. "She was gone before Vivian arrived. We sacked an innocent girl."

Aunt Louisa shrugged as she reached out a hand to trail her fingers over the smooth, wooden surface of the desk. "How long before word gets out about Lord Benedict's arrest...at this house?" Aunt Louisa cocked an eyebrow.

"I'll find out who it is. I'll speak to them," Margaret said.

"They need to be muzzled."

"I said, I'll find out. You needn't concern yourself."

Aunt Louisa raised her chin and smiled. She nodded and pursed her lips as she pondered Margaret's reassurance. "This used to be my father's desk," Aunt Louisa said. "Did you know that?"

Margaret shook her head.

"I was here the day your father had it brought over. Our father had passed the week before and your father was eager to begin his work as Earl of Montcliff." Aunt Louisa smiled as she looked at the high back chair pulled up to the desk. "They found a note in this drawer that my father had left. *Control thy passions lest they take vengeance upon you.* I do believe my brother took those words to heart. Over the years I saw him sour. It was as if all his enthusiasm for life were being sucked out of him."

She pulled the chair away from the desk and ran a hand along the arm before positioning herself in front of it. After taking a deep breath, Aunt Louisa closed her eyes and lowered herself into the seat. She rested her hands on the top of the desk and smiled when she looked to Margaret, who was inching toward her.

"Heavy is the head that wears the crown," Margaret offered.

"Oh balderdash." Aunt Louisa waved a dismissive hand. "He is a vindictive fool, just like our father before him. My only hope is that Daniel is different."

Margaret winced internally.

"How long have you known Daniel isn't Abraham's son?" Aunt Louisa asked, after seeing the look on Margaret's face.

"Several months."

Aunt Louisa nodded. "Daniel knows as well, then?"

Margaret shook her head. "I don't think so."

"And Peter? How has he taken the news? Is he angered?" Aunt Louisa lowered her chin and eyed Margaret.

"More like relieved," Margaret answered truthfully. "He has no interest in this desk, or this office. His work at the morgue is his true calling and he's thankful to be able to continue it."

"Good." Aunt Louisa patted the arms of the desk chair simultaneously and sprung to her feet. "Now if we can just get Mr. Thornton to propose then we shall be all set." She patted the side of Margaret's cheek and smiled like a doting mother to a docile child before heading for the door.

"If he did ask for my hand, I will not be accepting it," Margaret said as Aunt Louisa began to walk away.

"Say again?" she asked, turning to look at her niece. "I'm getting on in years and for a moment I thought you had said you wouldn't accept Mr. Thornton's offer of marriage."

Margaret nodded, and felt every muscle in her body clench. She knew such a conversation was coming and had prepared innumerable retorts to any objections her aunt would undoubtedly have, all which evaporated now that the conversation was well at hand.

"He will be a duke—"

"But I am no duchess," Margaret said, aware of the shaking in her voice. "I saw my mother marry a man out of duty. I saw how it not only destroyed her spirit but my entire family as well. Those who do not learn the lessons of the past are doomed to repeat it. That is a past which is not worth repeating."

"Oh really, Margaret." Aunt Louisa raised a hand to her temple and closed her eyes. "This family can only handle so much. We will need a bit of good press after your father's illness and brother's promises to marry the maid!"

"And these things are my burden to bear?"

"My, my, Margaret, you are a right old bluestocking, now aren't you?"

Margaret huffed and turned her gaze away. "So what if I am?" She marched for the door and pushed past her aunt, who tried to bar her way. "It seems far better than being an interfering drunk."

Chapter 22

Julia and Lucy were installed in one of the finer guest bedrooms on the second floor. None of the family members complained, but the staff, who had been ordered to prepare the room, looked more than a little put out by the arrangements.

"Perhaps Miss Kemp would be more comfortable in one of the third-floor rooms. We can move Prudence to Lisle's room," Violetta suggested when Margaret ordered her to bring up some fresh linen.

Margaret's heart quickened when she realized there would be a confrontation. "Those rooms are hardly suitable for a baby," Margaret said calmly.

"Yes, but the child can sleep in the nursery with George and Hubert, and Miss Kemp can have her old room." Violetta gave a closed-mouth smile and tilted her head to one side.

"Miss Kemp is our guest and, as far as I am concerned, she will remain such for a good deal of time. My suggestion is if you or anyone else belowstairs has a problem with whom I chose to house under my father's roof there is a door to the street and you are all welcome to use it." Margaret brushed a loose strand of hair from her forehead. "Now, can you please send Maxwell up to speak with me? We're going to need the cot from the attic as well." Margaret flashed a dry smile as the dispirited maid ducked back into the hallway.

"Miss Margaret, please, it would be no trouble for us to sleep with the servants," Julia said once the three of them were alone. She clutched Lucy closer to her bosom and gently swayed back and forth to keep the child from waking.

"Nonsense, this room is empty and well suited for two people," Margaret said, as she pulled down the seam of her bodice. "Besides, I have no doubt we'll be moving you down the hall before long."

Julia blushed as her eyes darted to the floor.

"Now away with you, Peter," Margaret said, nearly pushing him out the door. "Aunt Louisa and I have our guest well taken care of. You shall see each other in the morning."

"It's not safe."

"Two constables are stationed right outside our front door. I've already ordered Maxwell to bring them coffee throughout the night." Margaret placed a hand on Ainsley's upper arm. "Go rest."

Ainsley nodded reluctantly, and looked over his sister as she ushered him out the door. "Summon me if you need anything."

"Goodness, there will be none of that," Margaret teased, pulling the door to close it.

"That's not precisely what I meant," Ainsley said, flashing a look of disappointment.

"You are all safe now."

He leaned on the doorframe, preventing Margaret from closing the door fully.

"How assured are you of that?" he asked, keeping his voice low.

Margaret hesitated. "If I admitted to my true feelings on the subject I may never sleep again," she said, as she slowly pressed the door into the frame.

"I do not mean to cause any quarrels," Julia said, biting into her lower lip. "Your family shouldn't have to suffer," she said, "for what I've done. I've brought this to your door."

Margaret's shoulders sank when she heard Julia's voice so defeated and resigned. "Heaven's no. You are no more responsible for the deeds of a madman any more than I am," Margaret said. Without thinking, she raised her hand to the scar at her throat. "We all bear our scars," she said after a moment.

"I have to tell you, Lady Margaret," Julia said. "I have to tell you who I really am and what I've done."

"You've done nothing, nothing at all to deserve this." Margaret went straight to her and gathered up the sleeping Lucy in her arms.

"I wish that were so." Julia closed her eyes but it was

too late. A tear slipped from her eyelids and rolled down her cheek.

"Your husband's choices are not your choices," Margaret said, trying to reassure her maid.

"There's more. Please, Lady Margaret, let me tell you all of it." Julia reached out with one hand and took Margaret's hand. "I was young and reckless when I agreed to marry him," she began. "He possessed everything I lacked: money, power, a future. I knew his business was illegal but I didn't know the extent. I was happy to have food and shelter and protection. And my brother encouraged it. In a way, I had no choice. I had thought I was happy but I know now that I was simply scared." She licked her lips and wiped away a tear as Margaret gathered Lucy from her arms. "He...he hit me often and he told me it was my fault, that I needed to be trained."

When Margaret saw the tears in Julia's eyes, and heard the words she spoke, she choked up and found herself unable to speak.

"His brother, Edgar, was far worse," Julia continued. "His wife, Ida, lost a baby by his hand. She had come to me to help her stop the bleeding, but I couldn't. There was so much blood. It was everywhere. I was so afraid she'd die and that they would blame me."

Margaret took in a deep breath and raised a hand to her face. "Oh." She turned to the bed and slowly lowered Lucy into the middle. Gingerly, she positioned pillows on both sides of the babe and then pulled a blanket from the chair behind her to cover the child.

"She knew she couldn't stay with him. She wanted me to come with her but I was too scared. I couldn't imagine a life by myself. In many ways, she was much stronger than me."

"What happened to her?" Margaret asked reluctantly.

"Edgar found her and slit her throat, and threw her in the Thames, just as he threatened to do many times."

Margaret gasped and nearly fell back into the chair beside the bed. "Oh, Julia."

"I started carrying a knife with me wherever I went, just in case. And then one night he came to me, drunk and angry. He said I had ruined his marriage and killed his baby. He ranted and raged, for nearly an hour. He threw things about and hit the walls. He wouldn't let me leave and it was just getting worse and worse. And then he lunged at me. He had me against the wall and was choking me, both hands clasped at my throat. I had no choice." Julia reached up and touched her neck, pained at the memory. "Somehow I found the strength to drive my knife into the side of his neck. Even as he bled out he held tightly to my throat, determined to kill me as he died. He nearly succeeded."

The room went dead silent as Margaret digested what Julia had just described.

"I dragged his body to the yard and cleaned up the room as best I could. I wanted it to look like he died in some brawl or something. That night I ran to Mrs. Holliwell and a week later she found me a place here. I thought it worked until I saw that man tied to the lamppost. I knew then that they had found me."

Margaret sat in silence as Julia went for the window. Pulling back the drapes she peered outside to the street below. "I've seen all that you and Peter have been through and I've wished so many times it didn't have to be like this. They know where I am now. And I'm afraid what happened to my sister-in-law Mary is just the beginning."

"Why do you say that?" Margaret asked.

"Thaddeus is like a cat," Julia explained, turning to look at Margaret. "He likes to play with his prey before finishing it off."

Chapter 23

Ainsley had no intentions of sleeping and found no rest in the confines of his room. The house grew quiet and then the streets below followed suit as he sat at his desk, flipping through his sketchbook. He searched for the images he drew of Julia, finally able to look at them now that he knew she was close to him again. He had meant what he said on the street earlier. He had thought of marriage briefly before but such thoughts were always tethered to the reality of their differences in class. He had never permitted anything but a fleeting thought on the matter, but now he could not deny that it was the single most desirous thing imaginable to him.

Allowing his feelings such open rein over his senses felt liberating and absolutely terrifying at the same time. It was as if a piece of his body would always remain outside of him, wandering the streets vulnerable and yet bolstered by his love. The thought brought a smile to his lips as he leaned into his upturned palm, his elbow propped on the desk.

A noise downstairs alerted him and he sat upright. He listened intently to subtle sounds in the foyer and then came three loud knocks from the front door.

Look. Look.

The voices circled about him in an eerie funnel cloud, layers upon layers of undecipherable whispers and chants.

Not him. Not him. Look. Look.

Shaking them off, Ainsley stood and marched for his window. He could see nothing below. He was at the top of the stairs by the time Margaret's and Julia's doors opened. Margaret tightened her housecoat.

"Who is it?" she asked, groggily.

Ainsley shook his head and raised his finger to his lips, entreating her to be quiet. Julia inched toward him in the dark. "Stay here," he said.

As he came down the stairs he saw a shadow move

through the frosted glass of the front door. The streetlamp cast a dim glow onto whoever it was on the portico.

"Careful, Peter," Margaret cautioned from the second-floor landing.

Ainsley was halfway down the stairs when he heard another bedroom door open, and then another. Margaret was successful at keeping everyone from coming down with him, except Nathaniel, who tiptoed down the stairs.

"Do you think it may be *him*?" Nathaniel said as he appeared behind Ainsley.

He didn't care to answer and grabbed the only conceivable weapon at hand, a gold-plated candlestick. Nathaniel was quick to take up its twin.

So much time had passed since the initial knock that it seemed odd there was no other. The shadow at the door moved but no sound was heard. As Ainsley inched for the door he motioned for Nathaniel to stay back.

"State your business!" Ainsley yelled through the thick, exterior door. No reply came except an eerie, high-pitched scratch.

After turning the lock, he curled his hand around the brass handle, giving a quick glance to ensure Margaret and Julia were safe on the landing, before yanking the door wide open.

A black mass greeted them, solid and unmoving. A scream echoed through the hall as Ainsley swung the candlestick, striking the figure square on the chest. The being buckled backward but made no sound, and he realized he had hit something softer than flesh.

A light behind him grew brighter as he stood there. Suddenly the mass took shape and form, mimicking a man, hung from the portico ceiling, still swaying from Ainsley's blow, the rope creaking against the beam of the portico.

A terrified shriek came from the top of the stairs.

Ainsley gasped for breath and heaved himself up from the chair. He was in his room with the oil lamp dim and his sketchbook pages scattered about the floor. It took a moment for him to catch his breath from the fright.

"It's all right," he told himself. "It's not real."

Chapter 24

Barely a word was said as they filed into breakfast the next morning. For the first time, Julia was invited to sit with the family for the meal, but she graciously refused.

"I think I will sit with your father for a spell," she said when Ainsley tried to coax her to the dining room. "Perhaps he would like meet Lucy."

Ainsley highly doubted it. Their father had little concern for them when they were younger and seemed to groan with relief once all his offspring came of age. He said nothing of the sort to Julia, however, who was most likely looking for any excuse not to overstep her station too soon. Ainsley knew it was better to ease everyone into it, despite his desire to have their relationship out in the open at last.

Aunt Louisa gave a look of surprise when she saw that Julia would not be dining with them but it was Nathaniel who commented first.

"Perhaps her table manners require further tutelage," he offered.

"Perhaps she knows she will be scrutinized mercilessly," Margaret said with a growl.

Aunt Louisa shot her son a look, as if cautioning him from speaking further. It was a warning he chose to ignore.

"She's causing strain on an already precarious predicament," he said, glancing to Maxwell, who stood dutifully next to the sideboard. Nathaniel lowered his voice. "Don't you see? Imagine having to serve one of your own? The staff are close to revolt."

"Let them," Ainsley said unsympathetically.

"It is not very different from the underservants serving the housekeeper and butler," Margaret said casually, not wanting to entirely commit to furthering such a doomed conversation.

"I should say there is much difference," Nathaniel laughed. "Does this mean anyone can improve their station simply by connecting with the right people?"

"Is that not the foundation of the British peerage?" Ainsley asked, still coming to terms that he was having such a conversation.

"Besides, Julia is more a family member than I think you realize," Margaret said.

"Oh really?" Nathaniel pushed the food around on his plate. "How long has Cousin Peter been sneaking her into his bedroom then?"

A fork clattered onto a plate as Ainsley stood. Margaret, who had been seated next to him, stood and placed herself between him and their cousin across the table. "Peter," she said cautiously.

"When will The Briar's improvements be completed, Aunt Louisa?" Ainsley asked, without taking his eyes from Nathaniel, who had pulled as far back from the table as his chair would allow.

Margaret slowly pulled away but kept a hold of Ainsley's sleeve.

"Only another week or so," Aunt Louisa answered. She turned to her son beside her, slapped his thigh and gave him a stern look.

"Don't let us keep you here any longer than necessary," Ainsley said, pulling his chair toward him.

The rest of the meal was eaten in near-silence, each person lost in thought and silenced by the obvious strain. Ainsley barely touched his food and instead found himself moving it about the plate with his fork. The room had grown so quiet nearly everyone jumped when the doorbell sounded, shattering the tension. Aunt Louisa raised a hand to her head as she tried to steady her breathing.

Maxwell left the room to answer the door but curiosity got the better of Ainsley, who followed the butler out into the hall. The two constables stationed in the foyer stood erect and waited as Maxwell walked to the door.

"Good day, sir. Please inform Mr. Marshall and Ms. Crandall that their presence is requested at Scotland Yard." Sergeant Fisher hopped up on his toes as he spoke.

"What is it, Sergeant?" Ainsley asked.

The sergeant nodded. "Inspector Simms has something to show you, sir," he said. His eyes darted to the side. "Ms. Crandall, if you please?"

When Ainsley turned he saw that Julia had come to the top of the stairs holding Lucy.

Julia reached the bottom of the stairs just as Aunt Louisa and Margaret came toward the door. "I'm afraid I cannot leave my niece."

"It's all right," Aunt Louisa said, reaching out to take the baby. "I'll see she is taken care of." She grabbed Ainsley's sleeve and pulled him toward her. "Pay no heed to what Nathaniel said. He has much to learn."

Ainsley nodded before bending over and kissing her softly on the cheek. "We won't be long, Aunt Louisa."

A few moments later, Julia and Ainsley were installed in a waiting carriage with a plush, velvet bench and smooth privacy curtains. Ainsley could feel the movement in the carriage as the sergeant climbed up beside the driver. A few minutes from the house, Ainsley pulled back the curtains and noticed they were on Westminster Bridge, heading in the opposite direction of the Yard.

"Didn't he say we are requested at Scotland Yard?" Ainsley asked.

"He called me Ms. Crandall," Julia pointed out, looking over his shoulder.

Ainsley ran his hand over the bench cushion. "This isn't a police carriage," he said, his mind instantly recalling the one he had ridden when he was arrested recently.

"Thaddeus." Julia breathed the name that was on both of their minds.

"We have to get out of this carriage," Ainsley said.

The traffic was light, which allowed the carriage to move steadily through the streets, heading directly for Southwark. Ainsley tugged on the door handle, but found the mechanism latched and locked. He leaned back onto the bench seat and used his feet to kick at the latch. Each blow sent the carriage box rocking. It wouldn't take long before Sergeant Fisher and the driver noticed. The door bowed, but would not give.

"Aim for the window!" Julia cried out.

"Cover your face!" Ainsley pulled back his feet and gave one swift kick with the heel of his shoe. The glass shattered instantly, some cascading down on to the floor of the carriage. By the time Ainsley caught himself Julia had her arm through the opening and was pulling at the latch from the outside. The carriage slowed and was pulling over to the side of the road.

Before Sergeant Fisher could clamour down Ainsley and Julia were on the pavement running in the opposite direction.

A gunshot rang out and screams erupted from the intrigued crowd as Peter and Julia ducked into a narrow alley.

"Good God man, not in broad daylight!"

When Ainsley glanced back he saw Sergeant Fisher giving the driver a thump with the back of his hand before jumping from his perch.

"He's coming!" Ainsley urged Julia further down the alley and grabbed her hand as he passed her. They passed a doorway and she pulled him back, slipping into the shadows.

"What is this place?" Ainsley asked, feeling the dust churn about them as they scurried to the opposite side of a very large, dimly lit room. It was there that Ainsley could smell a hint of the Thames.

"It's the building where Thaddeus keeps all his carriages," Julia said, "and sometimes other things."

Ainsley knocked his knee into the large wheel of a disabled cart and bit down on his tongue to keep himself from crying out in pain. Julia let go of his hand and disappeared into the gloom.

"Julia!" Ainsley dared not bring his voice above a whisper. He followed the sound of her footsteps and came to the bottom of a set of stairs.

"Follow me," she said, "I'm up here."

He clamoured up and breathed a sigh of relief when he found her at the top.

"This door leads to the roof," she said, "We can jump to one of the neighbouring buildings but once I—"

The alley door opened suddenly and Sergeant Fisher appeared. Ainsley could see the glint of the pistol in his hands as he scanned the room.

"Come now, doctor," he said, "let's not get too hasty. They only want to talk to you."

Ainsley reached for the doorknob behind Julia but her

hand stopped him from turning it. In the dim light he could see her shaking her head. She was waiting for the right time.

"It's the girl they want, not you. Give 'er to us and you can go back to that nice, elegant home of yours." Sergeant Fisher's voice grew distant as he walked to the opposite side of the building. Suddenly, Julia pulled the door open, splashing light into the room.

"There!"

Together they darted onto the roof, running along the narrow bit of flat roof before clamouring up to the peak and sliding down the other side. At the top Ainsley caught sight of the Thames, Blackfriars Bridge, and the Tower on the other side. The roof was flat on the next building and they were able to run. And then the roof ended. They stood at the edge looking down onto an alley littered with garbage and broken bits of wood.

"If we can get to the bridge we can hire a hansom," Julia said.

She led him to the corner of the building and pointed to a wooden landing nine feet below. The stairs would lead them to the alley but only if they could make it to the landing, which looked weatherworn and unstable, hardly capable of supporting a kitten, let alone two adults at the same time.

"It's not safe," he said, turning away.

"We have to," Julia said, forcing him to look at her.

"I'm not going first and leaving you here for that madman, and I'm not sure I want to see it collapse under you." Ainsley drew his hand through his hair, pained by the choice in front of him.

She clasped both hands on the side of his face and kissed him. "I love you," she said, before turning and crouching over the edge. She held on to the ledge as long as she could before dropping down. The wood swayed slightly but did not collapse and she started down the stairs.

"Come on!" she yelled, as she looked up.

Ainsley nodded and swung his feet over. She was halfway down before he decided he could do it.

"Easy there, pal!"

Ainsley felt a metal chain slip over his head and set at

his neck. He looked up to see the carriage driver flashing a black-toothed grin. "Jump now and I can promise you a slow, painful death."

Behind him Ainsley could see Sergeant Fisher catching up, heaving from exhaustion and relieved to see Ainsley had been caught.

"London's elite, eh?" the driver sneered.

"The girl?" Sergeant Fisher asked.

They all looked over the ledge and saw a deserted alley.

"Don't worry," the driver said, tightening the chain somewhat. "She won't leave without Prince Charming here."

Chapter 25

With his hands tied in front of him, Ainsley was brought to the courtyard behind Thaddeus's warehouse building. He had been pushed along by Sergeant Fisher and the carriage driver, who showed little concern for the pedestrians watching their march down the street. Their fear of Thaddeus appeared well established. After they pushed Ainsley into the courtyard, the carriage-high gate groaned and reverberated as it was eased back into place.

Ainsley's eyes went to the window of Thaddeus's office, expecting to see the man himself, but the panes were black and empty. Thaddeus's mother smiled from the breezeway entrance.

"Good of you to join us again, Dr. Ainsley," she said, as she walked toward them. "Glad to see you are healing nicely." She turned to Fisher. "The girl?"

"She got away, ma'am."

Her shoulders sank as she heaved a sigh and turned her attention back to Ainsley. "Had I known you were harbouring Ms. Crandall our last meeting wouldn't have ended so quickly."

"Why does she matter to you so much?" Ainsley asked.

"She killed my son, Dr. Ainsley. I think even you can understand there can be no forgiveness for that."

It was then that Ainsley realized where he knew her from. "Shall I call you Mrs. Calvin or do you prefer Mrs. Wagner?"

The woman smiled as she pulled the same handkerchief Ainsley remembered from her sleeve. Her face contorted into a pout and she feigned a sniffle.

"Goodness, Doctor, I'm flattered you'd remember," she said, taking on the very same tone of voice she had used while supposedly looking for her daughter in Ainsley's morgue. "So gullible." She turned to Sergeant Fisher. "He can be useful until we find the girl." She jerked her chin toward one of the buildings to the side. "Check with

Delaney for now. I'll send out a group for Julia."

Ainsley was pushed to one of the doors. Sergeant Fisher opened it to find a man seated on the stairs.

"Is that the doctor?" a man asked, scrambling to his feet.

Sergeant snickered. "Doctor of the dead. You Delaney?"

The man nodded. "Bring him up here."

Sergeant Fisher took hold of Ainsley's upper arm and shoved him in the door. Inside, there was a long, narrow hallway with a set of stairs at the very end. Only one other door was on the ground floor, which Ainsley guessed led to the pub he had seen on his earlier visit but on the opposite side. A window, tinted brown by silt and age, illuminated the stairwell, which consisted of warped wood that had been beaten and bowed by heavy foot traffic.

The man led the way, springing ahead. Ainsley glanced up the stairwell before stepping onto the first board. He felt a sudden shove from behind him, so strong he almost fell onto the stairs.

"Get on with you now!" the sergeant boomed.

"Keep your voice down," Delaney hissed from above them. "The girls are sleeping."

Ainsley walked, but only with the knowledge that he could not fight off both of them, especially with his hands tied. The second floor had more doors and was laid out similar to a hotel but Ainsley was only permitted a quick glance before he was urged up to the third floor. At the first door, a woman stood smiling as her body hugged a doorframe.

"Well hello," she said.

Delaney pushed the woman back into the room. "Close the door," he said with a pointed finger.

The door was closing as Ainsley passed. The woman snarled at him, revealing a severely chipped front tooth and an empty space beside it.

They passed an open door with no one inside. Ainsley saw a narrow metal bed, a bare mattress, and washstand.

A brothel.

Ainsley suddenly felt ill at the thought of being brought here to treat an unfortunate woman who had been injured, diseased, or worse. Ainsley had no interest in helping these men continue their illicit business venture, especially if it exposed him to the many diseases they were known to carry.

At the end of the hall, the man opened the door and gestured for Ainsley to get inside. At the door Ainsley closed his eyes and titled his head to the side, not believing what he was asked to do.

"See what you can do for him, doctor," the man said.

Ainsley opened his eyes and was surprised to see a man, curled up on the bed. His clothes were wet with sweat and blood had caked into the fibers.

The doctor stepped into the room and turned to his captors, presenting his hands, which were fastened at the wrists. "And what do you expect me to do with my hands bound?" he asked.

Delaney reached into his pocket and pulled out a knife.

"No," Sergeant Fisher said, grabbing the man's wrist and nearly taking the knife from him. "He escaped once. Make him do it like that."

Ainsley laughed. "Then there is nothing I can do," he said with a shrug.

Delaney shook his hand from the sergeant's grasp and cut the rope.

Rubbing his wrists, Ainsley turned to the man in the bed.

"You have a medical bag, I presume?" When neither of the men in the hall responded, Ainsley turned to them. "I'm not a miracle worker. I need the proper supplies."

"I'll see what I can find," Sergeant Fisher said. "You watch him."

Delaney stayed at the door as Ainsley moved farther into the room, rolling up his sleeves as he looked over the injured man on the bed. He looked as if he'd been beaten in a similar manner that Ainsley had. Ainsley wondered why they were bothering to treat his injuries.

Ainsley leaned over to look at the man's back, and rolled him gently as he touched his lower back. Then he knelt down at the side of the bed to look at the man's face. A flash of recognition came to the man's eyes, but he said nothing. The man's cheek was swollen on the left side with a sizeable cut on his cheekbone that Ainsley could hardly see for all the blood that had caked onto the man's face. He shuddered as Ainsley pulled down his lower lids. The right eye showed signs of damage, with broken blood vessels and a pool of blood blotting the white of his eye.

When Ainsley looked to the man's hands he saw numerous scrapes and bruises, along with a few swollen fingers on his left hand. Ainsley tried to force them to flex but the man just recoiled from the pain.

A few seconds later, Sergeant Fisher appeared with a dusty medical bag Ainsley thought was better suited for a display case than actual use.

"This was from the other doctor," Fisher said. He dropped it on the foot of the bed.

"What happened to him?" Ainsley dared to ask as he stood to look over his offered tools.

"Same thing that happens to all of them," Fisher said with a smile.

The clasp nearly broke off the bag as Ainsley pulled on it. Inside he found a number of bottles, opium mainly, some laudanum and alcohol, but no carbolic acid or soap. "It appears your other doctor had an addiction," Ainsley said. "Or he had a lot of female patients."

"Never mind that. What does he need?" Delaney asked, jerking his chin to the man on the bed.

"He needs a hospital," Ainsley said matter-of-factly. "Surgery, probably."

He pulled out the leather tool case he found at the bottom of the bag and unwound the straps. He laid it out on the bed.

"Shit."

The scissors, scalpels, pliers, tweezers and knives were rusted and corroded beyond repair. Most likely they had been neglected regular care, were hardly ever washed, and certainly not dried before being put away.

Any hope of him being able to help this man evaporated.

"He probably has a punctured lung," Ainsley said without bothering to look up. "I can't operate on him here."

Delaney opened his mouth to say something, but a

commotion outside in the courtyard drew his attention. He crossed the room to the window and peered outside. "Let's go."

Ainsley had no time to react before Delaney was closing the door from the hallway. The iron key gave a muted groan and clink and then the hallway went quiet.

Ainsley went to the window but couldn't see what everyone was running toward.

"You're the one Julia told me about," the man in the bed said suddenly, wincing as he turned to face Ainsley. "The doctor she works for."

"Robert Crandall?"

The broken man in the bed nodded and then closed his eyes. "They made me fight him."

Ainsley circled the bed, his mind reeling with every possibility to make an escape but now he had an invalid to slow him down. He began to pull out everything from the doctor's bag, searching for anything he could use to the break the lock.

"They told me to fall in the eighth round, or they'd kill Mary and Lucy."

Ainsley felt his heart stop at the mention of Robert's wife and the image that flooded his mind.

"That fighter did me in good," he said, folding into his fetal position. "I didn't think I'd make it out of this room."

Ainsley pulled out a brown bottle and gave a quick sniff. Chloroform.

"Can you walk?" he asked, pulling at a rip in the bare mattress. He edged out a sizeable piece of cloth and put it in his pocket along with the chloroform.

Robert started to move, at first pushing himself from the bed and then swung his legs over the edge. He looked as if he could scream out in pain at any moment but didn't. The man was to be commended for that.

Ainsley knelt down so that Robert could wrap his arm over his shoulders and use his body to stand. Once on his feet Ainsley guided him to the door.

The sound of numerous men and their thunderous boots marched the full height of the stairwell, passing the floor Ainsley and Robert were on. Then the noise reverberated through the length of the hall above, only now it was laced with the tiny, muffled screams of a female.

"They found her." Robert covered his face and looked as if he could weep.

Ainsley tried to look out the keyhole but found the opening dark, which meant the key was still in the lock. He guided Robert to the metal footing of the bed and went to the doctor's bag. He pulled tweezers from the pouch and tried to use it to turn the key. Slowly he positioned the tool to clasp the key but each time the tweezers touched the iron of the key hole and sound rung out.

He pulled the tweezers away at the sound of Sergeant Fisher and Delaney returning.

"I thought she was gone for good," Delaney said. "Or at least she will be when Thaddeus finds out we caught up to her."

Above them Ainsley could hear sobbing, as if someone were crying directly into the floorboards above them. He looked to Robert, who swallowed nervously. Ainsley strained to listen, wondering if there was anything in the woman's voice that resembled Julia's.

"When they open this door, I need you to rush at them," Ainsley said quietly, pulling the cloths and chloroform from his pocket. He doused the fabric with a healthy amount of liquid before replacing the stopper and putting it back in his pocket. "Can you do it?"

Robert nodded but the look on his face betrayed his doubt. The pain must have been immense and any exertion was putting him at death's door. Ainsley handed him one of the cloths and a pair of pointed scissors.

They waited a few more minutes before the sound of boot steps on the floorboards in the hall signaled that someone was coming. Ainsley stood poised with the rusty scalpel in one hand and a chloroform rag in the other. The men stared at each other as they listened. The footsteps stopped just outside the door and then there was nothing.

Ainsley leaned closer to the door, wanting desperately to hear what was happening on the other side. A floorboard creaked under his weight. He froze.

Come in, you bastard. Come in.

The lock turned and the door swung open. Together Ainsley and Robert lunged into the hall, attacking Sergeant

Fisher. Ainsley was quick to press the cloth to his mouth as he pushed the officer back into the opposite wall. Defensively, he pulled at Sergeant Fisher's hands and pressed the cloth to his mouth with such force Ainsley was sure he'd suffocate. Not that he didn't deserve it.

Robert growled as he pushed his entire body against their opponent and collapsed on the floor when he realized Ainsley had the cloth over Fisher's mouth.

The sergeant fainted rather quickly. The struggle was over as he slumped to the floor. Ainsley checked for a pulse. "We don't have much time."

He scooped Robert up and together they limped for the stairwell. They both went for the third floor.

The floor layout was different than the storeys below. Instead of a long hall with rooms at each side, just a single door greeted them at the top of the stairs.

Discouraged by the sight of their new obstacle, Robert fell and moved his body to sit at the highest step. "Go get Julia," he said breathlessly. "I'll wait here."

Ainsley didn't argue. The door was locked, and this time no key was left. Ainsley began ramming the door, placing all his weight in the iron knob and lock. A succession of female screams rose up from inside the room as Ainsley felt the frame crack. Then the door burst open, revealing a dark, attic room and a number of young women housed inside. Some stood on guard as if ready to defend themselves while others cowered, either behind the stronger ones or on mattress-like bedding arranged on the dirty, wooden floor.

"Not another step," one of the women sneered, readying her fist.

"He's not one of them," another one said. "I haven't seen him before."

It's not him. Not him.

"They brought a woman here, moments ago," Ainsley said, raising his hands in front of him to show he intended no harm. "Where is she?"

The woman, twenty of them or so, stood and stared for a moment, exchanging glances and licking their lips as if unsure. Finally, one of them stepped aside, and then another. As the women moved apart they revealed a path into the attic that allowed Ainsley in. As he drew closer, he could hear a woman crying and then realized he was in the part of the attic that was directly above Robert's room.

When the woman looked up Ainsley could see it wasn't Julia at all, but rather a slight, black-haired young woman, who sniffled into the hem of her ripped dress. When she saw him her entire body began to shake.

"Please don't kill me! Please!" she yelped. She held out her bruised and lacerated hands to keep him away.

"Who are you?" Ainsley asked.

"Nelly Macdonald," she said, slowly taking her hands down.

"Avery Adams."

"Jennifer Smith."

"Maybel..."

"Victoria..."

The names grew into a chorus and came at him so quickly he wasn't able to put a face to the voices. He closed his eyes as the list rolled on and then realized these were the voices that had been following him for days.

"I don't understand. What are you doing here?" He turned back to the woman cowering in the heap of blankets and did a quick visual check of her injuries. She had been beaten, but the extent of her injuries couldn't be seen in the dark room.

"Those men, they snatched me in Camden Town two weeks ago." The woman raised her head, hope brightening her eyes as she stared at him. "I have a mother and a sister. I work at the market on Fridays—"

"They snatched us all and brought us here."

"We don't know what they plan to do with us."

"Don't be daft. We know bloody well what they intend to do with us!"

A quick glance to the door revealed Robert had come in, closed the door behind him and now sat on the floorboards with his back to the door. The expression on his face mirrored the disgust Ainsley felt.

"Why did they beat you just now?" Ainsley asked, looking at the woman on the floor.

"She escaped."

"She was our last hope."

"They are sending us away tomorrow."

Nelly smiled through a fat lip and fattening cheek. "We made a secret passage through the attic. I almost made it," she said. "But there were so many out in the neighbourhood. More than usual. I think they are looking for someone else."

"They would have killed her, you know," said a voice behind him. "They do it to all the other girls."

"Shh! You don't know that."

"We don't see them no more, do we?"

"They slit their throats and toss them in the river," Robert said, straining his voice to be heard over the whispers amongst the women. "I saw it once. He made me watch."

Nelly began to sob uncontrollably as if the realization dawned on her of how close she had come to the list of dead women pulled from the Thames. She raised a hand to her gaping mouth as the fear griped her, revealing knuckles that had been scraped nearly to the bone. The sound of her cries fell into the back of her throat, silencing the room for a moment before bursting forward with a gasp.

"Shh...it's all right," he said, trying to hush her.

She fell onto the bedding and covered her swollen face with her hands.

"Do you know if they found the woman they were looking for? A woman named Julia?" he asked. He looked to the group when no immediate answer came. No one said anything.

"They will be coming soon," Robert said, pulling himself to his feet. "We have to go."

"You can't leave us."

"You must take us with you."

Ainsley and Robert's eyes met, both aware that such a large group would not be able to move about the neighbourhood without being spotted.

"I have to get to Thaddeus' office. He has something that belongs to me. I can't leave it in his possession." Ainsley paused. "And I think it will help us get out of here."

Robert nodded, an understanding passing between them.

"There's an opening," one of the women said. "That's

how Nelly got out."

"Show us."

The room sprang into action. Two women guided Ainsley and Robert to the far side of the attic. The rafters were so low the men were forced to crouch to avoid hitting their heads. Almost at the wall, the leading woman stopped and ran her fingers along the mortar of a brick wall that would lead into the next building. When she pulled a loose brick away she revealed an empty space. Brick after brick was removed, perhaps ten in total, before the round opening was completely revealed.

"We worked on this for weeks," she said.

Ainsley leaned in and looked into the adjoining attic space, which had no floorboards and even less light.

"There's another opening on the far side," the woman said, pointing. "And then that attic is the one directly over the public house."

"And Thaddeus' office," Robert said from behind them.

Ainsley nodded as his heart quickened. Everything inside him told him to run for the nearest door and get the hell out of there. He tried to convince himself that Julia was able to get far away from Southwark and possibly to Simms for help. He had to fight his urge to flee because he knew he couldn't allow that pistol to remain in this man's possession. The only way forward was getting that weapon back.

"Are you all right to come with me?" Ainsley asked Robert, who had slumped onto the floor in pain. The man gave a quick nod and moved to get closer to the opening.

"You can't leave us," one of the women said, pulling on Ainsley's arm.

Ainsley grabbed her hand and held it as he looked her in the eye. "I have to get this man to a hospital. My friend with Scotland Yard will be here for you by nightfall," he said slowly. "Keep that door closed. Be very quiet and they will have no reason to come up here." He licked his lips. "I'm planning on having all attention on me anyway."

Chapter 26

Margaret sat in a chair in the nursery with Lucy cradled in her arms. Prudence, pulled from her work in the kitchens, played on the floor with George and Hubert on the other side of the room.

Despite the presence of a stand-in nanny, Margaret dismissed all of Prudence's reminders that she could see to Lucy. It calmed Margaret considerably to sit and hum. It provided enough of a change from her constant concern for her father.

"Did Violetta bring those nappies from the scullery I requested?" Margaret asked, mindful of her volume.

"No, my lady," Prudence said. "Should I go gather them for you?"

"It's all right," Margaret said, slipping from the chair slowly. "I'll go." She went to the perambulator near the door and gently laid Lucy inside. "Can you mind Lucy?"

"Of course."

Margaret made her way to the back stairs and went down to the kitchens where the scullery, pantry, and butler's office was located. Mrs. Aster, the cook, raised her head as soon as Margaret entered.

"Good morning, Lady Margaret," she said, somewhat surprised. She dropped the spoon in the bowl in front of her and wiped her hands on her apron. "Is there something I can help you with?"

"I asked Violetta to bring me some nappies for Lucy," Margaret said, absentmindedly glancing about the room.

"Did she then?" As Mrs. Aster crossed the room, she pointed a finger to the maid at the stove. "Don't forget the bread in the oven then," she said. The maid nodded, but said nothing as the cook left the room with Margaret.

They walked the length of the hall and ducked into the scullery. Mrs. Aster searched each cupboard in turn before spotting a pile of folded white fabric. "Here they are then," the cook said, happily. "Shall I bring them up for you?" She pulled the fabric out and placed them on a table near the door.

"No, I can manage. Thank you."

Mrs. Aster smiled and retreated to her kitchen. As Margaret bent forward to scoop up the nappies, her stomach lurched and she felt as if she were going to throw up. She closed her eyes and raised her hand to her mouth while she waited for the feeling to pass. Out of the corner of her eye she saw Violetta pass her in the hallway, heading from the front servant's door.

Peering around the doorframe, Margaret watched as Violetta slowly opened the servant's door. A dark figure stood on the other side but, from where Margaret stood, she could not see who it was.

She watched as Violetta pulled an envelope from her skirt pocket.

"Again in two days?" a familiar voice asked. The figure handed Violetta some folded bank notes, which the maid promptly slipped into her pocket.

"As always," Violetta said softly.

By the time the maid closed the door and turned back into the house, Margaret was standing in the middle of the hall. "Who was that?"

Violetta's eyes widened at the sight of her employer. "Lady Margaret. I didn't realize you were down here. I'll bring those nappies to you now." Her tone was far more amiable than in recent days.

"I asked who that was."

Violetta hesitated. She glanced to the door behind her while stammering. "I...don't..."

Margaret darted past her and snapped open the door just in time to see Theodore Fenton, reporter with the Daily Telegraph and Courier, step from the metal stair to the pavement in front of Marshall House.

"It was you all this time," Margaret said, closing the door and stepping back inside. "You've been selling family secrets to the society pages."

Violetta started to back away slowly. "Now my lady, I haven't the faintest idea what you are talking about."

"I just saw Theodore Fenton leaving," Margaret said, inching toward her. "I saw you give him something. What was it?"

Instinctively, Violetta's hand went to the folds of her skirt, where her pocket was stitched into the fabric. "Nothing."

Margaret charged for her just as Maxwell came down the stairs. Violetta let out a shriek when Margaret reached her. Grabbing Violetta's hands, and pulling them away from her pockets, Margaret grappled with the maid, which sent them to the floor. Margaret could feel Maxwell behind her, trying to pull them apart, but Margaret was too filled with anger to end it just then.

"Hand it over," she shouted as Violetta shrieked.

"Oh, get her off me, Maxwell. See her for the vicious vixen she is!" Violetta cried, trying to keep Margaret's hands away from her.

Soon Mrs. Aster and her assistant were in the hallway as well.

"Goodness, my lady."

Eventually, Margaret pressed the weight of her entire body into Violetta and was able to squeeze her hand into the maid's pocket. Violetta struck her hand as Margaret caught hold of the money, which sent the individual bills into the air and littering the ground around them as they fell.

"How dare you! My father trusted you," Margaret yelled. "I should have you horsewhipped."

She fought off Maxwell's hands while trying to subdue Violetta.

"Lady Margaret, please," Maxwell called.

It was only when Aunt Louisa and Nathaniel rushed down the stairs that Margaret stopped. She was straddling Violetta, who was lying on the floor and sobbing uncontrollably.

"I'm so sorry, my lady," Violetta said. "I only needed the money for my sister."

Margaret found herself unable to believe the pathetic reasoning. She loosened her grip on Violetta's wrists and looked down at her piteously. "You could have asked for the money," she said with disgust. "Does twenty-five years of service to my mother count for nothing?"

Margaret allowed Maxwell to help her stand.

"What is this then?" Aunt Louisa asked.

"I discovered Violetta selling father's secrets to Mr. Fenton, of the Telegraph and Courier."

Aunt Louisa's face soured.

Maxwell helped Violetta to stand.

Heaving heavily to catch her breath, Margaret spoke. "You will leave this house at once," she demanded, brushing away strands of hair that cascaded over her face.

"But Lady Margaret—"

"At once."

Violetta choked back tears as she turned from the gathering and headed for the servants' stairs, which would take her to her room, using the wall to hold herself upright.

Margaret turned to Maxwell. "See that this money is cleaned up," she said. "You may take it to her in a short time."

"Are you sure, Lady Margaret?" Maxwell asked.

Margaret surveyed the scene, each person looking at her in dismay. "Yes, she'll need it."

"As you wish."

Margaret walked for the scullery and quickly collapsed in the first chair she spotted. Aunt Louisa and Nathaniel promptly came to her.

"Are you all right?" Aunt Louisa asked.

For some reason, Margaret couldn't catch her breath. "Yes. I don't know what came over me," she said, closing her eyes. "I was just so angry."

"Your reaction is understandable," Nathaniel said, glancing to the door.

"How could I have been so blind?" Margaret asked. "She was doing this right under our noses."

"Do not blame yourself, my dear," Aunt Louisa said, reaching over and taking Margaret's shaking hands in hers. "I will say this, however—you certainly remind me of your mother."

Half an hour later, Margaret entered Great Scotland Yard on a quest to find Peter. He had a right to know what had happened and what she had done, even if he wasn't able to affect a better outcome. Besides, getting out of the house seemed a likely solution to calm her nerves.

At the front desk sat a constable she remembered from before. "Cooper, is it?" she asked as she approached.

The young man smiled with surprise when he saw her and then took on a more professional expression. "Yes, ma'am, may I help you?"

"I'm seeking Inspector Simms. He's working with my brother, Dr. Ainsley, but I don't recall where they were to meet."

"Inspector Simms is in his office, ma'am," Cooper said, with slight hesitation. "Dr. Ainsley has not been in today."

"What do you mean? Sergeant Fisher came to the house to collect him and one of our maids, Julia. He said Simms wished to discuss the case." Margaret leaned into the desk. "Are you sure he didn't leave at some point."

Just then, Simms approached the desk, an open folder held in front of him. He looked up in surprise when he saw Margaret. "Lady Marshall, what are you doing here?"

"This young woman says you sent Sergeant Fisher to bring Dr. Ainsley in and a young woman—"

"Julia," Margaret interjected.

Simms shook his head. "Not at all. I haven't seen your brother all morning."

Margaret's expression fell.

"I know what's happened," Simms said suddenly. "Cooper, assemble all you can. We must get to Southwark, quickly."

Chapter 27

The attic was a maze of wood planks and beams with low trusses and scarcely any light. Robert trailed slowly behind Ainsley, who was acutely aware of each breath and tiny moan from Robert. Halfway to their target, Ainsley wondered if it would have been better to have left Robert with Nelly and the other women. He was in a tremendous amount of pain and the crouching and crawling through the attic void would only be doing further harm to Robert's already injured organs.

Finally, Ainsley stopped and turned to Julia's brother. "I can take you back," he said, pausing below a truss and holding onto the beam with one hand.

Robert shook his head and wiped some sweat from his brow. The attic was stifling hot, without any movement of air. Each breath was hard for Ainsley to pull and must have been excruciating for Robert in his present condition.

"Keep going," Robert gasped. "Don't pay any mind to me."

Five minutes later they were crouched at an opening in the floor, indicated by a thin line of light that bordered a rectangular piece of wood. A tin box, about the size of a loaf of bread, was sitting on the opposite side of the attic opening. Curious, Ainsley reached for it but froze when the beam of light turned dark. Squinting, Ainsley could see someone below them, walking around in Thaddeus's office.

Ainsley raised a finger to his lips and looked to Robert, who nodded in acknowledgement. The sweat dripped wildly from their faces as the heat threatened to cook them like a Christmas goose. Ainsley prayed Thaddeus would leave his office soon so that they could get some fresh air at last. His prayer was answered when moments later the light beam returned and the sound of determined footfalls made their way across the room below. They strained their ears and concentrated on the sound of Thaddeus's door closing, the latch of the knob tapping into place.

Gingerly, Ainsley pulled at the board and stole a peek into the room. Empty. Feet first, he lowered himself down and stood on the solid desk in the middle of the room. "Hand me that tin," he said to Robert before he was able to follow him. Robert passed it down, careful not to let the metal box drop, and then moved to slide through the gap himself.

Ainsley saw Robert wince as he stepped down from the desk and then the man doubled over with an arm pressing into his left side.

"Robert?" Ainsley crouched down on the desk before jumping to the floor.

Robert waved him away and a moment later he was standing upright again.

The lid of the tin box opened easily and inside Ainsley found a few pocket-size notebooks, with tiny, detailed writing inside.

"These are his books," Robert said, flipping through one. "He writes everything in here."

Ainsley had to fight the urge to read them then and there and instead slipped the books into his inside pocket. "Watch the door," he said, nudging his chin to Robert.

Robert went without argument and stood at the centre of the door with his ear to the wood. Hurriedly, Ainsley opened each of the desk drawers and even reached up under the bottoms. Nothing. He dropped to his hands and knees and looked beneath the shelves as well as under Thaddeus's chair and still he found nothing.

Ainsley balled his hand into a fist, supressing the urge to yell. He couldn't be so close and leave empty-handed. The man could singlehandedly destroy his life by revealing that gun to the authorities. More than enough witnesses had seen him use it. By itself the pistol was enough to bring an investigation to his door that even Simms could not ignore.

And then Ainsley saw it, an iron grate screwed into the floor just under a table behind Thaddeus's desk. When Ainsley moved closer he could see the screws were missing and that simply lifting the grate was enough to access the void. He wasn't able to look directly into the hold but he could reach his arm in up to his elbow and felt around.

"Yes!" His exuberant hiss was muted by the fact that his face was pressed into the hardwood floor.

Ainsley heard the door open.

Robert landed a quick jab to Thaddeus's face before pulling the man in and closing the door. Although caught off guard, Thaddeus fought back, landing a right hook into Robert's side.

"You fucking bastard."

Thaddeus growled as he tried to push Robert to the floor but Robert stood his ground and was able to shake Thaddeus off him with enough force to send him into a shelf along the wall. The shelf teetered but didn't fall. Thaddeus scowled and took a step toward Robert but Ainsley cocked the pistol and pressed it into Thaddeus's temple.

"I will not hesitate," he said.

Thaddeus put up his hands slowly. "I don't doubt it."

"Where is she?" Ainsley asked, moving to face Thaddeus, who only shook his head. The expression on his face betrayed his confusion.

"Who?"

"Julia!" Ainsley stepped forward, pressing the gun into the front of Thaddeus's cheek.

"I have no idea what you are talking about."

Ainsley kicked up his elbow and landed a hit to Thaddeus's jaw.

Thaddeus faltered and stumbled. "I told you, I haven't seen my wife in a year!" He raised a hand to his lip and patted at the blood.

"You sent a carriage for us this morning," Ainsley yelled, stepping closer and pressing the barrel of the gun into Thaddeus's cheek. "Sergeant Fisher, he works for you."

"Yes, but"—Thaddeus let out a breath, looked to Robert and then back to Ainsley—"I never sent him for you. I told you I haven't see Julia in months. She left me. I don't chase after women."

Ainsley gave a sideways look to Robert, who looked equally confused. "You picked me up and forced me to fight in your ring," Robert said. "That wasn't to force Julia to come find me?"

"You owed me," Thaddeus said, his mouth folding into

a sneer. "And I needed someone I haven't used in a while."

Ainsley's heart raced as he stood there, keeping Thaddeus in the corner. All this time he had thought Thaddeus was trying to pull Julia out of the shadows. He figured it was some sick plan for revenge.

"Who killed that man in Belgravia?" Ainsley pressed.

"Jeremiah," Robert offered. "My friend. You sent your boys to my house. You scared my wife. They told me you called in my debt. Why?"

"Look it wasn't me, all right? Perhaps you don't understand, I don't give a fuck for that woman. She killed my brother and I don't blame her for that, but I certainly ain't going to share my bed with her anymore. When she walked out that door I knew she was as good as dead. It's a miracle no one else killed her just to get to me." Thaddeus pushed the barrel of the gun away. "Are we done here?"

Ainsley pulled the trigger. A bullet ripped into the wall over Thaddeus's shoulder as Ainsley pushed him back. "I told you I'm not bluffing." He glanced to Robert, who despite much cooler temperatures compared to the attic, was still dripping sweat from his brow and hairline. Ainsley needed to get him to the hospital or he would surely die.

"Let's go." Ainsley gestured for the door, and pulled Thaddeus away from the wall by the collar. With the pistol pressed firmly in between Thaddeus's shoulder blades, Ainsley guided him out into the empty hall and led him toward the stairs.

They reached the bottom of the stairs and made their way across the courtyard to the main gate. A quick scan of the place revealed only a handful of people, all easily subdued once Thaddeus instructed them to lower their weapons. He said nothing, only signalled with his hands, and they all obeyed.

"I told you I don't know anything," Thaddeus said, allowing them to guide him to the main door at the side of the gate. There's no need for the gun. I'm not going to hurt you."

Ainsley could hear him smiling through his words. "Like the last time you said I could go?"

"That was just so you knew who was boss." Thaddeus pivoted, grabbed Ainsley's wrist, and pushed his arm to the ground. Ainsley used his free hand to hit Thaddeus in the face and then pushed up his chin before taking hold of his throat.

Without letting go of Ainsley's arm, Thaddeus used his body to block Ainsley's hits. The struggle brought them to the ground, and sent the firearm sliding across the cobbles.

Only able to pull one arm from his body, Robert tried to pull Thaddeus away, but was clocked in the face and sent backward into the brick wall. The pair were a mess of elbows and fists, each man fighting for control, sending dust into the air about them. Ainsley tried to crawl for the gun and felt the desperate hands of Thaddeus pulling at his body, pinching his arms in a vise-like grip and hitting his kidneys wildly.

Ainsley could feel the metal of the gun just inches from his grasp but the gun kept sliding from his fingers. He used his legs, kneeing Thaddeus in the stomach and then groin, while growling his frustration.

Men with guns drawn began to stream out from various doors heading into the courtyard.

Click.

Ainsley brought the butt down into Thaddeus's face and scrambled to his feet.

Below him, Thaddeus writhed in pain. Blood gathered above his eye, where Ainsley had hit him. Thaddeus's men, Fisher and Delaney included, glanced to each other, unsure how to handle the threat.

"To your knees," Ainsley yelled, glancing up at the gathered crowd. "I said, to your knees!" He pressed the barrel into Thaddeus's temple just beside his gash.

Thaddeus laughed as he pushed himself to his knees. Allowing the gun to slide over his blood-streaked faced, Thaddeus turned to reveal a wide smile. "Do it, Doctor." He erupted in laughter and inched closer to Ainsley, pressing his forehead into the gun. "I said, do it!"

"Peter, we should go," Robert said. "We need to get help."

Ainsley pulled at Thaddeus's collar, dragging him to his feet. "Let us leave," Ainsley said, addressing the crowd, "And I won't have to kill him."

The men with guns, four by Ainsley's count, resighted

him but remained where they were.

Robert skirted ahead, still clutching his lower ribs, and unlatched the main door.

"Walk." With his back to the door, Ainsley guided Thaddeus backward, away from the group and toward the alley that would allow them to go free.

Before they could walk through the door, Julia appeared. With her hands up in front of her, her eyes darted to the side. Delilah appeared behind her through the doorway.

"Julia?" Ainsley's heart skipped at the sight of her.

Delilah made Julia walk ahead and then gave a half turn to close the door, her movement revealing a small, derringer pistol pressed into the small of Julia's back.

The maid had her hands raised in front of her, her palms open, but her expression remained solid until her eyes met Ainsley's and then they only faltered for a second.

Delilah guided her, with a hand clutching a clump of hair at the base of Julia's skull and the gun pressed into her side. Using Julia as a shield, Delilah inched forward. "Look who I found lurking out front."

"I'm sorry, Peter."

"Delilah, go home." Thaddeus shook his head, no doubt ashamed at the way her hand shook and her voice trembled when she spoke.

"I can do this," she answered defiantly, stepping closer, pushing Julia ahead.

"One more step and your brother doesn't make it," Ainsley warned.

"And I'll shoot Little Miss here before my brother hits the ground." She reached up with her free hand and tightened a fist around Julia's hair.

Julia let out a tiny yelp and jerked her head back slightly.

Mrs. Calvin appeared at one of the doors to the courtyard. "Thaddeus?" She inched closer to the scene and glanced to the men, who still had their weapons pointed to Ainsley. "What's going on?"

"This doesn't concern you, Mother," Thaddeus said, through gritted teeth.

"Delilah, what are you doing?"

Delilah raised her chin at the sight of her mother. "I can do it," she proclaimed yet again.

"Tell her to stop, Mother," Thaddeus said. "Tell her to lower her weapon and make a trade."

Ainsley licked his dry lips as Mrs. Calvin inched toward Delilah with her hand outstretched. "Listen to your family, sweetie," she said. "Do the right thing. For all of us."

On the other side of Thaddeus, Robert looked up to Ainsley. All colour had vanished from his face and Ainsley could tell it was a struggle for him to remain upright. "Promise me you'll take care of my girls," he said in a whisper.

It was clear they were not all getting out of there alive. Thaddeus was only bidding his time.

"Don't do anything stupid, Robert," Ainsley said softly. He could see Robert steeling himself against what he believed he needed to do.

"I'm not going to make it," Robert said, the muscle in his cheek twitching.

"I can still get you to a hospital. Guy's is just around the corner."

"Delilah, put the gun down," Thaddeus warned. "Delilah!"

The young woman trembled, as her heart quickened beneath her tight bodice. "We have to do this, Thad." Her eyes darted to their mother and then back again. She recommitted herself by raising her gun so that now it pressed into the flesh of Julia's temple. "Let my brother go!" she demanded.

Betting on Delilah's lack of fortitude, Ainsley shook his head.

Delilah's naive features betrayed her shock for a few seconds before she corrected herself. "You haven't a clue how long we have wanted Julia dead," she said with a scowl. "Don't give me another reason to pull this trigger."

"Take Robert and go," Julia said. "He needs a doctor." A tear trailed down her cheek as she closed her eyes for a second as if to will any others away.

"I'm not leaving without you." Ainsley moved his gaze between Thaddeus, Delilah, and Robert. He knew Delilah was nervous. He could see as much by the way her skirt shifted. He imagined she was shifting her weight from one side to the next. Earlier, she tried to convince her brother that she was capable. She was clearly comfortable holding her tiny gun, had probably done so many times, but he doubted she had ever pulled the trigger.

In that instant, Ainsley's gaze met Robert's and he realized what Julia's brother intended to do.

"Remember what I said."

He charged for Delilah, cutting through the space between them and tackling her to the ground. With Delilah's fist still clutching her hair Julia was pulled to the ground in the tussle as Mrs. Calvin sprung to help her daughter. A cloud of dust erupted around them as they rolled about.

Thaddeus rounded on Ainsley and tried to wrestle the gun from his grasp. Face to face they struggled, each growling and grunting with the gun raised in the air. With his free arm, Ainsley threw his elbow and landed a hit to Thaddeus's face. He kicked Thaddeus's feet out from under him and then threw his body weight onto him. He pressed Thaddeus's face into the cobblestones and thrust his gun into his back.

A high-pitched shriek came from Delilah.

BANG.

At the same time, Ainsley could hear the sounds of horses' hooves on the other side of the gate, as if a thousand or so had converged on the small side street. A second later the gate was forced open and a dozen constables stormed through, readying their billy clubs as they spread out into the yard. Thaddeus's men ran in countless directions, barring doors behind them as they scattered.

Simms appeared at Ainsley's side. "I hope you weren't intending to use that."

Ainsley didn't answer him. His focus had turned to Robert and Julia, both lying on the cobbles, a pool of blood spreading out between them.

"Julia?" Ainsley stumbled as he tried to run to her, and ended up crawling the rest of the way. "Julia!"

Ainsley pulled her into his arms, ignoring the blood that caked into the fabric of her dress. The bullet had hit her shoulder, dangerously close to her heart.

"Bring a carriage!" Simms yelled. "A carriage, you fool!"

Robert moaned as he rolled, revealing a grisly wound to his stomach. Delilah sat in shock for a few seconds as she pulled herself away, snatching the gun from the blood on the cobbles.

"You killed her," Robert said, inching toward the woman who was desperate to get away. "You were supposed to kill me, not her!"

Mrs. Calvin reached out for her daughter.

"Stay away from me," Delilah commanded, struggling to keep the gun from slipping in her hands.

Robert continued forward.

"I said stay away from me!" She pulled the trigger once as Robert caught up to her and missed. He wrapped her hands around her throat but Delilah shot again, this time getting him in the chest.

"Arrest her," Simms said. "Peter?"

But Ainsley was already on his feet, Julia cradled in his arms. He passed all the police carriages and ran as fast as he could muster for Guy's. Her pulse was weak and he couldn't know how much blood she had lost on the ground of the courtyard.

"Fight for me, Julia. Fight for me," he begged through gritted teeth.

By the time he reached the front doors of the hospital the words had morphed into a marching song that he repeated again and again even as the attending surgeon rushed him to the nearest surgical bed. "Save her, damn you, save her," he said as he backed away.

"Dr. Ainsley, you must let the surgeon do his work," the nurse said as she guided Ainsley away from the surgical table.

Ainsley looked to her, startled that she had called him by name. No one forced him to leave the room and instead he stood back and watched as the nursing staff rallied and the surgeon barked out his orders.

"Is she going to be all right?" Ainsley heard himself saying.

No one answered him.

Chapter 28

Two hours later Ainsley pulled his head away from his hands and realized he was sitting in the hall at Guy's Hospital. He thought he was all alone until he glanced down the corridor and saw Simms and Margaret talking. They were too far away for Ainsley to hear what they were saying but Margaret looked unwell, as if she had been sobbing for some time.

She turned her head toward Ainsley and then lowered her gaze. A few seconds later she walked toward him slowly, as if approaching an injured animal that could startle at any given moment. Brushing the tears from his cheeks, Ainsley stood and wiped his wet hands on his trousers.

"What's happened?" he asked, choking back the urge to pepper her with questions.

It took her a long time to raise her gaze to him and even then she bit her lower lip hard. "Robert succumbed to his injuries," she started.

Ainsley could see how much it was a struggle for her to speak. Tears graced the lids of her eyes and already her nose was turning pale pink.

"And Julia? She's in recovery, yes?"

Margaret let out a deep breath and closed her eyes. "Peter—"

His legs rocked slightly and he reached out to the wall to steady himself. "Don't say it," he begged, tears coming freely. "I couldn't bear it. Please, Margaret...say I'm only dreaming."

She reached out to him, but he turned from her in an effort to hide his tears.

"She lost too much blood," she continued, even as Ainsley leaned further into the wall. Amidst his internal wailing, his throat closed and he found himself gasping for air. He felt himself collapsing, as if his entire world had shifted and he could not fight the force of it. The wall was the only thing keeping him upright.

Oh, how he loved her. The curls that framed her face. The tiny laugh she offered him when he kissed her neck. The stern look she gave him when he had said something insensitive. Since the day he had met her she had been the driving force in his life, the strength by which he bettered himself. She was, without a doubt, *his* Julia and always would be.

"Peter?" Margaret touched his arm but he shook her off. His hands were already curled at his side. He did not give her another chance to call out to him. He was charging down the hall, out the door and into the sunny street before his first tear even hit the floor.

The murmur at 4 Whitehall Place died instantly when Ainsley entered the front door. He ignored the piteous stares and sideways glances, and instead made his way down the hall. Two uniformed officers stood outside one closed door and he knew that was where they were.

Inspector Simms, who had struggled to keep pace with him all the way from the hospital, jogged up beside him.

"You found the women in the attic?" Ainsley asked, without turning to look at him.

"Yes. They are all safe now. But, Peter, you need to stop." Simms tugged at his arm. "Peter, don't."

Ainsley jerked his arm away and pushed past the officers who were caught off guard by Ainsley's bold behaviour.

Inside, Delilah sat at the desk, sobbing into a lace handkerchief while her mother leaned into the desk talking to her. Startled, they pulled away from each other and Mrs. Calvin stood. Thaddeus, holding a cloth to the wound on his forehead, was the only one who looked wholly unconcerned by Ainsley's sudden appearance. He even smiled when he saw Ainsley step toward his mother.

"You can't come in here," she said, placing herself between her daughter and Ainsley. "Haven't you already done enough?"

"My anguish ends when Delilah and Thaddeus hang from the gallows."

Delilah's eyes widened when Ainsley pointed at her.

"Hanged?" She looked genuinely shocked at the

prospect.

"You killed her!" Ainsley growled and fought each effort Simms made to remove him from the room. "You killed her and I will not rest until she sees justice."

Thaddeus uncrossed his legs and sat up. "Julia is dead?"

"She killed my son," Mrs. Calvin said uncaringly. "Edgar was my miracle child. As far as I am concerned, my daughter was only doing right by us all by taking care of that murderess."

A quick glance to Delilah revealed far less confidence in her actions.

"Don't let them hang me, Mama," she said, tugging on her mother's sleeve as if she were eight years old once more.

Simms pulled at Ainsley, coaxing him away, but Ainsley stood steadfast. His eyes were locked on Mrs. Calvin, who stood defiant and proud. What had she said to Delilah?

Listen to your family, sweetie.

Do the right thing. For all of us.

That woman had stood in his very morgue, supposedly weeping over the loss of her daughter, a domestic servant serving a house in the city's west end.

"It was you," Ainsley said.

Mrs. Calvin turned her head slightly, but never broke the stare.

An overwhelming feeling of disgust rolled over him. He finally saw her for what she really was: manipulative and conniving. "You told Delilah to kill her. You gave her the derringer."

"Mama?"

"Quiet." Her voice was sharp. "My daughter is in deep mourning for her brother, Edgar. It is perfectly understandable upon seeing her brother's murderer she would seek vengeance." She averted her gaze then, turning to her meek daughter seated next to her. She cradled Delilah's chin between her thumb and her forefinger and smiled. "I commend her for her bravery."

An awkward smile, half pleasure, half pain, touched Delilah's face as confusion set in.

"Your baby that almost died. That wasn't Thaddeus. That was Edgar. You made him into the monster who killed his own child and wife." The pieces slid together in Ainsley's mind, formulating a clear picture of the Calvins' distorted world and cruel outlook. "You put her up to this!" Ainsley said, pulling Mrs. Calvin's hand away from Delilah. "Horses and tethers, Thaddeus, is that how your mother raised you? Horses and tethers?"

Simms began pulling Ainsley out the door. "All right, that's enough, Peter."

Soon another constable joined him and Ainsley found himself no match between the two of them. He pawed at arms that hooked around him and fought them until they stood in the hall, on the other side of the office door.

"She did it, Simms. She put that poor girl up to it and now she will hang in her mother's stead." Ainsley ran a hand through his hair as he paced the hall. He could see Delilah, Mrs. Calvin, and Thaddeus through the glass door, which only angered him more.

"It's done," Simms said with resignation.

"You can't let her get away with it."

Simms shook his head, a pained look on his face. "There's nothing I can do. I have twenty witnesses that saw Delilah pull the trigger."

"And Thaddeus?"

The detective hesitated.

"The women in the attic?"

"Who were all abducted by his men. Most of them had never even seen Thaddeus at the warehouse."

"The women in the Thames?"

"Again, probably someone in his employ."

"You have to try."

"I will try. The investigation is ongoing. I haven't interviewed everyone yet. But it's just as I've said before, it's like he doesn't exist." Simms clasped a hand on Ainsley's shoulder and looked him in the eye. "Go home and rest, Peter. It's been one hell of a day." Simms began walking down the hall. Three steps away he turned back when he realized Ainsley was locked in place.

"Home?" Ainsley's voice shook as he spoke. "My home is nothing but ashes."

When Ainsley walked by Margaret's room he could hear her crying. He peeked inside and saw her seated at her toilette table, staring absently at her own reflection. How cruel fate had been to both of them. Ainsley struggled to find words of consolation but nothing seemed appropriate. In shock himself, he stood there for many minutes before the murmured cries of Lucy pulled his attention away. Only then did Margaret's eyes focus and finally see him at the door.

"Peter?"

But he had turned away, continued down the hall to the nursery. Prudence sat on the floor, slumped toward the side of the bed, her head slouched into the soft covers that draped over the edge. A tiny snore left her as Lucy played contently nearby.

Ainsley tiptoed past and reached down to scoop her from the floor.

"Oh goodness, my apologies, Mr. Marshall." The maid rubbed her weary eyes and moved to stand.

"It's all right," he said, holding Lucy on his hip. "She's probably been running you off your feet." He smiled and bounced the baby up and down.

"Yes sir," the young girl answered.

"She can come sit with me for a while. You rest." He didn't give the maid any chance to protest and simply left the room with Lucy gurgling at his side. Nothing in particular propelled him to his father's room. He passed the door and at the last second decided to go in.

Aunt Louisa wept at the mantel, rubbing the bottom of her nose with her purple handkerchief. She stopped suddenly when Ainsley entered. "Oh Peter, it's just awful."

Someone had put Lord Marshall in a deep, cushioned chair near the window. Lucy pointed to him as they crossed the room and then clapped her hands joyfully.

"I think she likes you," Ainsley said, avoiding Aunt Louisa's pleading gaze.

Pulling a chair from the bedside, Ainsley sat opposite his father. He placed the baby at the very edge of his knee and instantly she pulled against his grip wanting to get closer to Lord Marshall.

The patriarch sat unsure for many seconds before raising his good arm and beckoning Ainsley to bring her closer. Lucy sat upright on Lord Marshall's lap, cradled somewhat on his paralyzed side, and took hold of the finger on his good arm. She giggled as she forced his hand up and down. A smile touched Lord Marshall's lips.

"Poor sprite," Aunt Louisa sniffed. "She has no one in the world now."

Lord Marshall's eyes welled up slightly, causing him to turn his head away.

"I know it's extraordinary," Ainsley said, licking his lips and willing a fresh wave of tears away, "but I've decided to take Lucy in as my own." Ainsley focused on the movements of the little girl, somewhat scared of his father's reaction to such news. "It's the least I can do for Julia." He sniffled. "I haven't told Margaret yet."

The decision was not a hard one to make. Both her parents had been murdered and her aunt had been very dear to him.

"Oh my," Aunt Louisa said. She came up alongside Lord Marshall's chair.

"I don't know anything about babies or raising children..." Ainsley chuckled at the idea of him adopting a daughter. His expression sobered when he saw the terrified look on his father's face. "You won't be able to talk me out of it," Ainsley said, running his hand through his hair. "I'll purchase a place of my own if it isn't agreeable to you, but you won't be able to stop me."

Slowly, Lord Marshall formed his lips, parting them and closing them as if struggling to say something. Ainsley waited, suspecting his father wanted to end the notion. Had he been capable, Ainsley had no doubt they'd already be locked in a heated exchange, typical of their contentious relationship. For the first time, Ainsley was thankful his father was incapable of communicating. Defying him was so much easier when Ainsley couldn't hear the disappointment in his voice.

"S—st—st—st—" Lord Marshall gave up, balling his hand in a fist in frustration.

Ainsley met his father's gaze. "Stay?"

Lord Marshall nodded in that jerky, single nod they

had come to recognize.

"You want Lucy and I to stay?"

Aunt Louisa clapped her hands together. She grabbed hold of Ainsley and shook him a little. "Did you hear that?" she exclaimed.

Ainsley sat stunned as his aunt jostled about in excitement. Lucy was more than happy to join the revelry as Aunt Louisa snatched her up gleefully. The seconds of joy ended quickly when Daniel entered the room. He carried the stench of wine and brandy upon his breath and clothes.

"What's this?" he asked, stopping at the door.

Ainsley noticed his aunt retreat quickly, giving a forced smile in Daniel's direction, but not looking at him squarely. "Are you dining with us again tonight?" Ainsley asked innocently.

Daniel did not reply immediately, only shrugged as if he preferred to skirt the subject. "Why should I not? Am I not welcome in my own home?"

The tension between brothers was palpable and Ainsley would rather have had the conversation away from their ailing father. Ainsley gestured for the hall, inviting Daniel to come join him before sliding past. Several paces from the door Ainsley turned to face him.

"Perhaps you have not heard—"

"Oh, I've heard," Daniel said with a sneer. "Nathaniel had the wherewithal to bring the news to me."

Behind him, Nathaniel came up the last step and stopped with his hand on the newel post, the look on his face giving away his utter disdain.

As if bolstered by his accomplice, Daniel took a step closer to Ainsley. "I've heard all the rumours about you and that servant girl, Margaret's lady's maid. It's disgusting."

Ainsley winced at his brother's choice of words. "You only find it disgusting because you had wanted her first." There was no need to mince words. Daniel seemed to be spoiling for a fight and Ainsley was in no mood to step down on the matter.

Behind Daniel, Ainsley saw Margaret at the doorframe of her room looking on.

"Am I not permitted to look?" Daniel asked indignantly.

"You are a married man."

Daniel laughed. "Since when have you been the moral compass for this family?"

There was so much Ainsley wished to say and bit his tongue against. He could see Margaret, with her tearstained eyes and red nose, and knew she expected him to rise above Daniel's drunkenness.

"You need rest," Ainsley said. He reached out a relaxed hand and clasped his brother on the upper arm. He made a point to look Daniel squarely in the eye. Daniel appeared ready to concede when Aunt Louisa came out of Lord Marshall's room. Lucy was quiet and observant in her arms.

"What's this?" Daniel staggered back toward them. Apparently he hadn't noticed the baby when he first came into the room. "The guttersnipe from Bethnal Green."

"Daniel." Margaret's voice gave a resigned sigh.

"What? What did I say?" He rounded quickly and almost lost his balance.

Ainsley fought back his anger at hearing Julia's niece referred to as a guttersnipe.

"She should be taken to the foundling home at first light."

Instinctively, Aunt Louisa raised a hand protectively over Lucy's head and turned her from the scene.

"Oh no..." A look of confusion washed over Daniel's face as he watched Aunt Louisa carry Lucy down the hall to her room. "Have we a little pet? Another plaything for Margaret?"

"Daniel, stop." Margaret walked toward him but stopped suddenly when he turned to her. Ainsley tried to signal for her to go back to her room but she did not look at him.

Turning to Ainsley, Daniel straightened his stance as best he could in his current condition. "Get rid of her."

"No."

Daniel took one step closer to Ainsley and pointed a finger at the carpet between them. "As leader of this family—"

"You're not the leader of this family! Father still lives." Ainsley could not soften the clenching of his jaw, nor the rapid beating of his heart. Their patriarch was in the next room, his ability to hear just as sharp as ever, and Ainsley had no doubt he was listening as they argued. It seemed deplorable that Daniel should behave so, to treat their father as more an object and less of a man now that he was injured.

Ainsley stepped up and placed himself in front of his brother. He lowered his voice so their father could not hear. "You will have your wealth and title soon enough, but until then you command no one in this house."

Years of rivalry haunted them even with their feet firmly planted in adulthood. How he wished his brother weren't so competitive. It was this part of Daniel's nature that pitted brother against brother. It planted a wedge between them from the very beginning and it was a rivalry Daniel seemed loathed to be rid of. Ainsley had accepted his place as second son years before, and enjoyed the freedom it afforded him. Daniel, however, never missed the opportunity to lord over his two younger siblings.

Daniel snorted, licked his lips, and bent to Ainsley's ear. "It still kills you that I am the eldest son."

Ainsley closed his eyes and pressed his lips together hard. "But you are not *his* son."

Margaret gasped and Daniel's face hardened. Behind them Nathaniel looked confused.

"What did you say?"

"Mother had a lover, remember?" Ainsley continued to speak even as the confusion and fear flashed over his brother's face. "Father agreed to marry Mother even though his true firstborn would never be heir. Your father is a surgeon...like me."

"Peter, that's enough." Margaret pulled at Ainsley's sleeve. "He's drunk."

Daniel turned to Margaret. "You knew about this?"

"We never wanted you to know."

Ainsley readied himself, as did Margaret, for the storm that was sure to come. Daniel had been raised believing he was Lord Marshall's son and heir, and adopted his role early on. He learned to mimic their father's demeanor, voice, and stance, even his quick temper and penchant for drink.

Daniel and Ainsley stood, eyes locked, for some time. At first, Daniel's expression was hardened and rueful. Ainsley was sure that at any moment he would fly into a rage, smash the closest object, and deny the accusation emphatically.

Surprisingly, he did not.

Suddenly sober, his chest heaved, but he said nothing at first as his mind turned over what Ainsley had said. As the moments passed the muscles in his face relaxed and his gaze drifted away from Ainsley.

"What do you want? The title? A larger portion of the trust? What?" With each question, Daniel grew impatient for an answer.

For the first time in a long time, Ainsley felt sorry for him. Daniel's greatest fear was losing what mattered most to him—the life he had been preparing for and felt assured of receiving. Ainsley, however, never begrudged him his inheritance because he had other desires.

"I don't want anything from you," Ainsley answered forcefully. "You can have *all* the money, the house, and your damn titles. I just want my family!" His eyes began to sting as he spoke, mourning the loss of the woman who he wanted to give him such a gift.

Margaret began openly weeping and circled her arms around him. Ainsley wrapped one arm around her and tilted his head toward her embrace. At the same time he held out his right hand to his brother. "You are my only brother," he said. "I wish for nothing but your blessing."

Daniel eyed Ainsley's outstretched hand cautiously before taking hold of it and nodding a silent consent.

Chapter 29

The following day at midday, when he could cry no more, Ainsley placed a decanter of brandy in the middle of his desk and then spent the next hour sitting in his chair staring at it. It had been a long while since he sought the comfort of drink. For a time he had believed he could live a life without it. But by suppertime he was drunk and remained so for several days.

He made sure he was sober the day of Delilah's trial, however. Summoned as a witness, Ainsley went as Mr. Peter Marshall, son of the Earl of Montcliff, speaking on behalf of his father, who had hired the lady's maid, and himself, who had befriended her. As he sat in the witness box, giving testimony, he kept his gaze locked on Delilah, who wept. She was sure to hang.

Behind her in the gallery sat Mrs. Calvin and Thaddeus, both stoic and unaffected, even as the judge placed the black cloth over his wig and delivered his judgement. The terrified shrieks from Delilah were not enough to move her mother to tears.

Simms was waiting for Ainsley outside the Old Bailey, staying clear of the mass exodus of people, who had come for the entertainment only a murder trial could provide.

"It is done then?" Simms asked, tucking his notebook into an inside pocket.

"Not to my liking," Ainsley answered. He scanned the crowd that milled about and spotted Thaddeus helping his mother into the carriage at the kerb. "He should have to die in the same manner in which he killed those women."

"If only it were that simple," Simms said. "An hour after you left the station a man arrived claiming he had done the entire thing himself, with Sergeant Fisher's help. The shoeprint Margaret found matches Sergeant Fisher's. He confessed that Thaddeus knew nothing of his little side business."

"But the women in the attic?"

"I showed them all pictures. None of them recognized Thaddeus. They knew of him and there were rumours of what he was doing but none were witnesses to it. He has that entire street locked in by his charm."

"You mean his money."

Simms shrugged. "That too."

"And Cooper? Is he torn up about Delilah?"

"He swears he knew nothing. Says she asked him a lot of questions about his work but he assures me he said nothing. Thaddeus may have been preparing to pay him off too." Simms slipped his hands into his trouser pockets and looked to the skyline, where the dome of St. Paul's peeked out over the courthouse. "Cooper's been transferred out of the city, where I have people keeping an eye on him just to be sure. He may be back one day."

Ainsley nodded.

"There's something else, Peter." Simms stopped short and scratched his temple with his thumbnail.

"What is it?" He could tell there was something more, something serious the detective wished to say. Ainsley followed his gaze and saw that Thaddeus had never entered his carriage. Instead, he stood there on the pavement, watching them without any care if they saw.

Simms squinted against the sun and turned to walk away. "Follow me."

They walked two blocks before turning a corner and heading down a narrow side street. Trolleys of coal, buckets of ash, and piles of misshapen iron littered the cobbles outside a large arched door. The heat of the place radiated out to the inspector and doctor as they slowed their pace. With sweat forming on his temples, Simms turned and pulled his hand from his pocket.

Ainsley's heart skipped at the sight of the G. & J. Deane pistol.

"I picked this up at the warehouse," Simms said. He held it flat in his palm and offered it to Ainsley. "Thought you'd like to have it back."

For a moment Ainsley just looked at it, afraid of what would happen if he held it once again. The pistol had shattered his life twice. Having it so close again quickened his heart rate and made him queasy.

Slowly, Ainsley reached out his hand for it and then realized what Simms had intended him to do.

With the pistol in his hands, Ainsley nodded to the workman, who tipped his cap at Simms and then stepped aside from his hot, roaring furnace. Simms stood back as Ainsley stepped forward, still staring at the weapon in his hands. The first time he had held it, the etched pictures on the side of the metal looked benign and almost whimsical, but now, in the shadowy, orange light, they looked maniacal and sinister. The steel, brass, and wood in his hand had been responsible for wounding one person and killing another. And its very existence continued to plague him.

With a hard swallow, Ainsley tossed it into the furnace's open gate and watched the yellow and orange flames consumed it whole.

With that, the gun was gone.

A few weeks later, Margaret insisted they retreat to The Briar. "Now that the improvements are finished," she said, "a gathering of friends will be just the thing to make it a lovely home for Aunt Louisa and her boys. I don't intend for it to be extravagant, but I've invited a few friends for a small dinner party."

Ainsley wasn't pleased at the idea but did not fight it. His only stipulation was that Lucy must go with them as well.

"Of course," Margaret said with a soft smile.

The improvements made to the Marshalls' country home had exceeded expectations. The new roof, wallpapers, and plaster had transformed a very weary country home into its full splendor once again. The transition had done a great deal to erase the tragedies of the past and remake the Marshall's house anew.

At first, Ainsley hid in his room. The only obligation that succeeded in pulling him from his sorrow was Lucy, who gave him much joy and satisfaction to the daily sadness he faced.

One week after their arrival, Margaret stopped suddenly at his door. "The dinner gong has sounded."

Ainsley and Lucy were sprawled out on the floor with a set of wooden blocks to entertain them.

"You haven't dressed," Margaret said from the door. She glanced to the suit Cutter had freshly pressed and laid out for him. "Our friends have started arriving."

"I apologize, but your *soiree* is of no interest to me. That is a very fetching gown, however. Did you invite Blair?"

"Oh my goodness, Peter, what a way to divert the conversation."

A chambermaid arrived at the door behind her. Margaret pointed her to Lucy and the maid immediately went to her and scooped her up.

"Don't—"

"Lucy has to make an appearance too and she needs to get dressed." Margaret tilted her head to the side. "Please, just come for half an hour. If you don't like the conversation or the guests you can just leave."

"Goodness." Ainsley pulled himself up from the floor.

"Oh, just do it. I don't want to hear another word about it."

As he dressed, Ainsley became suspicious of his sister's insistence. When he spied Winifred Talbot in the foyer as he came down the stairs he suspected the entire dinner was a plot to get them reacquainted. The thought alone was enough to want to make Ainsley turn on his heels and head back upstairs. Only a month had passed since Julia's death and his ability to function as he had before still eluded him.

"Hello, Peter," Winifred said as he neared the bottom of the stairs. "Margaret said you would be here."

"I'm not sure what Margaret told you to expect but I'm—"

"Still in mourning? I know." Winifred smiled at her own cleverness. "She was just a maid, though, yes?"

It pained him to think Julia could be seen so plainly. She was more than just a maid, at least to him. He decided to change the subject. "I'd like to apologize for my behaviour last year," he began, keeping his voice low. "It was never my intention to hurt you."

Her features hardened somewhat and she looked away to show her disinterest.

Ainsley scanned the room and saw Nathaniel step out of the library and adjust his tie. "Will you allow me to introduce you to someone?" he asked.

Ainsley led her to Nathaniel. "Winifred Talbot, this is my cousin, Nathaniel Banks."

Within minutes, Ainsley was allowed to leave them to their own conversation and he started toward the dining room. Aunt Louisa was standing next to the door when he walked in.

"Oh, there you are," she said, placing a gloved hand on the small of his back.

"So many people," he said, adjusting his collar. "I'm not sure I am ready for such a gathering."

"Well, yes, but...there is one guest in particular who is very eager to meet you." Aunt Louisa smiled wryly and raised her eyebrows as she gestured to one side.

There, standing next to Margaret, dressed in an elaborate frock of silk and lace, stood a woman who looked like Julia. Ainsley closed his eyes and turned away, convinced he was only seeing things. Her ghost had yet to haunt him as he wished she would. Aunt Louisa guided him closer and he was forced to greet the spectre.

"Allow me to introduce Miss Cassandra Dare." Aunt Louisa and Margaret smiled expectantly, but Ainsley had resolved to simply be polite and nothing more.

"Good evening, Mr. Marshall."

Ainsley's eyes focused at the sound of her voice.

"Miss Dare has been away from England, exploring the continent for some time before, unfortunately, her family drowned during a ferry mishap in Russia about a month ago," Aunt Louisa explained slowly. "She will be staying with me...for the time being until her inheritance is settled."

The confusion was overwhelming. Everything about this woman mirrored Julia in every way, her hair, her eyes, the angle of her jaw, and yet here she was presented to him as an heiress.

"Aren't you going to say hello, Peter?" Margaret asked.

Ainsley stammered. "Forgive me," he said. "What did you say your name was?"

"Cassandra Dare," she said, trying hard to hide her smile.

Ainsley took his sister's hand with a noticeable tremble. "Margaret, a word with you in the library, please?"

"Perhaps I should come as well," Aunt Louisa offered.

"Miss Dare, would you care to join us in another few minutes?" Ainsley said evenly. "We cannot all leave at the same time and arouse suspicion."

"An excellent notion, Peter," Aunt Louisa said. "You two head on over. Miss Dare and I will join you shortly."

Ainsley pulled at his sister's arm tightly.

"You are hurting me," she whispered as they made their way back through the maze of people crowded into their dining hall.

"You deserve a little pain after what you have all put me through," Ainsley hissed.

Ainsley closed the library door immediately after entering it and then ran both of his hands through his hair in exasperation. "How could you not tell me?" he demanded.

"You have no idea how many times I wanted to," Margaret begged. "Forgive me, please. It was Simms's idea and I thought it was best."

"Simms?"

The library door opened a crack. Margaret and Ainsley ducked behind it so none of the party guests in the hall would see them.

"*The Iliad*? Perhaps you'd be interested in borrowing our copy." Aunt Louisa showed Julia in and closed the door. She smiled broadly and balled her hands into excited fists. "We did it. Everyone thinks she's the Dare heiress."

Ainsley turned from them and took a few steps. "Are you both out of your minds? Do you have any idea what you three have put me through?" When he turned back to them his eyes were glazed over and his cheeks were red. "I stood at your grave weeping. I've spent hours writing love letters saying all the things I wished I said while you lived. I started...I started drinking again."

"Oh, I know," Margaret said. "It killed me to see you in such a state, but we couldn't, we just couldn't. You have to believe us."

Julia stepped forward, licking her lips. "I'm sorry," she said softly. "When I woke in the hospital it had all been decided. I had no choice."

"You had already confronted Thaddeus and told them she was dead," Margaret explained. "That's what Simms had hoped you'd do."

Ainsley closed his eyes, as his mind returned to that day. "That's why he never stopped me. He and those constables let me go right in there."

Margaret nodded. "Yes. It had to be believable. They'd know if you were lying. We had to convince them Julia was dead so they would stop coming after her."

Julia pulled at Ainsley's hand, cupping it in both of hers. "I wept as well, thinking of the anguish all of this was causing you."

Ainsley placed a hand on the side of her face and rubbed her cheek with his thumb.

"Simms knew Thaddeus would never stand trial and we needed to protect Julia," Margaret explained.

"It's been a month," Ainsley said, closing his eyes. "An entire month."

"Simms found out Thaddeus was watching us," Margaret said. "We couldn't tell you too soon because then he'd know."

"But, who is Cassandra Dare?"

"I am," Julia teased.

"Simms fixed everything—"

"Cassandra Dare passed away nearly three weeks ago, while travelling with her family," Aunt Louisa interjected.

"Everyone died," Margaret said, "and the Dares never spent that much time in one place, so no one will know that our Cassandra isn't the real Cassandra."

"Anyone who wants to look deeper will still find her birth and christening records here in England," Aunt Louisa added.

"But Miss Dare must have been buried somewhere." Ainsley was trying hard to keep up as his aunt and sister laid out the details.

"They requested to be buried in India. Don't you see, Peter, it's perfect. A second chance at a happily ever after." Aunt Louisa looked as if she were going to break out in tears as she came toward them to pull Julia into a tight hug.

Ainsley rubbed the back of his neck. "This is going to take some getting used to."

"Oh, stuff and nonsense, you've been pretending to be two people for years now. You can lie some more to save this lovely woman's life." Aunt Louisa slapped his chest playfully with the back of her hand. "Come now, Margaret, let us leave these two lovebirds. If we don't allow them some time to get to know one another, how are we ever going to explain their sudden infatuation?" Aunt Louisa winked as she reached for the door. She and Margaret left under a cloud of excitement.

For a second Ainsley couldn't bring himself to look at Julia, afraid he'd wake up and find it was all a dream.

"Are you mad at me?" she asked.

"Mad at you?" Ainsley exhaled. "No, I'm not mad." He closed his eyes against the tears. "Happy beyond measure." He looked her over, tracing the outline of her face. "I never want to let you out of my sight again."

"That will be difficult," Julia said with a chuckle.

"Come here." He placed his hand at the back of her neck, weaving a finger or two into the curls of her hair, and pulled her toward him. The kiss they shared was soft and slow, every effort was made to savour the sensation of it. Julia's eyelashes tickled the crest of his cheeks, forcing him to smile, but did not pull them apart. He realized then that each embrace prior had been taken for granted and the only way to rectify his arrogance was to make a personal vow to relish each moment with slow, deliberate passion.

Everyone thought it best if Cassandra remain unseen for a prescribed period of time. Gossip began to spread regarding Miss Dare's return to London, and much speculation arose from it. Careful appearances would be planned at a later date, Aunt Louisa decided, in which Ainsley would be able to publically display his interest in the fetching heiress.

Great care must be taken for the following months, Simms cautioned. He warned that Thaddeus would be keeping an eye on them for some time, and that Ainsley should never let his guard down.

Simms's warnings came to the forefront of Ainsley's

mind one night in October when he, Margaret, and Aunt Louisa were leaving the theatre. A feeling of unease overtook him all at once, sending stomach bile up into his throat and causing his heart to race.

"Do you think it may be Lucy?" Margaret asked, as he rushed them out of the theatre.

"I'm not sure," Ainsley answered honestly. The panic he felt, dry and gnawing, couldn't be traced to a specific event or thought. While they rode home he knew something waited for them there. He thought of Thaddeus and tried in vain to push down the fear that threatened to envelop him.

By the time the carriage pulled up in front of the house, Ainsley was jumping out of his skin. He was the first to step out onto the pavement. The street was dark. The gas lamps above shed little to no light and the cold kept biting at him as he stood beside the carriage steps.

A shadow moved beside the front steps of the house. Slowly, it morphed into the silhouette of a man, broad and tall. Ainsley could not see his face for the dark.

"Do not take another step," Ainsley commanded. Behind him, he heard Aunt Louisa gasp as the shadow grew larger. Margaret clutched at his arm, more to pull Ainsley back than seek protection.

"Who are you and what is your business here?" Ainsley feared it was Thaddeus, or one of his men, come to exact their own form of street justice. He tried to shield Margaret and Aunt Louisa. Running for the front door was out of the question. There simply wasn't enough room between them and the shadow.

Behind them the horse team stomped impatiently at the kerb, releasing a heavy, nasal whinny. Ainsley could hear the reins, clasps, and buckles clinking amongst the leather of the halters and bridle. He wasn't sure where Jacob stood, but the loyal servant hadn't abandoned them. Ignoring Ainsley's command to stay, the shadow moved closer.

"Peter?" Aunt Louisa called but remained close to the carriage.

"Announce yourself!" Ainsley said. This was the first time Ainsley wished he still had that G. & J. Deane pistol.

Ainsley watched as the form stopped a few paces from

them. There was something familiar in its stance, something Ainsley had not noticed until then.

"Have you no patience," the stranger asked, "for an old friend?" The figure pulled at his hat and allowed the lamppost to bathe him in soft light.

"Jonas?"

Margaret pulled back on Ainsley but he ignored her.

A rush of relief gave way to joy as he took in the sight of his friend and medical school colleague. With arms open wide for an overdue embrace, Ainsley went to him but stopped suddenly at the sight of something black, no crimson, glistening over Jonas's white shirt.

"What's happened here?" Ainsley asked, afraid to commit to the embrace.

Weary and pained, Jonas looked to Ainsley, his eyes pleading. "You have to help me, friend," he said. "Something terrible has happened."

"What? What is it? What do you need me to do?"

Ainsley would have done anything for the man, his friend.

Jonas stood still for many moments. His face twisted into a painful grimace. His eyes became unfocused. His shoulders slouched.

"Come inside," Ainsley pleaded. "I can help you."

Margaret came alongside Ainsley, pulling her shawl tighter over her shoulders. "What is he saying, Peter?"

Ainsley shook his head, wondering how Margaret had not heard Jonas's plea for help. "He's saying he needs help," Ainsley said. "But he won't come inside." He turned back to Jonas. "I don't understand."

Something wasn't right. This didn't seem like Jonas at all.

At the sound of Ainsley's voice, Jonas turned and started down the pavement, carrying his hat at his side.

"Jonas, wait!"

"What's happening?" Margaret asked, frightened. She clutched Ainsley's sleeve tighter, preventing him from running ahead.

"He's leaving. Don't you see?" Ainsley finally looked to Margaret and saw the fear embedded in her eyes. "It's Jonas. He's right there."

"We..." she swallowed hard, "we don't see anything."

When Ainsley turned back, his friend was gone, swallowed by the black night of London.

About Tracy L. Ward

A former journalist and graduate from Humber College's School for Writers, Tracy L. Ward has been hard at work developing her favourite protagonist, Peter Ainsley, and chronicling his adventures as a morgue surgeon in Victorian England. She is currently working on the sixth book in the Marshall House Mystery series set for release in 2017. To find out more about Tracy's books follow her on www.facebook.com/TracyWard.Author or visit her website at www.gothicmysterywriter.blogspot.com

www.ingramcontent.com/pod-product-compliance
Lightning Source LLC
Chambersburg PA
CBHW051106030726
47504CB00006B/1806